Advance Praise for
My Bonney Lies Under

"Original, engaging, suspenseful and charming!
I loved this book—the rich historical setting, the sparkling array of characters, the balance of action and luscious descriptions. And, most of all, the smart, spunky young protagonist, Keridec Rees who faces a complicated shipboard murder plot. What more can a reader ask of the start of a new mystery series?"
— Anne Hillerman, Author of the New York Times best selling Leaphorn Chee Manuelito mysteries

"Miller is a master of the mystery genre, a scholar of women writers breaking barriers in the 19th century, and a poet who manipulates language in magical ways to further her plot. She and I and the remarkable Elizabeth Gunn were part of a critique group that published more than thirty novels over a couple of decades. Thanks, Susan, for continuing to carry our torch with the introduction of this delightful new sleuth!"
— J. M. Hayes, author of *The Grey Pilgrim* and *The Spirit and the Skull*

"In *My Bonney Lies Under*, Cummins Miller has created a beautifully written and captivating historical adventure with a crew of intriguing characters pitted against an unknown but powerful adversary—all at sea, aboard a steamship headed for San Francisco. Already in mourning, 15-year-old Keridec Rees undergoes yet another loss and then must fight to stay alive and discover who wants her dead. Analytic and gutsy, Keridec is an intelligent female heroine you'll want to see more of. I know I do! "
— Kathy McIntosh, Author of the Adventure Calls Mysteries

T0321329

"Susan Cummins Miller is an award-winning poet and her prose is lyrical and detailed, with beautiful descriptions of characters, the movements of the ship, the weather, the food, and serious attention to historical details—including adherence to the diction of the times, class divisions and racial tensions. We are privy to Keri Rees's innermost thoughts and emotions. I gulped the novel in almost one sitting (I had to go to bed!), and by the end, Keri had transformed through grief and smarts into an independent young woman, though still so very young. A very compelling and satisfying read. "

— Liza Porter, winner of the 2024 Faulkner/Wisdom Writing Competition in nonfiction and author of *Del Bac*, *Keep the Singing*, and *Red Stain*

"Rich descriptions grace this series launch from Susan Cummins Miller. The author deftly brings us into a new world as we meet Keridec Rees and learn of her misadventures as she crosses the Pacific on the *Oceanic* in 1885. Our heroine may only be fourteen, but she's traveled more than most of us and in dire circumstances that have taught her how to be suspicious and defensive. She's the perfect guide to a lethal but mesmerizing journey into the past."

— D.R. Ransdell, author of *Party Wine*

Additional works by Susan Cummins Miller

The Frankie MacFarlane, Geologist, Mysteries
Death Assemblage
Detachment Fault
Quarry
Hoodoo
Fracture
Chasm

Nonfiction
A Sweet, Separate Intimacy: Women Writers of the
American Frontier, 1800-1922

Poetry
Making Silent Stones Sing: Poems
Deciphering the Desert: A Book of Poems

MY BONNEY LIES UNDER

A Keridec Rees Historical Mystery

SUSAN CUMMINS MILLER

Artemesia
Publishing

ISBN: 978-1-951122-99-7 (paperback)
ISBN: 978-1-963832-02-0 (ebook)
LCCN: 2024941869
Copyright © 2025 by Susan Cummins Miller
Cover Illustration and Design © 2024 Ian Bristow

Artemesia Publishing
9 Mockingbird Hill Rd
Tijeras, New Mexico 87059
www.apbooks.net
info@artemesiapublishing.com

Dedication

To my parents, who first introduced me to the mystery, history, and natural beauty of the West, and who first took me sailing off the Pacific coast.

Prologue

On board Occidental and Oriental Company's Steamship
Oceanic
Northern Pacific Ocean
Saturday, August 1, 1885

"I know not whose offspring it is..."
— Lao Tzu, Tao Tê Ching IV (trans. Frederic Henry
Balfour, Shanghai and London, 1884)

10:00 p.m.

THE YOUNG MAN LAY on his back in the deepest shadow he could find: a cleft between the bulkhead, the curved bottom of a lifeboat, and the deck. He'd found his hiding place while the passengers were at supper, after the crew had lit the lamps to mark entrances and ladders. He waited for his target, dagger in his right hand, small rubber ball in his left, aware that only one person on this ship knew of his existence.

Yet he did not feel lonely. His earliest memories were of confined dark spaces where he was alone. He had never seen the sea, mountains, streams, or lakes, at least in the light of day. He had never seen a sunrise, never witnessed a sunset or the moon grow fat and round at the edge of the world. His horizons had been a square of sky in the northern slant of a tiled roof. He could look up and out, but not down. The jingling harnesses, clacking cartwheels, snapping whips, odors of livestock and cooking, laughter and shouts had told him his prison sat along a road traveled by those with business. But he had never seen Shanghai's streets, nor glimpsed those people who were free to travel the roadways.

His prison had only two occupants, himself and a succession of tutors—men who'd fallen into debt and been sold to the masters. Those tutors had given him the world through books, languages, and conversation. But freedom in any sense had eluded him until tonight, aboard this ship sailing east across the Pacific Ocean.

He inhaled the sea breeze, salty and clean. Felt the night air on his face. Touched the metal bulkhead, satisfying in its solidity. Fragments of poetry and song flashed across his mind. If he were truly free, he decided, he would become a wondering poet, beholden to no man... One could dream. During the worst times, he'd had his dreams. Perhaps, after this assignment and voyage were finished, he could find a way to escape into the unknown land ahead.

In the meantime, he had a smaller, floating world to explore. He'd read all about ships. Now he was on one. Sounds came from all directions. The constant thrumming of the steam engine turning the massive screw that helped drive hundreds of feet of iron, steel, and wood through the water. The flapping of sails and rigging on four masts. Bells and whistles and conversations in a dozen languages carried by the singing wind. Shouted orders from officers to sailors. Distant music. A whistled tune. All unfamiliar, fresh, intensely exciting. His heart beat faster. So this was what freedom sounded like.

A few passengers began their nightly circuits of the deck. A part of his mind listened for conversations in English, one of five languages he could speak and write. His effectiveness as a tool depended on language skills, and he had worked hard. Each task had been rewarded with another day, another week, another year of life.

His tutors had filled the empty vessel of his mind with the miracles of numbers, writing, languages, and the mind-to-mind thought transference found only in books. None of the teachers lasted long, except for an old soldier tasked with instructing him in martial arts. The others disappeared in the night. But it hardly mattered, for they left their books behind. And what he heard or read once, he remembered.

As he waited, he perused his mental library, finally settling on a teaching aid his last tutor, an American, had employed: the memoir *Two Years Before the Mast*. "The fourteenth of August was the day fixed upon for the sailing of the brig *Pilgrim*, on her voyage from Boston, round Cape Horn, to the Western coast of North America."

The opening words seemed a propitious sign. The author had set sail on the very day this ship was scheduled to reach San Francisco.

The young man heard voices speaking English. A trio of men. *No.* Several couples passed more slowly. *No.* Two women, approaching at a rapid pace, almost trotting. He focused, listening for verbal markers that would identify the speakers.

"Boyle's Law states that for a given mass of gas kept at a constant temperature, the pressure, P, and the volume, V, are inversely proportional. For example, as the pressure decreases by half, the volume doubles. And vice versa." American accent with overtones of Britain. Good diction—precise and clear.

"I'll take your word for it, Miss Keri." Irish accent. Undertones of humor and affection.

He knew nothing of science, except for a smattering of facts he'd picked up by chance. His masters had deemed the knowledge unnecessary for the work of the tool they were honing.

"Next question?" Miss Keri said.

But their voices faded as the women, one tall, one short, passed by his hiding place. He would have to follow them a ways to confirm their identity.

He crept out of the protective shadows, making no sound, and fell in behind them. The shorter one, perhaps twice the age of the taller one, walked double-time to keep up with her companion's longer legs. Dim lanterns hanging from the bulkhead revealed other passengers, all walking clockwise, as if it were an unspoken rule aboard ships.

He slowed when he reached the stern, awed by the huge sky, black as ink and pierced by stars. Their light, broken and distorted, reflected off the black water. He had seen only a handful of stars before tonight. His heart seemed to swell with the limitless expanse around him. The exuberant lightness reached to his toes. He wondered if the heavens would be this clear in San Francisco.

He pulled his mind back from dreamland, refocused on his quarry, increased his pace. He was a weapon, kept alive and launched by his masters. Trained to dispatch a target or overhear and memorize private conversations. Knowledge could be sold, problems removed. He was the remover.

His masters did not speak in terms of right and wrong. Those were ethical concepts that he had read about in books. For him there was only success or failure. He would complete his task tonight. His reward would be to watch the sunrise from some hidden vantage point.

He trotted like a steward in a hurry, closing the gap. A lantern's light showed that the women wore simple dark dresses. Miss Keri, a girl not much younger than himself, wore a light summer jacket of some gauzy material. A short shawl draped the older woman's shoulders. She waved a white card.

The girl said, "Wait, Annie—that's not one of mine. Did Phineas slip that into the stack?"

"Mr. Quade said the examination will cover literature, history, and philosophy, too," Annie said. "So, you might as well be prepared."

Miss Keri shrugged. "Point taken. The question was something Shakespearean... *Hamlet*? Couldn't Uncle P have chosen a more cheerful subject? I've had enough of death."

"Name me one historian, poet, or playwright that didn't write about death."

The girl was silent. Then, "Again, point taken. Lay on, MacDuff."

Annie lifted her shawl to cover her hair. "You're to find similarities between the advice Polonius gives Laertes and the *Meditations* of Marcus Aurelius."

"But that will take *all night*. What say we compromise—limit it to five observations. If Uncle P wants more, he can badger me at breakfast."

The young man had never heard of Marcus Aurelius. He'd tried to read William Shakespeare's plays. He'd found the language dense and confusing. But none of that mattered now. He'd heard enough.

He glanced around, saw that no one was walking nearby. The women were focused on Miss Keri's summation. He tossed the ball so it rolled by their feet, silver wash flickering in the starlight.

Annie stopped short. The girl slammed into her. He stabbed with his dagger as they started to fall. Felt the blade enter layers of fabric and catch on something. The ship lurched, and he almost lost hold of the knife. He yanked it free, scooped up the ball, and dashed around the corner, out of sight.

He felt a momentary panic. Had his blade pierced flesh as well as cloth? Or had he failed?

Taking a deep breath, he slid the dagger into a leather sheath at his waist. His hiding place was not far away. There would be food and water there. And the comfort of books. He'd seen a copy of William Shakespeare's plays on one of the shelves. Perhaps he'd try again to make sense of *Hamlet*...

He would have another chance at the target tomorrow. Thirteen more days and nights of chances. Time was on his side.

They were on a ship far out at sea. She could not elude him forever.

* * *

10:30 p.m.

My companion, confidante, and lady's maid lay half under me on the deck, muttering Gaelic imprecations. People paused, then hurried away, as if embarrassed for us, or wanting to give us privacy. Oddly, no one offered to help.

"I'm sorry, Annie," I said, struggling to my knees. "Are you all right?" I patted her back, followed her shoulder to her arm, searching for her hand.

A figure detached itself from the broken shadows thrown by a ladder a bit farther along the deck. A man holding a pipe and dressed in plain workman's garb. A trespasser from Third Class. He walked to the rail and tapped the pipe, releasing fragrant tobacco into the wind. Tucking the pipe in his vest pocket, he said, "Allow me, ladies."

He held out his right hand. Lamplight showed his left was missing.

I accepted the hand. Felt him lift me up. I stepped aside so that he could assist Annie. With my weight off, she'd managed to push herself to her knees. She brushed her mane of red hair out of her face, straightened her shawl, and stared. "You're from the old country."

He grinned. "Indeed. Michael McGinn from Limerick, at your service." He lifted her as if she'd been light as pumice. "And you?"

"Anne Bonney, from Cork."

Her hand was still in his. They'd forgotten I was there. Static electricity raised the hair on my arms and neck. I'd read about such a thing, but hadn't witnessed it before—hadn't believed it was real.

"I'll be chased away in a minute, Anne Bonney," he said. "Not allowed up here. But I'd like to see you again."

Even in the dim light I saw a flush suffuse her pale cheeks. She withdrew her hand and pulled her shawl up to cover her hair. "Yes."

One simple word sealed her fate.

"Tomorrow night, same time, Miss Bonney?"

"Tomorrow night, Mr. McGinn."

He merged with the darkness again. Annie and I turned and walked sedately toward the entrance to our passageway.

In the well-lit cabin, Annie stared at her hand as if she might not wash it for a month of Sundays.

"Annie? What caused you to stop?"

She pulled a hanger from the closet, still with the bemused expression. "A rat. Leastways, I think it was." She helped me off with my jacket and slid it over the crochet-covered wood. "What's this?"

Her entire hand fit through a rent in the cloth. I felt my back. The silk jacket had swung freely enough that something sharp had only nicked my dress. But the slit was a horizontal line on the left side, where a blade could have slid between my ribs and found my heart.

When I said as much, Annie clucked and shook her head, dismissing my suggestion. "You must have snagged something as we fell. Don't worry, I'll mend it good as new."

I didn't recall seeing any sharp objects in the vicinity of our tumble, although the deck lay in shadow. But there had been no mistaking the tug on my jacket, the footsteps running away... and the hand snatching an object from the deck.

Annie was wrong. It hadn't been a rat passing by. Wrong shape. Someone had rolled a ball past our feet.

I found my father's hunting knife. Slid it under my pillow. And I made sure the cabin door was locked before I drew the curtains around my berth.

* * *

I described the incident to my guardians when they joined Annie and me on our dawn promenade. Phineas Quade and Toru Nakagawa, my father's partners, were escorting me home from the Orient. For the past two years they, Father, and I had been exploring mining prospects. Home, for all of us, was San Francisco, the headquarters of our company.

Nothing untoward happened that day or the next. I chalked the first night's incident up to my imagination, and let down my guard.

So did Annie.

Part I

On board the O&OL Oceanic, northern Pacific Ocean
Monday, August 3, 1885

"Which of the gods was it, who snatched you from us... ?"
— Virgil, The Aeneid VI (translated by James Lonsdale
and Samuel Lee, 1871)

Chapter 1

THE INVITATION HAD BEEN delivered to my door on the coffee tray that morning. *Captain Helmut Stowall requests the company of Miss Keridec Rees at supper this evening.*

The captain, I knew, hosted small dinner parties in an alcove off the main salon. He was working his way through the list of First-Class passengers, in no particular order that I could discern. After three days at sea, he'd reached my name. I accepted, though it meant I'd have to dress formally, right down to the dreaded corset and bustle. I found it difficult to breathe, much less eat, while wearing the equivalent of a boa constrictor about my ribs.

Perhaps I could have gotten by *sans le corset*, as I was twelve days shy of my fifteenth birthday. Between two worlds, in so many ways. Capable of looking after myself, yet still viewed as a girl requiring guardians to protect me from a world that gave no quarter.

I had witnessed that world firsthand three years ago, while fleeing a war in which Chile, Bolivia, and Peru tore into each other like feral dogs disputing territory. The War in the Pacific, they'd named it. My father, my pregnant mother, and I dashed from desert to the closest harbor with a ship, *any* ship that might carry us to safety. Our route led us along tracks and roadways where cadavers filled ditches and slumped against pockmarked walls. The stuff of nightmares.

I bathed away the morbid thoughts and called Annie to help me dress. Truth be told, I would have preferred another quiet evening alone, reading in our cabin.

Annie lifted my mother's pearls from their velvet

pouch. A single strand of perfection, long enough to loop twice around my slender neck. My father had given them to my mother on my first birthday. I felt tears threaten to breach the dam.

"There," Annie said, stepping back after fastening the necklace. "You look quite grown up." She handed me a fresh handkerchief. "No tears tonight. Tonight is special."

I dabbed the corners of my eyes. "I shall hate to lose you to Mr. McGinn."

"Mister or no mister, you'll never lose me, Miss Keri. Don't you know that by now?"

Her voice rang with sincerity. So why did I doubt her words?

Because Father promised the same thing not four weeks ago. And he was dead before morning.

I stood, feeling the great ship breach a strong swell. Hours earlier, the *Oceanic* had turned northeast to skirt the edge of a storm, the first rough weather since we'd set sail from Yokohama. I smelled no rain through the open porthole, but the freshening wind brought lower temperatures and scudding clouds.

It would be a lovely night for Annie and Michael McGinn.

Chapter 2

A FEW MINUTES BEFORE eight o'clock, Toru Nakagawa arrived to escort me to the alcove off the dining salon. Uncle T's formal attire, fashioned of black silk by the best tailors in Tokyo, sat easily on his shoulders. His father, a Japanese silk merchant and exporter, had his hand in businesses of all kinds, including tailor shops.

I had stayed at the Nakagawa town estate during the months my father had struggled to recover in hospital. His pelvis and femurs had been crushed in a rockslide on the stark upper slopes of Mount Fuji. I'd pleaded with my father to let me make the hike with him and Toru. Only in the last quarter-century had women been allowed to climb the sacred mountain. I didn't know if I'd ever get another chance. Father refused, thinking it might be too dangerous because they were climbing the lower slopes in the dark.

Thus, I'd remained in Tokyo with Phineas Quade, who had contracted consumption during our exploration work in the Philippines. Uncle P couldn't handle the volcano's altitude or the strenuous climb. The decision to remain behind may have saved his life. And mine.

"Phineas will dine in his cabin," Toru said from the doorway.

I wasn't surprised. The clean sea air was helping, but, as yet, Phineas had neither the strength nor the inclination to mix with fellow passengers. He'd barely slipped through the doctor's physical examination prior to boarding.

"Ready?" Toru asked.

I nodded, as nervous as my mother must have been at her debutante ball in Paris. But my shipboard debut would be far from joyful. I smoothed the skirt of the

13

simple watered-silk evening dress that Toru's family had insisted on fashioning for me after my father died. The cloth was halfway between indigo and charcoal. Mourning dress.

Annie blotted tears from my cheeks and tucked the handkerchief into my *réticule*. "Just remember not to monopolize the conversation," she said, draping a matching shawl over my shoulders. "You'll be fine."

I kissed her cheek, straightened up, and took a shallow breath.

"You look perfect," Toru said, placing my right hand in the crook of his elbow. "And do not worry—we have faced far more daunting situations than this."

I gripped his arm. "You won't leave me alone?"

He smiled. "I would not dare. Phineas would never forgive me."

We entered the flow in the passageway. More than a thousand travelers and several hundred crew made their temporary home on the dowager of the Pacific, although only one hundred and sixty or so were traveling in First Class, which the steamship company called Saloon Class. We had our own dining salon, library, men's smoking room, and deck space. There was no Second Class. The rest of the passengers, like Michael McGinn, traveled Third Class—single men fore, single women and families aft. I felt as if I were perched atop a beehive.

I'd sailed on the *Oceanic* twice before, when the passenger ship plied the north Atlantic between New York and Liverpool as a White Star Line vessel. I was six years old then, and my parents had hoped to find a boarding school in Europe that would challenge their only child and foster my passions for the sciences, art, and mathematics. When nothing suited, we'd returned to the Western Hemisphere and a succession of tutors, including my mother, father, and his partners. But with my mother's passing two years ago, and my father's recent death, only Phineas and Toru remained to guide me.

Toru's gloved hand patted mine as we reached the dining salon. This meal was, in effect, supper. I had passed up the mid-day dinner of around eleven courses, most of them meat dishes, knowing this lighter fare would be served in the evening.

I preceded Toru around the perimeter to the captain's alcove, where silver, crystal, and porcelain glittered on an oval table set for ten. Toru and I found our place cards. Parchment menus listed tonight's courses: onion soup, filet de sole amandine, filet de boeuf en croute with new potatoes in butter and parsley, green salad, citrus mousse topped with slices of gooseberry. And coffee, tea, or port with a cheese plate. The descriptions made my mouth water, but, due to the corset, I doubted I'd be able to do more than sample each course.

Captain Stowall arrived last. A portly man a few inches taller than I, with graying-blond hair, neatly trimmed mustache and beard, and heavy-lidded blue eyes. He took the chair on my right, at the head of the table.

Toru seated me and then moved to a place opposite, two down on the captain's right. The wine server half-filled our glasses with a light, crisp chardonnay. He was Japanese, as were all the servers in the First Class dining room. This contrasted with the rest of the ship, staffed by Chinese. Only the officers were British.

Over the next half-hour, the captain kept a fatherly eye on the level in my wine glass and topped off my water from a carafe he asked the waiter to set between us. I was silent during the first two courses, watching Toru converse with the women on either side, the widowed Mrs. Pomfrew and her daughter, Priscilla. Toru's English was fluent, although accented. He had been educated at an English-speaking school in Tokyo, and later in the United States and England. He was tall for a Japanese, nearly six feet, with a high forehead, square face and jaw, and midnight-dark eyes that smiled often. Silver frosted the temples of his smooth black hair, but not his mustache, though he was over forty.

Mother Pomfrew's eyes had lit up when Toru had been introduced as "Dr. Nakagawa," until he clarified that he was a geologist and professor, not a medical doctor. I smiled behind my napkin, having observed this dance

15

before. Toru's intelligence, demeanor, and quiet charm drew people in. Especially women. The Pomfrews were no exception. The mother, a large woman, wore heavy black silk. A graduated sequence of polished jet beads dangled from the neckline. When waiters served the third course, the beads brushed butter from the potatoes each time she leaned toward Uncle T.

Captain Stowall turned to me from Mrs. Pomfrew, who wasn't holding up her end of the conversation. "You're very quiet."

I said, "My parents advised me—more than once, I'm afraid—that it's impossible to learn anything of value while the lips are moving and the ears are resting." I refrained from looking at Madame Pomfrew, but I saw the captain's eyes crinkle around the edges.

"Your parents are wise," he said. "Yet, they let you cross the ocean alone?"

"My parents are dead, Captain. Now I have Mr. Quade and Dr. Nakagawa to guide me." I gestured with a tilt of the head to Toru, who was listening to three conversations at once. "And Anne Bonney, my companion. They see that I don't cause too much mayhem."

"You've known your guardians long?"

"All my life. Uncle Phineas studied geology and mining engineering with my father in Paris and Freiburg. They worked for other companies for a few years, then started their own mining and exploration company. Dr. Nakagawa joined their main office in San Francisco the year I was born, and later became a partner."

The captain cut a bite of beef and chewed it slowly. "Keridec... Unusual. Is it a saint's name?"

I took a sip of water, stalling. Because my father had gathered information for various governments during the course of his field work, I'd been coached not to reveal unnecessary details of my life. The captain's question seemed harmless enough, but the situation was complicated.

My birth certificate showed, in formal script, *Winifred Constance Sabine Marie-Jeanne d'Annecy Keridec Glendower Rees.* Enough names to appease the ancestors on both sides of the family. My mother, Sabine de Keridec

Rees, had been born in Brittany. My father, Gawain Glendower Rees, in Wales. Hence, I possessed three passports. None carried my full name, a precaution of my parents in case I found myself in some political situation that might favor a citizen of another country. My American passport, which I was using on this voyage home, listed only *Keridec Rees*. No saint's name. No middle name. No middle initial. Blessedly simple.

"Well, Miss Rees?" Mrs. Pomfrew's voice was loud enough to make the captain wince. She cocked her head, waiting. As if on cue, the other conversations ceased.

I set down the water glass and offered what I hoped was a generous smile. "Keridec is a Breton name, Mrs. Pomfrew. A place name. To field scientists such as my parents, place has special import. I'm just grateful they didn't name me after the highest navigable lake in the world."

The captain made a choking sound. His face reddened with the effort of holding back a laugh. He reached for his wine glass.

Toru glanced toward the heavens and closed his eyes. My other tablemates frowned in confusion—except for one man: Gideon Lamb. Or at least that was the name he'd used a few years ago when we'd shared passage from San Francisco to South America. I'd missed his name during the captain's introductions, being focused on removing my evening gloves without sending them sailing onto Mrs. Pomfrew's diamond tiara.

When I'd entered the room tonight on Toru's arm, Lamb had reacted like a foxhound catching a scent. I wasn't sure which of us Lamb recognized, my guardian or me, or what it meant. I'd been a child when our paths had crossed before, so I doubted I'd made an impression. But Toru had been with us as far as Ecuador.

Lamb's type was common among the speculators I'd met who were making and losing fortunes gambling on land, mining, and railroads. On that eastern Pacific voyage, Lamb, in his late thirties then, had played cards with my father and Phineas. I recalled the strong, well-fashioned visage, the lean build of a fencer, the exquisite taste in clothes. A professional gambler, rootless as an air plant, Toru had described him. The kind of man that triggered a mother's instinct to lock up her daughter and throw away the key, Phineas had added. I doubted Lamb had changed in five years.

My fingers itched to try to capture the man in pen and ink. But I no longer carried a sketchbook everywhere I went, whiling away hours in a quiet corner as my father and his partners conducted business. The shock of my father's death had driven me to put away childish things. No more sitting in corners. I had taken my place at the table. Literally.

Toru followed my gaze, noting Priscilla Pomfrew's parallel focus. He studied Lamb while Mrs. Pomfrew questioned the captain about the largest lake in South America. Toru had confessed once that Caucasian faces all looked alike when he'd first left Japan to study in Europe and America. He'd had to work hard to adapt to western ways—not only absorbing customs, but refraining from automatic bows and frequent apologies. He likened it to learning a new language, one full of glottal stops, tongue clicks, and consonants rolling forever in the throat, where a word can have a hundred different meanings. He'd mastered several new languages, but still had trouble identifying Europeans and Americans he'd met briefly, and in a different setting, years before.

I caught the moment he recognized Lamb. Toru stiffened and opened his mouth as if to speak. I forestalled him with "Titicaca—"

Mrs. Pomfrew gasped and clutched her jet beads.

I fought a smile and started again. "Lake Titicaca is the highest navigable lake in the world, and one of the two largest lakes in South America—at least that they've discovered so far. Isn't that correct, Captain Stowall?"

"Spot on, Miss Rees."

Toru reached for the cobalt-blue glass salt cellar with its sturdy silver feet and tiny silver spoon. "I can attest that your parents considered naming you after flowering plants or minerals. I recall suggesting 'Chrysanthemum,' a favored flower in Japan and China. Mr. Quade proposed 'Malachite,' a copper mineral mined for millennia in your father's native Wales." Toru turned to Stowall. "Given the options, sir, my ward got off lightly."

The captain laughed aloud. "So it appears."

I flashed a smile of thanks at Toru as servers set the green salad before us, following the continental tradition. Mrs. Pomfrew waited till the coast was clear, then leaned forward, beads dragging through the dressing. "Dr. Nakagawa was telling us that your mother accompanied your father on his geological excursions. She must have been extraordinarily devoted to him."

Mrs. Pomfrew's tone implied that such devotion was not a desirable attribute in a wife.

"My mother was a scientist in her own right, Mrs. Pomfrew. She collected, described, and illustrated the flora wherever we went. She loved field work. And luckily, I was a portable child, more content out of doors than in."

I paused. Mrs. Pomfrew munched contentedly on her greens. Her daughter and Lamb exchanged glances. The captain emptied his wineglass. A staid gathering. My father, who had a black sense of humor and abhorred dull gatherings, would have dropped some kind of verbal bomb into the conversation. I decided to honor his memory.

I assumed an air of innocence, something Annie had been trying to teach me, and glanced at Toru. He swallowed, set down his knife and fork, and awaited the inevitable. "But I admit, Mrs. Pomfrew," I said, "that conditions can be hard on women, which is why so many of the exploration geologists wait to marry and have children until they're older and more settled. And many never do."

Toru looked resigned. I'd offered a convincing reason why he and Phineas were still eligible bachelors, but I'd also tossed them to the Pomfrew wolves.

Mrs. Pomfrew took the proffered bait and turned her attention to my guardian. "Priscilla studied science—botany, wasn't it, dear?—at finishing school. In Geneva. Switzerland, of course, not New York. I can't remember, dear, did you also study geology, since the Alps were in your back yard? You did? Why, you and Dr. Nakagawa have so much in common."

"Mother." The word held a warning.

Priscilla, a slender, whey-faced woman of perhaps nineteen must have failed to find a mate during her debutante year. Long oceanic voyages, which placed passengers in close proximity with no means of escape outside their cabins, provided worried parents another chance at the gold ring. But this daughter had a mind of her own. Gideon Lamb seemed to be her preferred target.

Mrs. Pomfrew launched into a description of the Grand Tour she'd taken with her husband before his death six months ago. The arrival of the dessert cart interrupted her saga. I thought I heard a small sigh of relief escape the captain's lips as he turned again to me. "What will you do when you reach San Francisco, Miss Rees? Continue with your schooling there?"

I dabbed my lips with the serviette. "If my grandmother has her way, I'll be packed off to a finishing school in France till I'm of marriageable age."

"Surely your parents left directives for your education."

"Not exactly."

His expression said quite plainly, *Explain, please.* I hesitated.

Toru smiled, and I knew something was coming. "Miss Rees, working with a variety of tutors, has satisfied the requirements for university matriculation. She is presently preparing to prove that in oral and written examinations. In the estimation of Mr. Quade and myself, she is ready for post-graduate work in any of four fields of study."

Colonel Grayson, the older gentleman sitting on Priscilla Pomfrew's right, snorted into his port. Conversation halted. My tablemates studied me like a newly discovered insect species. I felt a flush climb my cheeks. I lifted my water glass to salute Toru, and mouthed, "Touché," which he acknowledged with a slight bow. Honors even.

"Just how old are you, Miss Rees," Colonel Grayson said, "if that's not an impertinent question?"

It was, but now that the damage was done, I saw no

reason to hide my age. "I'll be fifteen in a few days."

"Not yet fifteen?" Grayson was staring at my bodice, much as he'd stared at Priscilla's chest all dinner long.

Beside me, the captain bristled. Toru leaned forward, but I forestalled them both by looking down and giving a little Gallic shrug I'd learned from my mother. "Ah, yes. *That.* I blame it on the corset, Colonel."

Mrs. Pomfrew said, "Well, I never!" Grayson, spider-veined cheeks turning an even brighter shade of claret, knocked over his wine glass. He was from Virginia, he'd said earlier, and had fought for the Confederacy during the War Between the States. He'd reminisced to Priscilla Pomfrew and Gideon Lamb about the antebellum South, when people knew their places. Presumably that included women, young and old.

Conversations resumed. Mrs. Pomfrew reclaimed the captain's attention. I wished I could loosen my stays, crawl under the table, and take a nap. I hoped Annie and her Michael were enjoying their evening more than I was. But then, how could they not?

An officer slipped into the room. His left hand clutched a woman's hat. The hat I'd given Annie this afternoon. My heart skipped a beat, then began slamming against my ribs.

The officer passed a note to Captain Stowall. He glanced at it, pushed back his chair, tapped cheese fork against water glass, and said, "Duty calls. Thank you all for dining with me. It's been the most, er, *interesting* meal I've enjoyed on this voyage. After-dinner beverages will be served in the saloons, as usual. Please excuse me."

Chairs scraped. Men rose to assist the women. The captain leaned toward Toru and said in a low voice, "Come, please. You and Miss Rees."

Toru and I followed Captain Stowall through the main dining room, which was being cleared for dancing, and into the small library.

Lamplight warmed the room. A long rack with periodicals clung to the wall between two deck-to-over-head bookcases, one with well-thumbed lighter works by Twain, Thackeray, Alcott, and Austen, the other with histories, biographies, travel books, and the classics, from

21

Homer and Virgil to Milton and Shakespeare. I'd examined the offerings my first day aboard and found that many of the classics, bound in leather and stamped in gold, had uncut pages. An ivory-handled letter opener dangled from a sturdy chain attached to the side of the bookcase. I suspected it had seldom been used.

The officer with the hat followed us in, closed the double doors, and sat at one of three small desks occupying the periphery of the room. He set the hat aside, opened a notebook, and dipped his pen in the inkwell. The captain and Toru headed to the armchairs grouped with a settee around a large coffee table in the center of the room. I crossed to stand at the open porthole, drinking in the fresh air, trying to fill my lungs and steady my nerves.

"Miss Rees?" the captain said.

I didn't turn. I couldn't. Fear flexed its claws deep inside my gut, and I knew it would show on my face. Showing fear was never a good thing, my father had taught me. Fear gave the advantage to your opponent. Fear needed to be faced, fought, and subdued.

I slid my fingers over my mother's pearls and forced words through tight throat muscles. "What happened to Annie?"

"We don't know. We're searching the ship for Miss Bonney now."

"Where did you find the hat?"

"We didn't. The passenger who reported her missing—"

He must have turned to his officer for help because I heard the rustle of paper before a new voice said, "Mr. Michael McGinn, sir. He said he found the hat on the after deck, near the railing."

"Annie planned to meet him," I said. "At ten o'clock. I helped her get ready before I left for dinner."

"Does she often wear a hat at night?" Stowall asked.

"She usually pulls a shawl over her hair when we take a turn around the deck. But her hair is thick and wild and escapes even that. She didn't want it blowing in her face tonight, so I gave her the hat. It matched her coat." I clamped my lips together to halt the babbling. But when I tried to take a deep breath, the corset fought me.

No one spoke. The lamps in the room seemed to dim for a moment. *Not Annie. Please, not my Annie...*

Toru was beside me. "Perhaps you could fetch the ship's doctor," he said to someone.

"I don't need a doctor." My voice came low, fierce. I sensed him retreat, although he didn't move.

My heart tapped out a rhythm, over and over, as my breathing shallowed. *Not Annie. Not Annie. I couldn't bear to lose Annie, too.*

The lamps coalesced into a single pinpoint of light before dissolving altogether.

Chapter 3

I *SURFACED IN MY* own cabin, lying on my side on the lower bunk. Dr. Doyle held my wrist, fingers over pulse, pocket watch in his left hand.

He looked up when I moved. "How are you feeling, my dear?"

"Annie?"

His eyes grew serious. "We've no word, yet. I'm sorry." He patted my hand and stood, repeating, "How are you feeling?"

I realized I still wore my evening dress. The bustle precluded my turning onto my back. Taking an experimental breath, I found I could fill my lungs without impediment.

"I took the liberty of unlacing your corset," Doyle said. "Left the bustle to you. Why women wear the damned things—pardon my French—I'll never know. You should be fine now."

Toru sat with Phineas Quade at the small table by the starboard bulkhead. Uncle P wore a smoking jacket of burgundy silk, though he hadn't smoked in months. A white silk scarf covered the lower half of his face. A doctor in Japan had suggested that a mask might help prevent the worsening and spread of his illness during the voyage home.

"I must have interrupted your game," I said to Phineas. He took his meals in his cabin, and Dr. Doyle checked on him every night after supper. Unless the doctor had a more pressing engagement, or Phineas was having a bad spell, the doctor stayed to play cards or a board game.

Uncle P's drawn face lightened. He'd known me all my life, and knew I'd never fainted before. This was uncharted territory. I imagined his lips curving into a smile behind the silk mask. "You rescued Doyle from a thrashing."

"Chess?" I asked.

"Backgammon."

"There's always tomorrow night," Doyle said. He picked up his medical bag. "Send the stewardess or your cabin boy for me if you have more problems, Miss Rees."

"I will. Thank you, Doctor." When the door closed behind him, I sat up, crossing my arms to hold my loosened gown in place. "We need to talk," I said to my guardians. "Please, while I change, would you ask Ah Jim to bring tea and biscuits?"

My guardians left. With the corset unfastened, I was able to shed the formal clothes in record time. I pulled on a silk chemise, a long tunic, a matching split skirt of my own design made from dark-blue cotton, and a quilted short kimono belted by a narrow *obi*. Three layers, and I still felt cold. Must be shock. I slipped my feet into black *tabi*. Better. The outfit gave me freedom of movement yet covered all the essentials.

Normally, Annie helped, so we hadn't had to avail ourselves of the single stewardess who attended all fifteen First-Class women passengers. She was a formidable Chinese woman who had yet to acknowledge me or smile when our paths crossed. What would I do if Annie had abandoned me?

My hair had come loose. I twisted it up and fixed it with a silver comb my mother had bought for me in Lima. I closed my eyes for a moment and composed my features, forcing fear about Annie into a remote recess of my mind. Squaring my shoulders, I opened the door.

Three men looked back at me. Unlike Ah Jim, the compact cabin steward of indeterminable age holding the tea tray, Toru and Phineas weren't smiling. Ah Jim set the tray on the table and bowed his way out.

"There's news?" My hand shook a little as I poured tea into a cup. I took a few cautious sips, then nibbled on a shortbread biscuit sprinkled with sugar as I carried the snack to my berth.

"Not yet. That's what worries us." Phineas pulled down his mask. He and Toru resumed their chairs at the table, eschewing tea in favor of brandy in teacups. A Mad Hatter's tea party.

Phineas glanced at my old hat, Annie's hat, resting on the dressing table. It hadn't been there when I'd been changing, only minutes before. "Captain Stowall said they searched the ship thoroughly, Keri." He nodded toward the hat. "That's the only sign of Annie they found."

I wiped my hands on a serviette, stood, and crossed to the dressing table. The hat and matching coat had been favorites of mine. I ran my fingers over soft felted wool the color of gentians, touched the contrasting grosgrain ribbon circling the crown and trapping a sprig of silk forget-me-nots. Strands of Annie's red hair were caught inside, under the brim.

"Did they find—" The words came out as a soft croak. I cleared my throat and tried again. "A hatpin?"

Phineas frowned. "The officer didn't mention it. Is it important?"

"Perhaps."

The hatpin was eight inches long and wickedly sharp. My mother's hatpin collection had come to me at her death. My father and Toru had shown me how the decorative jewelry could be used as weapons. I'd urged Annie to wear this pin tonight, although she shouldn't have had to use it. Michael McGinn would have been with her. But perhaps she'd misjudged Mr. McGinn's intentions. They'd only known each other a short time.

A knock on the cabin door. I laid the hat gently back on the dressing table and opened the door to find Ah Jim wearing his perpetual smile. I didn't trust people who hid their feelings behind insincere expressions. But then, my livelihood wasn't dependent on a pleasant, subservient expression.

"The captain wishes to see you, Miss—" Ah Jim stopped, glancing at the men in the room before returning his gaze to me. I thought he'd make another stab at my last name. So far, he'd butchered it in myriad ways. But he settled for, "Come now, please?"

He turned and took two steps down the narrow passageway, then paused, waiting for me to follow. I turned to Phineas. Another cough racked his body.

"Please get some rest, Uncle P. I'll need you sharp tomorrow... er, today." I kept my voice soft and low, as befitted the late hour and the open door. "Uncle Toru, would you mind coming with me?"

"You'd think the captain could wait until morning." Uncle P's irritation was born of exhaustion.

"No," I said. "There's the hat, you see. I wore it and the matching coat last night. The coat was too snug through the shoulders, so I gave it to Annie." *Tragedies can grow from the seeds of such small kindnesses.* "She spent all morning altering it."

Phineas and Toru looked at me blankly. Ah Jim cleared his throat in the passageway.

"If something's happened to Annie, whoever hurt her might have thought they were attacking me." I shivered. "And they'll likely try again."

The expressions on my guardians' faces changed as they recalled my tumble the first night, and the slash in my silk jacket.

"Then go you must," Phineas said. "And I hope you'll find good news awaits you." He kissed my forehead, said good night, and left.

"I'll just be a moment, Uncle T." I buttoned a matching cloth panel to the front of the skirt, disguising the split. But I left off the back panel. After a long and enervating night, decorum could only demand so much.

At the last moment, I took the silk jacket Annie had mended for me from the closet and my sketchbook from the nightstand drawer. I might need the comfort drawing provided.

Chapter 4

TORU PRECEDED ME INTO the passageway. Ah Jim set off at a fast trot, and we endeavored to keep up.

I wondered what Captain Stowall had to say that was so urgent it couldn't keep till morning. My chest and shoulders felt tight as guitar strings. I focused on my breathing, trying to ease the rigor of my muscles. The recent injury and death of my father had been both traumatic and wearying. But the last time I'd felt this sustained level of tension was when my parents and I raced to evacuate the war in South America. That anxiety abated only after we found berths on a merchant ship headed to Australia.

We hadn't cared about the delay of the round-about way home. It gave us time to recover from the nightmare of what we'd witnessed in Peru and Chile. My mother, four months pregnant, nearly lost the baby during our flight. She spent much of the voyage in our cabin, trying to protect the life growing inside her. But she walked ashore with her sketchbook when we put in to drop off supplies at Easter Island. I still had her sketches, hidden away in my San Francisco bedroom. Hidden from Grand-mère Constance.

My grandmother had never asked about her daughter's work. Nor had she ever shown an interest in *my* passions and talents. I couldn't recall her ever reading a book to me or walking with me in the hills of San Francisco. Her attention focused always on social status and attracting attention. Those elixirs sustained her. When she entered a room, conversation stopped. Lights seemed to dim around the periphery. She looked younger than her daughter, for life in mining camps and in the thin, dry air of deserts and mountains had aged my mother on the outside. But on the inside, she had been happy—an emotion I suspected Grand-mère had never experienced. Triumph, yes. Life for her was about winning.

The captain stood by one of the desks in the library, his shoulders stiff with fatigue.

I took one of the armchairs around the coffee table. Toru moved to face the porthole.

"You have news?" I stopped breathing, afraid of his answer.

"I'm sorry, no. But we need to ask some additional questions." Stowall tipped his head toward the officer sitting at a desk, pen poised above a blank page in the logbook—the same officer who had brought Annie's hat to the dinner room and escorted us to the library afterwards. "Mr. Arnold will witness and record our conversation."

"Is that necessary, Captain?"

"It's policy, although I still hope that we locate Miss Bonney alive and well—that we discover she was visiting acquaintances and lost track of time. It's happened."

Concern softened the stern visage. He didn't believe that scenario. Nor did I.

"Annie planned to spend the evening with Mr. McGinn. She'd dressed specially—"

"If you have information that might bear on the situation, you must tell me, child."

The captain's shoulders relaxed fractionally. He was not, I decided, a man accustomed to interacting with children, especially with one whose parents had treated her as a functional adult for most of her life. To him I was *mare incognitum*, an unknown sea.

I chose not to cause a disturbance, instead relating the odd occurrence of the first night, and summarizing what I'd told Toru and Phineas about the import of Annie's hat and coat. I handed him the light jacket and pointed out the mended tear. "I didn't report the incident to the purser because I wasn't sure what had happened. But with Annie's disappearance tonight..." I paused. Considered. Tried another tack. "I wore Annie's ensemble last night, when we circled the deck before retiring."

29

Toru crossed the library to stand beside me. We waited. The captain fingered the rent that Annie had mended with such care. I saw the moment comprehension dawned behind his eyes. He handed back my jacket.

"You're implying that your companion's disappearance might not have been an accident?" he said. "That someone intending to do you harm mistook Miss Bonney for you in the dark?"

"Exactly. And if so, her attacker might try again in the coming days," Toru said.

"But who? And why?"

"We do not know, Captain," Toru said. "But for the present, Mr. Quade, Miss Rees, and I would prefer to err on the side of caution."

The captain paced, hands behind his back, making circuits of the small room, his steps hypnotically regular.

"Captain?" I said.

The steps paused. His eyes took seconds to focus on me. He'd been far away. "Yes?"

"You requested my presence—something urgent."

"Ah, yes, of course. My apologies. The situation surrounding Miss Bonney's disappearance may be more complex than I first imagined." He gathered himself and continued, "Here's the long and the short of it, Miss Rees. Only one member of the crew noticed anything amiss tonight. Around 2200 hours, ten o'clock, a deck hand heard a cry or scream. Then he swears he saw someone fall past him, as if they'd jumped from the deck above."

I wanted to shout at him, to demand why he hadn't told us this immediately. But I stayed silent, fingernails digging into palms.

"Passengers do jump, you know, although it's rare." Stowall cleared his throat. "We've searched the entire ship once. Knocked on every door. Come the breakfast hour, while the passengers are in the dining salon, my crew will re-check their cabins. If the search turns up nothing, then we must solve the mystery of what transpired on the after deck."

Negative evidence was as strong as positive. If they hadn't found Annie, then Annie wouldn't be found—alive, at least. Add that to the testimony of a crew member witnessing a person falling overboard, and the news reduced hope to the flicker of a guttering candle.

"The deck hand grabbed a life preserver from the bulkhead and threw it into the water," Stowall said. "The night was too dark to make out anything but the waves, but he heard no calls for help."

I had been on deck at night. I was sensitive, even hypersensitive, to noise. A scream might have carried up from the dark water, but I doubted it. And even if it had, the rumbling of the great turbine motor and the racket of the wind-whipped rigging would have covered all but the loudest sounds.

In a forced, muted tone I said, "This new information raises more questions, Captain. But I require a minute to marshal my thoughts."

His eyebrows shot up. Toru gave a little shake of his head. I had trespassed on convention. Again. Passengers, especially girls in their teens, did not issue commands to captains.

"Please forgive my tone, Captain Stowall. I only meant that odd discrepancies in the tale are colliding in my brain. I need to sort them out. It will only take a minute or two, if you'll indulge me." I tried out a tentative smile.

His features softened. "Take as much time as you need, child. When you're ready, I will also require a detailed description of Miss Bonney. Mr. McGinn was distraught to the point of incoherence."

"Of course, Captain." I gave another, warmer smile, and decided to push my luck a fraction. "While I'm sorting out my questions, would it be possible to send one of the crew to bring your witness here? And also Mr. McGinn? I know it's late, but I doubt either man is sleeping tonight."

His answer was to turn and nod at Mr. Arnold. The wind outside had strengthened, and the big ship plowed through the waves, up the sides, over the crests, into the troughs. It felt like falling. I focused on the flame of a small lamp above Arnold's appropriated writing desk.

What did we know for certain? I took the small drawing pad and pencil from my pocket. Drawing and note-taking had been the constant companions of a childhood spent with an artistic, botanist mother and men who made maps above and below ground. As I made notes, I felt my pulse calm, my scattered thoughts become ordered.

When I looked up, perhaps five minutes had passed. "Annie stood about an inch over five feet," I said. "She had curly, long red hair. Last night she tucked it up under the hat, secured with a hatpin I lent her. Have you found the hatpin? It wasn't in the hat, and there was no sign that the hat had been ripped off during an attack. I examined it in my cabin. The pin holes are pristine, clean and round, not jagged and torn."

"You believe she removed the hatpin?" Stowall asked. "And that's important?"

"I do, Captain. Mr. Arnold said that Mr. McGinn found Annie's hat near the rail on the after deck. That suggests that he did not meet her as planned and escort her to their trysting place."

"Perhaps he was late," Toru said. "Or she was early and chose to walk a bit while she waited."

"Either way, if he is telling the truth, she must have ventured alone along the dark deck, or gone with someone untrustworthy. I'd loaned her the hatpin as much for protection as for functionality. It was much longer than her own."

"I see," Stowall said. "Other than that first night, had you encountered trouble?"

"Annie was accosted twice."

"Twice? Aboard *my* ship?"

"It shouldn't surprise you that many men consider women fair game, Captain Stowall. Especially maidservants and companions."

He sighed and rubbed a hand over his face. "The same man each time, Miss Rees?"

"Yes. Mr. Small. Edward Small. He was inebriated on both occasions, not that that is an excuse. As a result, I shared with Annie what I had learned from my father and Dr. Nakagawa about the use of hatpins as weapons."

"It sounds like we'll need to talk to Mr. Small, as well as to Mr. McGinn."

"Indeed. Here is my thinking, Captain. If Annie felt compelled to remove the hatpin to use against an attacker, the pin might be near the stern rail. And it might have done damage to..." I couldn't finish. Tears gathered behind my eyes as I faced the horror of that imagined scene.

The captain made no attempt to rush me. I took a deep, steadying breath. "Here, let me show you what to look for." I retreated into the safety of drawing.

"The shaft was about eight inches long and recently honed." I sketched the tapering outline of the pin. "The large bead at the top was of Murano glass the color of clearest quartz infused with flakes of gold leaf. Surrounding the glass bead were circlets of tiny diamonds and rubies, held in place by facetted jet beads." I shaded the beads to give a suggestion of depth and drew a scale on the bottom of the page to indicate that I'd reduced the size by fifty percent. In careful script I labeled the elements, hoping that viewers would mentally supply the colors of ruby and gold. Satisfied, I handed him the drawing pad.

The captain studied my sketch. "You've had training."

"My parents loved their work and shared it with me."

I felt the loss of them wash over me. If Annie was gone as well... I rubbed my eyes and wiped my nose with a handkerchief. The room seemed hot all of a sudden. I struggled to remove the kimono jacket. Toru eased it from my arms.

The captain handed me a glass of water. "May I take this drawing? I'll have the crew search for the hatpin once it's light."

"Of course."

He tore out the page and returned the sketchbook.

"Should I draw Annie?" I asked. "There's little hope, now, but you said you'll be completing your search in the morning."

"Yes, please do, Miss Rees. It will help."

I wondered if Toru noticed the captain had switched from calling me "child" to "Miss Rees." Unconsciously or consciously, Stowall now viewed me as an adult.

I began drawing Annie, as much for myself as for the

searchers. I heard the captain cross to Mr. Arnold and murmur something. I closed out the sounds in the room, the movement. When I drew, the process became my world. I started with the shape of the head, automatically calculating the vanishing point and angles of foreshortening that set the scope of the drawing, adding shading to suggest three dimensions. Nothing existed but my attempt to match the lines to the picture I carried in my head. The pencil moved as if of its own accord. I slipped into a near-trance, hearing nothing, but sensing people arriving, speaking, leaving.

Toru's hand on my shoulder broke my intense concentration. My parents had used that waking technique for years. Again, tears crowded my eyes.

"The witness and Mr. McGinn are here," Toru said.

Part II

*On board the O&OL Oceanic, northern Pacific Ocean
Tuesday, August 4, 1885*

*"Powers, who possess the realm of spirits, and ye, silent
shades, and ye, Chaos... may it be granted me, by your will,
to unfold truths buried... in darkness."*
— Virgil, The Aeneid VI (translated by James Lonsdale
and Samuel Lee, 1871)

Chapter 5

MICHAEL MCGINN STOOD, CAP in hand, just inside the door. His left arm ended at the wrist, the stump wrapped in a clean white cloth. Two Chinese sailors stood to his right. The captain ignored them all for a moment and held out his hand for my drawing of Annie.

He studied it. "I believe I saw her once," he said. He beckoned to the seamen and Michael McGinn. "A good likeness?" he asked Michael.

"That's Annie," Michael said, his voice crusty and hoarse, as if he'd been calling her name over and over through the night. He settled the cap on his dark curls and touched the drawing, tracing the lines of her cheek with a reverential finger. "That's my lass."

One of the sailors spoke English. He interpreted for the other, who had heard the cry in the night. The witness spoke rapidly, then gestured toward Annie's sketch.

"He says it was that woman who fell," the interpreter said. "He had seen her before last night." He turned to me. "Sometimes with you, miss, sometimes with that man." His chin lifted and pointed to Michael. "He noticed her hair—long and red. It caught the light of a deck lamp, just for an instant, as she fell."

"There must be a dozen women in steerage who have red hair," Toru said.

The interpreter translated the observation. The witness used his hands to draw in the air, then plucked at his uniform shirt as he answered. "He says steerage passengers would not be on the upper deck. Also, the woman with red hair walked by him a few minutes before she fell. Her coat was of fine material—finer than the clothes worn by the women in Third Class."

"What time did she pass him?" I asked.

The men consulted again. "Perhaps ten minutes before 2200 hours."

"She didn't wait for me," Michael said. Pain filled his voice. "Why didn't she wait for me?"

The question had no answer.

Captain Stowall put his hand on Michael's shoulder and asked the sailor, "At what time did he see the woman fall?"

Another discussion in rapid Chinese. Then, "The first watch port commander allows the deckhands a five-minute smoking break midway through the watch. Seaman Wu says he was just finishing. So, perhaps 2205 hours."

I had asked the captain to bring the witness here so I could see his eyes as he spoke, listen to the nuances in his tones, and judge for myself whether he was truthful or not. I was no expert, but the man seemed sincere.

Michael had retreated to the porthole and turned his back on the group. I knew Annie loved him from the moment they met. But that didn't mean he felt the same. Now, I hoped for both their sakes that the seaman was mistaken, that Annie had fainted and lay somewhere in a pool of shadow, and that she would be found come daylight.

I went to Michael and put a hand on his one good arm. Annie had told me his story. He'd been an engineer on a new steamship, a merchant ship trading between Canada, the west coast of the United States, and the Orient. His hand had been trapped when some equipment shifted in heavy seas. They couldn't save the hand. After he'd spent two months in hospital in Yokohama, the company paid his passage to San Francisco.

Annie and he had been making plans for after they landed. I'd offered to have them live at my home in San Francisco if Annie would continue as my maid and companion—at least for a while.

"Till the bairns start comin'," she'd said. She'd been very sure about her future with Michael.

"My Annie's lost, then," he said.

"Not for certain," I said, knowing it was a lie but refusing to extinguish the glimmer of hope. "What I do know, Mr. McGinn, is that your meeting tonight with Annie was the most important thing in the world to her. So, let's pray there's just a slight delay in your plans. If she's still on the ship, the crew will find her."

I turned to the captain. "I'd like to help with the search tomorrow."

"You may leave that task to us, Miss Rees." He removed something from the inside breast pocket of his dinner jacket. A slip of ship's stationary. I could see the crest, the lines of neat script. He ran his finger down the rows, nodding at each entry. A list of the questions he wanted to ask me? The finger stopped. He looked up. "Tell me, Miss Rees, was Miss Bonney in the habit of going out alone at night?"

I straightened. "No, Captain."

"Do you concur, Mr. McGinn?"

"When Annie would meet me, at least one other person would be with her. Dr. Nakagawa and Miss Rees the first time, and then the cabin steward." He tilted his head in our directions. "Then they would go their ways so we could spend some time alone. But tonight, you see, I was running behind time... a few minutes only. When I didn't find her at the door to the deck, I waited a bit before going to check the after deck. I thought perhaps she went on ahead, thinking I was there. Don't know why she didn't wait for me, Captain. May well be her steward knows."

Toru stepped into my line of sight. "Mr. Quade and I questioned Ah Jim. He said that he and Miss Bonney encountered the young couple that occupies the cabin next to Miss Rees. They engaged Miss Bonney in conversation. A deck hand told Ah Jim he was needed in one of the cabins, and Miss Bonney told him to go. When he left, she was still talking to the couple."

Mr. Arnold consulted a list of passengers and cabin numbers. "That would be Mr. Edward Small and his wife, sir. Their room was checked during the search. I have a note from one of the officers." He turned pages in the logbook until he found one that appeared to contain statements taken last night. The captain moved to look over Arnold's shoulder as he slid a ruler down the page.

The ruler stopped. "Ah, here it is, sir. The Smalls left Miss Bonney, at her request, just inside the door to the deck. They were expected in the gaming salon. Poker and whist, apparently. They'd only stopped to ask where Miss Bonney's hat had been fashioned. She told them Miss Rees bought the hat in San Francisco from a milliner by the name of Babcock."

Abcock, I silently corrected, although it didn't matter now.

"Once again we're left with more questions than answers," said Stowall. "Did Miss Bonney decide to walk unescorted to her rendezvous with Mr. McGinn, fully expecting him to meet her on the way? Or was she lured outside by someone she trusted, someone with whom she felt comfortable enough to have him, or them, accompany her to the stern?"

Silence in the library. The dance music had ended long ago. The card games had moved to quiet corners of the main saloon. A clock on the starboard bulkhead chimed the hour. One o'clock.

"There's a corollary to your first question, Captain," I said. I hadn't planned to speak. The words just slipped out. "If Annie decided to walk by herself, did she stumble on a situation, a scene so private or unlawful that someone would kill to prevent that secret from being revealed?"

Every eye in the room fixed on me. Even Mr. Arnold looked up from his note-taking. I heard the big turbine engine throb, the masts creak as the ship breasted a wave.

"Because I do know this, Captain. Annie practiced using the hatpin as a defensive weapon earlier today... um, yesterday. It made her feel safe. I believe that the pristine holes in the hat demonstrate that she had enough time to recognize danger, remove the pin, and attempt to fend off an attacker."

"Even if that's true," the captain said, "how does that help us discover what happened?"

"We're exploring two options: My friend's still on

board, or she isn't. I'm confident that Annie wouldn't have gone over the side without a struggle. Nor would she have submissively accompanied an abductor. In either situation, she might have left her mark with that hatpin."

"Ah, you wish us to examine any men who were seen out and about near the deck areas."

"Precisely. Look for scratches or gouges on their upper body. Annie would have been aiming for the head or neck. And..." I hesitated.

The captain sighed. "Yes, Miss Rees?"

"I wondered if you would check Ah Jim's alibi more closely. We only have his statement to Dr. Nakagawa that he received a message to attend another passenger."

"You don't trust your cabin steward?"

"I have no reason not to trust him. His service has been exemplary. But if Annie didn't step out alone, there are only a few people she would feel comfortable in using as an interim escort. Ah Jim's one."

"Don't worry, Miss Rees, we'll find the sailor who delivered the message. We'll also confirm Mr. McGinn's movements." He turned to Mr. Arnold, whose pen continued to move surely across the logbook.

The two Chinese sailors stood near the door, eyes closed, as if sleeping on their feet. But I'd lay odds the English-speaking one absorbed every word. Information was a valuable commodity both above and below decks. The captain, seeing the direction of my gaze, dismissed them.

Toru stood again by the porthole, staring out at the night. Michael had slumped down against the bulkhead, head back, eyes closed. Tears had left tracks on his cheek. As Stowall dictated a list of orders to Arnold, I sank down next to Michael and took his good right hand in both of mine.

"You were to be Annie's husband and thus a part of my life," I said to Michael. "I'd be honored if you'd still consider staying at my home in San Francisco until such time as you find a job and an accommodation that suits you better. It's a large house. We have plenty of room."

Mr. Arnold appeared beside me. He held out a glass

of brandy to Michael. "Do you imbibe, sir?"

"I'm Irish," Michael said. His eyes were red, his face haggard, but I detected a flash of a smile. "Thank you, sir, but I better not. I'm afraid if I start, I wouldn't care to stop."

He wiped his eyes with his sleeve, then rose to his feet with surprising grace. He extended his hand, thick with calluses, to me. A worker's hand. I took it and let him help me to my feet, as he'd done on that first night.

"If you're finished with me, Captain Stowall," Michael said, "I'll retire to me cabin for what's left o' the night."

"Any other questions can wait till the morning, Mr. McGinn."

Michael nodded to each of us and let himself out.

"I'll retire as well, Captain," I said. "But at first light I'd like to examine where Mr. McGinn found the hat. I'd like to... pay my respects." I felt tears crowding close to the surface.

Stowall made a ceremony out of putting an aromatic tobacco in the bowl of a carved ivory pipe and lighting it. He didn't ask me if I minded. "Agreed."

Toru said, "I'll escort Miss Rees back to her cabin. I assume you will have a watch set to prevent unwanted visitors."

"Is that necessary?" The captain rubbed his forehead, where the frown lines seemed to have deepened since dinner.

He was looking at Toru, but I answered. "I'll be alone in the cabin, Captain. And if the attack on Annie was meant for me..."

The captain turned to Mr. Arnold and ordered a guard for my door. I picked up my jackets and, escorted by Toru, returned to the sanctuary of my cabin.

Chapter 6

I AWOKE TO THE faintest predawn grayness barely two hours after I stretched out on my berth. At these latitudes the midsummer sun rose early and the nights were short.

The cabin that had seemed cramped when I shared it with Annie was spacious in her absence. She had a large personality, bright as a penny, voluble, and filled with seemingly boundless energy. After Mother died, whenever my father wasn't around, Annie acted as a filter between me and the world. And a crutch. She was quick to sense when I was overcome by the noise and clatter of a crowded place. She would find us a quiet spot in which to sit and sip water or tea from a flask she carried.

"There's always a park or a chapel nearby," she'd say. "Just ask for directions." She knew that if I had a map, even one crudely drawn, I could find my way. So we'd approach strangers—shopkeepers, buskers, street venders, or neighborhood children—and I'd draw a map as they talked. Making maps was my way of reducing the world to chunks I could digest. Without her I'd have to filter the world by myself.

Where are you, Anne Bonney? And why did you abandon me?

I wanted to look at the deck before any of the passengers were about. I sat up and swung my feet to the matting. My clothes of the night before, aired and pressed, hung from a hook inside the door. Ah Jim, bless him.

Before I went to bed, I had bathed to remove the pipe and cigar smoke that clung to hair, skin, and clothes as surely as did smuts from the smokestack. I'd brushed and plaited my damp hair, and now I sat before the dressing table mirror, released my mane, and repeated the process. The act of creating order from chaos soothed me. My mother had allowed me to brush and plait her hair when I was little, and I'd taught myself the art of constraining my thick, wild curtain of hair. But Annie had handled the more intricate styles with ease.

Tu me manques, Annie. I miss you.

As I worked, I studied my face in the mirror—something I rarely did when Annie worked with my hair. At those times I immersed myself in my lessons or listened with closed eyes as she expounded, in a rich Old-Country brogue, on the rules of etiquette in a proper society.

"Meet the eyes of the person you're speaking to, Miss Keri. And listen—that tells them you're interested in what they're saying, even if they are the most boring people on Earth. And smile occasionally—but stop short of laughing, even when some oddity strikes your funny bone... Yes, I know that Mrs. Sutcliffe has the face of a donkey and a bray to go with it. God cursed her features, right enough. No need for you to make it worse by drawing attention to it... Wait to be introduced before you engage in conversation, and wait for your elders to speak first. They're wiser and more experienced, though probably not smarter... And please, please remember to speak softly. You aren't trying to make yourself heard from one mountain peak to another, now, are you?"

I did try to modulate my tone, but had little success controlling my black sense of humor. It surfaced at the most inappropriate times. My parents and their scientist friends had indulged me. But now, except for Phineas and Toru, I was on my own. How would Annie's disappearance affect my carefully constructed plans?

A wave of panic washed over me. I dropped the braid, dug my fingernails into my palms, and focused on taking deep, regular breaths.

The swirling mist receded. I noticed the elements of my face reflected in the mirror. No excess flesh on the skull. Oval shape, spoiled by a strong chin and prominent cheekbones. A mouth neither thin nor full. Large brown eyes, slightly almond-shaped, made larger by the shadows of a near-sleepless night. Narrow nose, unremarkable except for a small bump at the bridge. High forehead. Black brows like tern wings. As I coiled the braid on the crown of my head and fixed it with pins, I wondered if I would grow into those eyes or if they would always appear outsized and vulnerable.

The entire face, I decided, was suspended between childhood and maturity. It hadn't yet decided what it would be, though I saw hints. But perhaps that would be up to me, in the end.

The captain had stationed one guard in the passageway and another outside, by my porthole. I supposed the deck guard could prevent a poisoned dart blown through a reed, or a silent arrow, or a pistol shot to my head. But those threats seemed unlikely.

I hadn't the heart to wake Toru and Phineas, so I asked the sailor in the passageway if he and the guard outside would escort me to the stern deck. We spoke in murmurs so we wouldn't disturb the occupants of the other cabins. He sent Ah Jim, dozing at his station, to get the required permission from the captain.

Closing the door, I hauled on my split skirt and tunic, added a silk shawl of bright blue, and a straw hat with a matching bow. Unconventional attire, but I no longer cared. Another of my mother's hatpins, this one crowned with lapis lazuli carved in the shape of a heart, secured the hat. My father had given the pin to my mother the day I was born. Every piece of jewelry I owned had a story.

A soft knock sounded. I faced the door. *One step at a time.* Toru had paraphrased a similar proverb the night before we left Tokyo: "A journey of ten thousand miles begins under your feet."

Time to take that first step. I opened the door.

Bowing, Ah Jim said all was arranged. I asked him to make up my cabin while I was gone and to have a light breakfast waiting for me when I returned. And then I set off, two sailors in tow, retracing the steps Annie took last night to her rendezvous with fate.

Behind and above me, smoke billowed from the single stack. Beneath me the deck vibrated with the turning of the screw. The sail lines hummed. Sheets flapped and whumped in the wind as if the heavens were driving us faster and faster toward land, farther and farther from where the sailor saw a red-haired woman fall from the ship.

On the eastern horizon, remnants of storm clouds glowed crimson. My guards pointed out where the hat was found, then turned their backs to give me privacy. I moved to the stern rail and stared down at the water churning in the *Oceanic's* wake. I sensed Annie's absence even more here, where the smell of brine infused the wind.

We don't truly understand how important a person is to our lives until they're gone. Annie had been substitute mother, sister, friend, advisor, confidante, teacher of social mores, rescuer. I'd known her for thirteen years, and we'd been constant companions for over two. I knew that, like me, she'd been orphaned at fourteen. A diphtheria epidemic had taken her parents and siblings. Left without money or prospects in Ireland, she'd written Mary Daly, a distant cousin in California. Tom and Mary Daly kept house for my parents. Trained lady's maids were scarce in San Francisco, they'd responded. They'd train her if she'd agree to work for them for three years. Room and board provided. Annie had arrived in due course—and stayed.

She'd never stopped learning, never stopped improving herself. She considered herself a work in progress. I'd loved her. But had I ever told her, shown her?

I pondered the past, needing reassurance. On her last birthday, Father and I had given Annie the weekend off and told her we'd pay for whatever she wanted to do, or whatever day trips she wanted to take. We were newly arrived in Tokyo, and she wanted to buy a few skeins of wool, take a lesson in Japanese flower arranging, and visit the Honjo Catholic Church to light candles in memory of her parents. Toru acted as guide that day. Among Annie's papers was a watercolor I'd done of her arrangement of deep-pink camellias. I'd signed it, *To Annie, with love, Keri.*

My vision blurred. I didn't know if the crew would find Annie in some cubbyhole on the ship today, but I thought not. Somewhere in the night I'd lost hope.

Abandoning me, leaving me unchaperoned, went against all Annie's instincts and training. It defied logic and the loving bond we shared. No, she wouldn't have left me voluntarily.

The sheets and lines beat out a rhythm that my memory set to music, a nursery song my father used to sing me. But now the rhythm had slowed to a dirge.

O dear, what can the matter be?
Dear, dear, what can the matter be?
O dear, what can the matter be?
Johnny's so long at the fair.

He promised he'd buy me a fairing should please me,
And then for a kiss, oh! he vowed he would tease me,
He promised he'd bring me a bunch of blue ribbons,
To tie up my bonny brown hair.

Annie had been hoping for more than blue ribbons when she'd gone to meet Michael last night. He seemed to have been hoping for the same. And now she'd left him waiting, perhaps forever.

Instead of ribbons, I had brought with me a few of the silk forget-me-nots from the bunch we'd tucked into her hatband yesterday. I tossed the flowers. The wind carried them up and away until I lost them against the sky. I wiped my eyes, blew my nose, then turned to begin my search of the deck.

I mentally recreated the scene as it would have looked in the dim light last night. Annie would have stood on the port side of the deck, where she could watch the route Michael would take. I crossed to the likely spot and put my hands where hers might have been. Whoever joined her must have come down the starboard side, otherwise she would have seen him—them?—coming. She must have heard or sensed a movement, despite the wind in the rigging and the rumbling engine below. She would have plucked the hatpin from her head as she turned.

I searched for the hatpin with my eyes first, exploring the nooks and crannies of the space, noting the deck's conformation, looking for hiding places. I began with the broad view, then focused as if I were looking through successive lenses of a microscope. 5-power... 10-power... 20-power... Found nothing.

I suddenly realized that not only was Annie's hatpin missing, but so was her handbag. It was not in our cabin, nor had it been recovered by searchers last night. I mentally emptied the small drawstring purse she always carried on her left wrist. A few coins: American, British, and Chinese. A small tablet of paper with a pencil for notes that I might dictate as we walked: things to do, things to remember. A white linen handkerchief I had embroidered with a fleur-de-lis for her last birthday. And a tiny phial of smelling salts.

For the first time I considered whether robbery might have been a motive in her disappearance, whether Annie's paltry belongings might have attracted the attention of someone with even less. A crew member, perhaps. If the attacker were after her bag, he would have brought a knife to cut the strings. And if a knife or the hatpin had drawn blood, there might be drops about.

Two Chinese sailors arrived, buckets and brushes in hand, to swab the deck. Their English was minimal. In pantomime, and with my guards' help, I requested that the cleaning be delayed until I finished my search, and I enlisted the sailors for my quest. I opened my notebook and quickly reproduced the hatpin drawing I'd made for the captain. I removed the lapis pin from my hat to show them the length of the needle. Then I drew a quick sketch of Annie's bag. They nodded, setting down their buckets with thumps that sloshed water onto the deck. I gestured to them to follow me to the aft portion of the deck. After more gestures and nods from me, the sailors dropped to their knees and began crawling over the rough boards.

Returning to the railing, I searched for traces of a violent altercation. A yard from where I'd been standing earlier, something dark and viscous had splashed the lower part of the railing and dripped down like dark honey to collect in the crease where the horizontal deck met the vertical railing. I dug in the join with my hatpin, and came up with a crumbly, damp, sorrel-colored substance. Sniffed it. Blood. Too much blood for a hatpin's work.

I took two deep, slow breaths. I wanted to sink onto the deck and allow the import to overwhelm me. But I could hear Annie's voice telling me to get on with it.

I turned back to the stain. Annie must have been stabbed with a knife and then, as there was no blood trail to suggest otherwise, lifted or shoved over the railing. The evidence couldn't prove the statement of the witness who'd reported seeing a woman fall, but the scenario seemed likely.

The deckhands continued their crawling search. I stood still, looking for places that might have captured a pin or purse flung or inadvertently cast off by Annie—or by her attacker. Movement in the shadows on the port side drew my eye. Phineas.

"Uncle P. I'm glad to see you up and about."

He moved out of the shadows to the port rail. The low light touched russet and gold strands in his dark brown hair. As I crossed to his side, he tugged his white neckerchief up to cover his nose and mouth. He looked like a clean, well-dressed version of a frontier bandit.

The neckerchief moved as he smiled, guessing my thoughts. The smile lit his eyes—striking eyes, the intense violet-blue of irises. Uncle P was as handsome as my father had been plain.

"It takes more than a bad night to keep me from my sunrise promenade," he said, the neckerchief muffling his voice. "Gives the steward a chance to straighten my cabin."

Walking before dawn also meant he wouldn't encounter other passengers.

Phineas cleared his throat and swallowed. "I presume you're looking for the hatpin? I caught the last part of your instructions to the hands."

So, he'd been there a while, keeping well out of sight. "The hatpin, Annie's purse, or perhaps a knife," I said. "She was stabbed, I think. I found..." I squeezed my eyes shut. Felt a hand on my shoulder.

"Stay here," he said softly. "I'll find it."

The hand dropped away. Soft footsteps moved off.

48

When I opened my eyes, he was bent over the stained rail. I looked out at the white-tipped waves. *My bonnie lies over the ocean*, sang a voice in my head. My father's baritone. "No," I corrected. "Anne Bonney lies *under* the ocean."

"Pardon?"

"Nothing. I'd better get back to my search."

Phineas put his hands behind his back and strolled over to peruse the lines tied to a mast. I aimed for the anchors with their coils of chain. The hollow centers of the massive links could hide an armory of small weapons. In one link I glimpsed a shape that was out of place.

Thirty seconds later I extricated the hatpin, unbroken, from its hiding place. Sunlight made the gold flakes in the glass bead shimmer. Blood traces, red-brown and dry, stained the lower inch of the shaft.

I handed the hatpin, wrapped in my handkerchief, to Phineas. He showed it to the guards and asked them to fetch the captain. They delegated to a deck hand.

While we waited, Phineas and I sat with our backs against the bulkhead. I sketched the after deck, marking the salient features, comforted by the act of drawing.

"Your mother was wearing that pin the day your father and I met her," Phineas said. "It was a gift from her father when she left for Paris. It had been his grandmother's, he told her, one of the few pieces of family jewelry to survive the Reign of Terror."

I leaned my head on his shoulder. I didn't have to say that I missed her, nor did he. We were silent, both of us, I surmised, recalling the times and places we'd spent with her. The good times. Phineas had loved her as much as my father and I had, though in a different way. Their friendship began in Paris, when she was studying art and botany at the Sorbonne and Phineas and my father were attending the École des Mines.

My mother told me she had discovered at a young age that art allows a quiet person to hide in plain sight. People ignore a woman with an easel. She becomes part of the scenery. They focus on the painting or sketch, not the artist herself. A woman alone is a curiosity. A woman with a sketchbook has a reason for being anywhere. I'd proved last night how true that was.

"You saw the blood on the pin," I said.

"How not?"

"What does it tell you?"

He opened my handkerchief to expose the pin and thought for a moment. "I think that either someone was waiting for Annie, someone followed her to this point, or she stumbled into a situation. It was dark, she was dressed in clothes you'd worn, and she could easily have been confused for you. I think that the splatter on the rail is her blood, and the blood on the hatpin is from her assailant. But how we'll find the perpetrator among the many crew and passengers on the ship, I don't know."

"Short of having them strip," I said, "neither do I. But perhaps the doctor might have some ideas. And if we spread the word that we're looking for someone who was scratched by a hatpin, then perhaps other passengers will help us narrow the search."

"Good idea." He refolded the handkerchief around the pin and handed it back to me.

"Did you talk to Toru last night?" I asked.

"No, the draught the doctor gave me put me right out. I didn't even hear Toru return to his cabin."

"You look better," I said. "There's color in your cheeks. And you seem to breathe more easily in the sea air."

"But I dread what will happen when we reach the fog of San Francisco."

"Then we must find you a sanitarium. Somewhere dry. Denver, perhaps. Or Arizona Territory."

"As long as it's near whatever school you attend. Otherwise, without you and Toru around, life will be quite boring."

"Toru will be picking up the slack in the company, doing the work of three. I doubt that we'll see much of him till things settle down."

The captain approached, walking briskly. He looked drawn. Even his mustache drooped.

I stood, brushed off my skirt, and helped Phineas up.

"You found something?" the captain said. His voice held a dubious note. He looked at Phineas, but I answered by leading the captain to the splotched wood on the deck and railing, still masked by morning shadow.

"Does this railing area line up with the place below where the deck hand saw Annie fall?"

"I will check."

I displayed the hatpin. Pointed to the anchor chain that had hidden it. Showed the captain the blood on the needle. Explained what Phineas and I thought had happened last night.

He nodded. "I think we can halt the onboard search for Miss Bonney. Now we must focus on protecting you and finding the culprit."

"And discovering why."

"Yes. My sincerest condolences on the loss of your friend, Miss Rees."

My eyes clouded. I always found adversity easier to deal with than kindness. "Thank you, sir." I handed him the handkerchief. "I will need the hatpin back when we reach port. It's a family heirloom."

"Of course."

I opened my notebook to the detailed, labeled, and self-explanatory sketch of the after deck. "For your official inquiry and report," I said. "The drawing's not to scale, but should suffice. Although I recommend you sign and date it as I have, to confirm that I accurately located the blood splashes and the area from which we recovered the hatpin."

He stared at me for a long moment before taking the sketchbook, visually inspecting the fidelity of my work, and signing the drawing. He tore out the page and handed back the book. "I won't rest until I discover who did this."

"Nor will I, Captain. I'll be in my quarters or with my guardians should you need me. And I'd very much appreciate updates as to how the investigation is proceeding."

He straightened, frowned, but said only, "As you wish, Miss Rees."

The seamen began scrubbing the deck and railing. I watched the captain, head bent as if in deep thought, proceed down the starboard side and melt away into the morning light.

We hadn't found Annie's purse. I showed the deckhands the drawing again, and then my guards started Phineas and me back toward the cabins. I couldn't read Uncle P's thoughts, but I suspected he was pondering how Annie's absence might affect the future of the company. I contemplated my own future.

I was at a pivot point in life. There is freedom in choosing a new course. But what course should I choose? What compass direction? I must decide with care, for the direction, once chosen, could not be reversed.

My personal freedom was limited. As he lay in hospital, my father and I had submitted my request for legal emancipation under California law. Our lawyer should have received the paperwork weeks ago and filed it with the courts. Yet, even if my request were granted, I would still be required to have a guardian until I reached my majority. Six years to go. *Six years.* Unless I married. It was legal to marry at fifteen in some states. But that would mean handing my inheritance and my independence over to someone else. I might be at a pivot point, but marriage wasn't a solution I'd entertain.

"Six years isn't forever, Keri," Phineas said, reading my thoughts. "It's just the next step in forever, however long or short that may be. So you might as well spend the time working at something you like."

"How do I narrow it down? How did you choose geology?"

"I liked rocks. I loved climbing peaks and exploring caves and mine workings. They were all around me in Cornwall, Devon, and Wales, where I grew up."

"I thought you were from Edinburgh?"

"I was born in Perthshire, actually. My mother's home. But my da was a mine supervisor. I first met your father in Wales—ran into Glen when I was exploring an old tin works. We decided it was more fun to go exploring together."

"Safer, too."

"There is that, lass." He smiled. "You're practical, like your mother."

"I've been thinking about Father lately," I said.

"Might have something to do with the urn in your cabin."

My father had made it clear early on, when he thought he would die from his injuries, that he preferred his remains return home as ashes. Luckily, unlike in the States, that was the mandated form of disposal for the dead in Tokyo prefecture. Toru had made the arrangements with one of the private companies that served the area. Toru, Phineas, and I together had chosen the brass ginger jar that would carry Papa's remains across the ocean.

"You haven't told anyone?" Anxiety made my voice rise.

He shook his head. "No need to feed people's superstitions."

"It's just, well, I like having the urn near me. Annie understood, or pretended she did." She had made the sign of the cross every time she entered the cabin.

I pictured my father as I'd seen him last—intelligent and talented, but nondescript. Brownish-black hair with auburn highlights. Eyes the color of lignite coal. Clean shaven face, when most men sported facial hair. He could change his appearance with ease when he needed to— add a mustache, muttonchops, a full beard. He could walk erect and stretch to his full five feet nine, wear lifts and boots that took him to six feet, or slouch, whiten his hair, wear a cap, and put on a local dialect, passing for a laborer. He was a natural actor, a chameleon, who drew people to him, effortlessly. I'd seen surly strangers open up to him, painfully shy women blossom. He had a gift. I'd studied him, trying to decipher his secret. But it was like catching sunlight in a bottle.

I liked to collect and sort and label the things I encountered. It helped me understand the world. Glen Rees hadn't fit neatly into any box except "*Homo sapiens*: Male; Sabine de Keridec's husband; Keridec's father." That used to be enough. It wasn't anymore. It didn't explain his magic.

"I miss him too, Keri. Deeply," Phineas said. "So does Toru." He watched the emotions play across my face. "It's no great mystery, lass," he said in his Welsh singer's voice, rich and warm and full-bodied even through the covering of his neckerchief. "Glen listened. He paid attention. He looked you in the eye. At that moment, you were the most important person or thing in the world, and what you were saying was important. You mattered. In a world that's constantly knocking us down, it's like water in the desert when someone listens, really listens. People told Glen all manner of private things. He never even had to ask."

Phineas dabbed at his forehead with a clean square of linen. "But it was more than just the listening, I think. Your da had a talent for making friends. People wanted to be *with* him. He loved to go adventuring, and they trusted that nothing could happen as long as he was in the lead." Phineas stopped. A shadow of pain slid across his face. He was thinking, I knew, of the ascent of Mount Fuji, when everything had gone wrong. "So unlike Glen," he said.

"He wasn't alone, Uncle P. Toru was with him."

"Not when the accident happened. Glen stopped to examine an outcrop and make some notes. Toru went ahead to the way station to arrange for a meal."

My father had told me that the trail would not open to pilgrims and climbers for a few days. The conditions were icy up top, and parts of the trail hadn't been checked. The men at the bottom thought the way stations were staffed, but there was some doubt as to whether or not they'd accommodate climbers.

"But Father would have planned for adversity. He was always prepared."

"They carried food and water. They would have been fine. But a cup of hot tea is welcome when the wind blows cold, as it was blowing that day. It was just ill luck that when the earthquake hit, they were apart."

Phineas and I hadn't discussed that day. He'd been so sick, and talking was such an effort, that I'd relied on a sketchy description from Toru. My father was no help. His memory was hazy, at best, as he'd been concussed, disoriented, and suffering from shock when Toru found him. Toru had had his hands full just keeping my father alive until help could reach them.

"When Glen was safely in hospital and Toru had

alerted you about the accident, he came to my room," Phineas said. "One thing was bothering him. The shaking seemed to be short, sharp, and extremely focused. No foreshocks or aftershocks."

"But enough of a jolt to cause a rockslide."

"A small one. With Glen right in its path. Thank God, Toru returned in time to pull him out."

I hadn't known that the earthquake was localized. Or that Toru wasn't with my father. I had an ugly feeling in the pit of my stomach that had nothing to do with the faint roll of the ship. "You and Toru think someone could have targeted my father. But how could anyone have known that they were climbing Mount Fuji that morning—known enough in advance, so they could purchase explosives and set up a trap?"

"A spy among the Nakagawa staff?"

"It's possible, I suppose. Did Toru question them?"

"All but one of the stable lads. He took sick and died about that time."

"So, a dead end."

"Literally."

I smiled in spite of myself. "Well, we've lots to discuss with Toru. How about breakfast in my cabin."

He nodded. "Twenty minutes?"

"I'll ask Ah Jim to order two more trays."

Chapter 7

MY *GUARDIANS AND I* sat around the small table in my cabin. I pushed away my barely touched breakfast plate, refilled my coffee cup, and said, "I need your help solving a minor problem."

"Minor?" Toru looked at Phineas.

"I'll need a lady's maid or companion for the remainder of the voyage."

Phineas sighed with relief. He must have thought some new catastrophe lurked in the wings, or that he'd have to explain "female issues." He said, "Can't you manage on your own for the next ten days?"

"Just dressing in these cursed clothes requires two people. And a single girl can't very well wander about the ship alone. Besides, I promised Mama I'd abide by convention, or as much as I was able. Annie served that function. As luck would have it, we suited each other."

"How about the stewardess?" Toru suggested.

"She'll do in a pinch, but I can't monopolize her time. She's attending to thirteen other women who are traveling without their maids."

"We should be able to find someone on a ship this size," Phineas said. "There must be two hundred women in Third Class."

"But how many are single?" I asked. "I suspect most of them have family commitments, or lack wardrobes necessary to interact with First-Class passengers. I wouldn't want her to feel out of place."

"I know of someone who might be appropriate," Toru said. "On an interim basis. Her grandfather represented my father's company in Shanghai."

Phineas straightened and set down his cup so briskly it landed on the edge of the saucer. Toru caught it. Phineas choked out a single syllable. "No."

My Bonney Lies Under

"It would be the easiest solution," Toru said. He ran thumb and forefinger down the crease in his trousers, face expressionless.

"You trust her?" Phineas asked.

"*Hé là*! I'm still here, gentlemen."

They started, shifted, and watched me with what seemed equal wariness on both their faces. I touched Uncle P's sleeve. "You know this young woman?"

"I've met her." The words seemed pulled from him.

"But you find her unsuitable."

"Not exactly."

I waited.

"We'll discuss it later, lass." The hybrid Scots-Welsh accent thickened. His ruddy skin flushed a darker red. He ran a hand through his short hair, erasing the neat center part.

Phineas could handle feuding mine workers, break miles of trail through a jungle, or fend off raiding parties of local bandits. He was a demanding science tutor, teacher of games, and now, guardian. But, except for my mother, he'd never been comfortable dealing with women. Girls, yes. Girls were a different species, and we'd always gotten on well. But suddenly he was looking at me as if I'd metamorphosed into something he didn't know how to manage.

"The subject is on the table. The relevant decision-makers are present," I said, voice soft as cotton-wrapped steel. "I propose we discuss it now."

"I second the motion," Toru said.

Phineas simultaneously shook his head and shrugged. "Her name is Hsu Lin."

I pronounced "Shoe Lin" back to him. When Toru nodded, I said, "Chinese." If that were the issue, I didn't see a problem. Unless she couldn't speak English, French, or Spanish.

"Eurasian," Toru said. "Her father was British."

"I haven't seen anyone like that aboard."

"She travels with a companion. They keep to themselves."

"Was she able to get a visa because she's part European?" The Chinese Exclusion Act of three years ago

57

had made it nearly impossible for Chinese natives to immigrate to America.

Toru frowned and twisted the jade signet ring he wore. "She is betrothed to a merchant in San Francisco. The wives of merchants are exempt. And yes, she speaks fluent English."

I looked from him to Phineas. "There's something you aren't telling me."

They studied their respective fingernails as if they held the secret of turning dross into gold.

"Does it have something to do with my father's business?" A reasonable guess.

Toru glanced at Phineas. This was progress.

"I'm a partner, a *full* partner, and an equal shareholder in the company. I've been involved with *all* my father's business decisions for the past two years. I know I'm a minor and that my age poses legal complications. We'll sort all that out once we reach San Francisco. But in the meantime, I propose we proceed with company matters as we've done since my father was injured."

More glances exchanged. Phineas yielded first. "She will find out soon enough, Toru, once she examines the books."

The books. My mind raced through all the possibilities, the ways the company might be connected with this Hsu Lin. I did not suspect that either Phineas or Toru had been involved with her. Their relationship was like that of an old married couple—solid and supportive, even when they were separated for long periods. Which left only one partner.

"Are you saying that my father had an affair with her?" This was not inconceivable. My father had been widowed for two years.

"Not exactly," Phineas repeated. He coughed into his handkerchief, giving himself time to find the words.

Toru rescued him. "Glen had a liaison with Hsu Lin's mother."

"It was years ago, before your parents wed," Phineas added. "Your father was working in Shanghai. He left China before Hsu Lin's mother discovered she was expecting. She died soon after childbirth."

It dawned on me, belatedly, why my guardians were uncomfortable with the subject of this girl. Hsu Lin was my half-sister.

"Hsu Lin is Eurasian, and hence impure," Toru said. "Her grandfather wished her exposed on the mountain. But her grandmother rescued her and sent word to Glen through my family. Your father agreed to pay for her care and education."

I moved to my berth and lay back, staring sightlessly overhead. This, on top of Annie's disappearance, was too much to absorb. My words tinged with wonder, I said, "Papa didn't think I needed to know."

"Not then. Perhaps not ever," Phineas said. "Glen and I slipped away to meet her when we were in Shanghai last year. Glen had to decide what would happen after she left school."

"*You* didn't think I needed to know?" No response. I persisted. "How old is she?"

"Seventeen."

This time I initiated the silence. Minutes ago I'd been an orphan, my only close relative a grandmother who had shown me no love. I felt confused, unsure how to react to this news of a half-sister only two years older than myself.

I knew that my father had made trips to the Orient long before I was born. He evaluated mine prospects, but also mined the areas for information of import to the governments of Britain and America. He had closed the door on that part of his past, seldom speaking of it, at least to me. But now that door had opened a crack.

My father's liaison with Hsu Lin's mother occurred before he and my mother reunited. Father had proposed to Sabine de Keridec when she visited him and Phineas in Freiburg. She wasn't ready to marry. He'd finished his studies and ventured to America to begin practicing his science with Phineas. But Glen and Sabine had continued their correspondence. When exploration opportunities had beckoned from Asia, he'd sailed west again. Which is why he was in Shanghai when my mother reconsidered his proposal and recalled him to San Francisco. After that, they were rarely apart. Even in my oldest memories, my family had travelled together.

I broke the silence. "Did my mother know?"

"I do not think so," Toru said. Phineas shook his head in support. But neither man was convincing.

Perhaps my mother had decided that the entire family should travel together precisely because she knew about Hsu Lin. And now I wondered: Were there other Hsu Lins in the circum-Pacific region or elsewhere? My father had studied and worked in Europe and crisscrossed America. I thought I'd known him. But I suspected no child ever knows her parents.

Toru poured another round of coffee and brought me a cup. We all sipped as I worked my way through a maze of emotions toward a solution to my original problem.

I shrugged, finally, and swung my feet onto the deck. "I have no other blood family— except a few distant cousins in Europe and my dear grandmama." I winced. My guardians smiled. "I might as well make this young woman's acquaintance. But please, do not tell her that I know about her relationship with my father. Let each of us learn about the other and draw our own conclusions. Once we reach San Francisco, we can part ways. Or not. That will be up to us. You say that she is getting married once we reach the States?"

"Her grandfather betrothed her to a widower," Toru said. "An importer. Much older, but well established, and willing to accept a woman of mixed blood. Chinese women are scarce as swan's teeth in America. Hsu Lin's grandfather hoped that she might have a better life there. Glen agreed."

"And he could keep track of her in San Francisco, perhaps see her occasionally."

"It would be like him," Phineas said.

"Does Hsu Lin wish this arranged marriage?"

"She was not consulted," said Toru.

May I never be in that position.

"I foresee a problem with Miss Hsu." Phineas slipped into his guardian's role. "She's only seventeen, and not married. Not old enough to act as an adult companion for an underage young woman."

I hadn't considered that. Nor had Toru. In China, girls were often married and became mothers quite young. That would have been suitable. Two underage single women was not.

"Her companion may have to join you," Toru said.

"The companion—what's her name?"

"Wei Xi." Toru didn't refer to notes or search his memory.

"My cabin's too small for three people."

"That's putting the cart before the horse." Phineas pulled up a fold of the scarf to cover his mouth and nose. "If Hsu Lin agrees to help us, we'll figure out the space problem."

"I'll meet them later this morning, if you can arrange it, Toru—unless, by some miracle, Annie appears in the meantime. It's only been a few hours."

"I will bring Miss Hsu here at ten thirty," Toru said.

That would give me over an hour to relax and change. "Fine. And after lunch let's hold a business meeting. We have much to discuss, especially given the events of last night."

My guardians frowned in unison.

"I must look to the future," I said. "If something happens to me, my third of the company would go to my grandmother. I won't have it. I need to hunt up someone who can draft a will for me without delay."

Phineas started several sentences, each one unfinished.

"I met someone," Toru said. "I will approach her."

"A woman lawyer?"

Toru smiled. "There are a few. Mrs. Phoebe Hartfield practices law in San Francisco."

"Perfect. Please explain the circumstances to her. And if she's inclined to assist me, invite her to the meeting."

Toru raised one eyebrow. "Which circumstances would those be, exactly?"

He was right. We needn't share everything about my complex situation with a prospective lawyer. Better to be precise—and simple.

"Please tell Mrs. Hartfield only that I require her help to protect my assets in the event that I do not survive the voyage to San Francisco."

"If you're looking to intrigue her," Phineas said, "that should do it."

Chapter 8

ALONE FOR THE FIRST time in hours, and functioning on only a thimbleful of sleep, I foundered. Exhaustion washed over me like a wave striking a ship. Too much noise, too many events and decisions assaulting me from all sides. I felt young, vulnerable, and not up to the tasks that lay ahead. I suppose I wanted my father to magically return and wrap his arms around me. Phineas needed to keep his distance. Toru was reticent by nature. Neither could fill my father's role.

Well, I could take a long nap later. For now, forty minutes of rest would have to suffice.

* * *

When I awoke, the morning air had grown hot and close, as if a storm were brewing. Shedding my wrinkled travel clothes, I washed, changed into a light frock of black linen (no corset), brushed and wove my hair into two long braids, and wrapped them around the crown of my head. Checking my reflection in the mirror, I straightened my shoulders, opened the door, and asked my new guard to accompany me to the library. He seemed grateful for the exercise. Protecting a young woman's door could be stultifying, I imagined.

"It's just you, then?" I said as we walked. "Early this morning there were two guards."

"We'll double up tonight. Miss Bonney went missing after dark."

The translated *Works of Virgil* still sat on the library shelf. Not surprising. Back in my cabin was my father's copy of *The Aeneid*, in Latin. I had read aloud to him, translating orally, while he was in hospital, and had continued the project with Toru and Phineas. We were determined I should finish Book XII by the time we reached port. Now, I wanted to see how my own translation compared with the experts from Oxford and Cambridge.

Virgil wasn't the author of choice on Pacific voyages. I took a few minutes to slit uncut pages with the dangling knife. My guard picked up an old copy of *St. Nicholas Magazine*, a popular children's monthly, and followed me in silence back to my cabin.

The door was ajar. The guard stepped in front of me and pushed it open. A young woman stood at the dressing table, her back to us. She seemed to be alone.

"Miss Hsu?" I said over the guard's shoulder.

As she turned to face us, the young woman's left hand slipped into the pocket of the long, high-collared jacket she wore over matching black trousers. Coiled buttons like crimson butterflies rested along her left collarbone. The lightweight, raw silk was free of embroidery, as if she, too, mourned the loss of our father.

Despite the ensemble, she looked more European than Asian, and I wondered if her mother had also been Eurasian. Our father's heritage was clear in the high forehead, the small hump on the bridge of a delicate nose, the faint dusting of freckles, the auburn lights in her hair. A few locks—wavy tendrils, not straight—had escaped the twisted figure eight at the back of her head. She'd inherited our father's curls, too.

To her Chinese friends and classmates, those waves would have set her apart and triggered ridicule. I wondered if she'd reacted by trying to pass for European. If so, that wasn't the case now.

"I am Hsu Lin," she said, taking a step toward me.

I slipped around the guard into the room. "Please put back whatever you, er, borrowed, Miss Hsu."

Perhaps if I'd held out my hand for the purloined objects, she might have protested her innocence. I'll never know. A slight frown of calculation touched the area between her brows, and then she did an about-face to the dresser. I heard the clink of heavy gold meeting porcelain. My father's signet ring.

"Miss Hsu's visit was arranged," I said to the guard.

He nodded and shut the door as he exited. I advanced into the room. "And the other."

Her back stiffened. From her left pocket she took a square jadeite pendant, carved with a dragon on both sides. The pendant dangled from a necklace of alternating beads of rose quartz and aventurine. The necklace joined the other jewelry in the dish.

"I'm Keridec Rees. I didn't expect to find you here alone."

Again, that frown, this time reflected in the mirror. I didn't know why she'd risked pinching my jewelry when she had far more expensive adornments in her hair. Exquisite butterflies, carved from palest jade, sat atop her hairpins.

I extended my hand and waited for her to cross the cabin. Lin was shorter than I by half a foot, with finer bones and a grace I'd never possess. She moved like my grandmother did, more akin to a glide than a series of steps. A dancer. I suspected she could have carried a glass of water on her head across two miles of rough terrain and not spilled a drop.

Her hand brushed mine, a feather's touch, but enough for me to sense the coldness in her. Whatever feelings she had would be locked down tight.

"I expected Dr. Nakagawa would be here with you and your companion," I said. "Why don't you ask her to come out and introduce herself."

Hsu Lin's eyes flicked to the folding wood and bamboo screen that created a private dressing area. Annie had draped her green shawl over the top. She hadn't needed it last night. She'd had my hat and coat.

My energy drained away. My heartbeats slowed. I didn't want anyone near Annie's things. I didn't want to share our cabin. Annie was still here, and I needed her to be here, just as I needed my father's ashes, sitting in their brass urn under my berth. I wasn't ready for a new companion. I must find another solution to the propriety demanded by a rigid system.

Reflection dulled my senses. Wei Xi stood close, half

of her thick body between Lin and me. I hadn't heard her move.

I shook myself like a dog emerging from a pond and focused my attention on the companion. This was no kindly *chaperone* such as I'd known in Mexico or South America, more formal companion than active protector. Quite the contrary. She reminded me of an oak barrel—round, squat, and banded with iron. I couldn't judge her age—somewhere between forty and sixty. Black eyes glittered below lids with strong epicanthic folds. A malevolent energy came off her in waves. But perhaps it was only fear of a situation she didn't understand.

I could see no family resemblance to Hsu Lin, whether in stature, carriage, or bone structure. A family retainer, perhaps. Or a watchdog sent by the intended bridegroom, worried his young fiancée might have second thoughts once free of her homeland.

"How did you know?" Hsu Lin asked.

"My guardians would never have left you here alone. And your companion wouldn't have allowed you to accompany Dr. Nakagawa without her."

I brought my hands together over my midriff and gave a slight formal bow to the older woman. I didn't know her marital status, so I omitted a title. "You must be Wei Xi."

She hesitated before returning the gesture, her body taut as stretched wire.

Lin, behind Xi's shoulder, made a slight grimace that Wei Xi missed. There was no love lost between them. The next ten days looked to be a dismal stretch.

"Does your companion speak English, Miss Hsu?"

"She does not," Lin said.

"Parlez-vous français?" I tried, my eyes fixed on Wei Xi's.

Not a flicker of response. I repeated it in Spanish and Japanese. I had only a smattering of Japanese phrases at my disposal, compliments of months spent in Tokyo, but I was curious to see how linguistically adept she was.

"My companion and I communicate in Wu or Mandarin. I will, of course, translate for you."

Which meant that I wouldn't know if my intent had

been conveyed correctly.

A knock at the door. I opened it to find the cabin steward with a tray of tea, coffee, and the ubiquitous biscuits. Toru stood behind him. "I apologize for my late arrival. Phineas needed me to make up more cough syrup."

"Will he be joining us?" I asked.

"He wishes to rest until our afternoon meeting."

The late night and strenuous morning must have taken their toll.

Ah Jim set the tray on the table, pulled the table out from the bulkhead, and set the stool from the dressing table on the fourth side. He gave a short bow, and sidled from the room.

I invited everyone to sit. Toru moved his chair back from the table a little way to give him room to cross his legs. The action also served to place him in the background. He was as good as saying that the interview was in my hands.

When we'd settled ourselves, I poured black tea into four white porcelain cups emblazoned with the *Oceanic*'s name and passed them round. I offered Hsu Lin a biscuit. Breaking bread together was both symbolic and practical, a sign of peace and community. An overture.

"Thank you, but I have eaten."

I waited her out. Her eyes—opaque, impenetrable, watchful—reminded me of a speckled cobra I'd once seen. But Hsu Lin's irises showed flecks of gold. Like mine. Like our father's. At last, she took a biscuit, broke it in two, and placed the halves in her saucer. Token acceptance.

Suddenly I was ravenous. I dipped a cookie in my tea, demolished it in three small bites, and took another. I said, "I understand your grandfather is acquainted with the Nakagawas."

"Yes. Our families have done business for generations." She spoke with only the faintest trace of an accent. "I come from a long line of silk merchants. We produce and export the finest cloth in Shanghai."

"Yet your family approved of your marrying a man so far away."

"My mother's father believes that my marriage will help our business interests in America."

"Establish *la prise pour le pied*, a toehold, as it were."

"No need to translate, Miss Rees. I speak French. And no, I will not be the first of my family to immigrate to America. My mother's brother opened a shop in San Francisco some years ago. My family provides the cloth that the Chinese tailors and seamstresses turn into clothing, curtains, and linens."

Her voice throughout this recitation was soft and expressionless. She had been sold to further the family business, putting her education to good use. Perhaps her family saw it as a return on my father's investment. Her Eurasian heritage and looks, however beautiful they might be to my eyes, would have been reminders of her mother's lapse in judgment. Or so I surmised.

"You have no brothers or sisters in Shanghai?"

She searched my face to see how much I knew of her story. When I gave a little shake of the head, she said, "My mother died three days after I was born. I was cared for in a Eurasian orphanage until your father... *our* father... was made aware of my existence. I was five when he entrusted my education to the nuns."

Somehow, the knowledge that my father had been unaware of her existence during her early years but had accepted the responsibility for educating her resolved my emotional confusion over learning I had a sister. We had both suffered tragedies, hers much more severe than mine. I would have to trust that we would come to accommodate this new relationship.

I moved to safer ground. "How many languages do you speak?"

"Mandarin, English, and French, as I said. Several dialects of Wu. And I can make myself understood in Spanish and Portuguese, although I am not fluent."

"Japanese?"

"A little." In French, she added, "If you wish to converse privately with me in front of my companion, I suggest speaking French. She knows a few words. Not many."

"*Bon*. There are things I will wish to ask you."

"And I, you."

I continued in French. "As you are here, I assume you are considering accepting a position as my paid companion for the duration of the voyage."

She smiled for the first time. "It would be a welcome change."

"Then what prefix should I use with your companion's name?"

"She never married, and is no relation to me. But she is my intended's sister, so I call her Honorable Aunt Xi."

"Where is your cabin?"

"Saloon, starboard side."

A few years ago, Asians would have been relegated to Third Class accommodations. This separation still applied below decks to the less affluent of all nationalities, but wealthy Asians could now book First Class cabins. The recent restrictions on Chinese immigration to the United States meant that only a few holding visas—such as wealthy merchants and those born in the United States—could disembark at American ports.

I drained the tepid tea from my cup. "Practically speaking, my cabin is too small for three adults. If you choose to act as my companion for the rest of the journey, would you and Miss Wei consider moving to a cabin closer to mine to facilitate the arrangement?"

"I would accept even a slightly smaller cabin, as long as it is on the port side."

The portholes on this side faced north on the journey home, and received shade for part of the day, even in high summer.

I turned to Toru for the first time. "Would you or Mr. Quade check with the purser about the availability of nearby cabins? One large enough for Miss Wei and Miss Hsu to share? I would, of course, recompense anyone who agreed to move to accommodate our needs."

"Of course. Excuse me for a moment." Toru stood and went out, leaving the cabin door open so the guard could keep an eye on me.

While we waited for Toru, I dumped the tepid tea from the cups into the sink, lifted the cozy from the teapot, and refilled the cups.

A rap on the open door announced the purser.

"Mr. and Mrs. Small, the young couple next door, wish a bigger cabin, even if it's on the starboard side," he said. "They are willing to exchange cabins with Miss Hsu and Miss Wei—after it's been thoroughly cleaned, of course."

Lin stiffened. The purser didn't notice.

"The Smalls accepted your kind offer to pay for the upgrade. However, considering the circumstances, the shipping line will bear the costs."

"I'm most grateful, sir," I said, surprised by the offer.

"The doors don't connect, Miss Rees, but you can pound on the bulkhead beside your berth in an emergency—or signal the guard outside your door."

I'd be alone, yet appease convention. A most satisfactory solution.

"Is the plan acceptable?" I asked Lin.

She conferred with Wei Xi, then said, "It is acceptable."

"To me also," I told the purser. "But I must receive my guardians' approval. Please tell the Smalls that I will give them a firm answer within the hour. And thank them for their flexibility."

The purser gave a brisk nod and left us.

"As my guardians helped facilitate the move, seeking their approval is *pro forma*," I said to Lin. "So, I suggest you have your steward start packing your belongings. I'll instruct Ah Jim to store your things here until the cabin next door is cleaned—if that suits you."

"As you wish," Lin said. And giving me slight bows, Lin and Wei Xi left me.

The cabin seemed much larger once Wei Xi's intense energy was gone. She reminded me of a tarantula rearing back in defense, pedipalps waving. I wondered how Lin survived in that atmosphere.

I rang the bell for Ah Jim. Made my request. Received assurance that the packing and moving would be accomplished as soon as I received confirmation of the plan from my guardians. He bowed and turned to leave.

I stopped him with a final question. "Did you unlock the door for Miss Hsu and Miss Wei?"

"Yes, missy."

"On whose authority?"

"They say you ask for meeting. They do not wish to wait in passageway."

"In future, unless you have a note from me or my guardians, please do not let anyone in when I'm not here."

He bowed his assent and left me alone.

Chapter 9

11:33 a.m.

TORU HAD SENT WORD that Mrs. Hartfield agreed to meet with us at four o'clock for tea. But I needed to talk to my guardians within the hour.

The guard followed me silently down the passageway to their adjoining cabins. I heard muffled coughing as we approached. Toru answered the door to Phineas' cabin.

"I am well protected here," I told my guard. "And we shall be a while. You're welcome to take a break for fifteen minutes."

The sailor looked undecided, then said, "I'll take five. But I'll be in shouting distance, miss, never fear." He was gone almost before he finished speaking.

I took a seat at the table. Toru relaxed back into his customary armchair. Phineas lay on the berth, a clean cravat covering his mouth. A coughing fit convulsed him. Toru took a small lacquer case from a vest pocket, shook a pill into Phineas' palm, and poured him a glass of water from the pitcher on the table.

I'd accompanied Toru to the apothecary's shop near the Nakagawa family compound in the old part of Tokyo, the core of ancient Edo. We bought a pill press from the equally ancient druggist, and he showed us how to measure out the opium, press it into convenient travel doses, and even turn it into a syrup.

The coughing fit subsided. "Tell me about your meeting with Hsu Lin," Phineas croaked. "Toru sensed some tension, but he wasn't sure what caused it."

I lowered my voice, in case someone lingered outside the open porthole. "When I arrived, Hsu Lin appeared to be alone, awaiting my arrival. But I discovered Wei Xi hiding behind a screen. Ah Jim let them in. He told me they'd refused to wait in the hall for me. And no, Uncle P, I wasn't late. They were early. I found it... unsettling."

"Naturally. Was that all?"

I shook my head. "According to Lin, Xi doesn't speak English. Yet she appeared to understand most, if not all of what we discussed. How well do you know her, Uncle T?"

"I met her for the first time this morning. But we didn't speak."

"Well, I don't think Lin is close to her. I think Lin tolerates her because she must. And there's something else." I described Lin's pocketing of my father's signet ring and my mother's jade necklace.

It was as if something sucked all the air out of the room. The color drained from Uncle P's already pale face—the part that wasn't covered. He sank back against the cushions.

Toru jumped to his feet and took a step toward the door. I stood and put a hand on his arm. "I handled it. She replaced them. I gave her no choice."

"I'm amazed that she'd risk it," Phineas said. "She must have known you'd catch her."

"Not necessarily," I said. "I would have questioned Ah Jim first. And I wouldn't necessarily have believed him if he protested his innocence."

"I will have a word with her," Toru said.

"Please don't. I'd rather ask her about it later, when we're alone."

Toru frowned. "If you are sure."

"I'm sure of one thing: If I don't find a companion for what remains of the journey, my own freedom will be limited."

"We don't care," Phineas said, "as long as you reach port safely."

I leaned down and smoothed the hair back from his forehead. The skin felt hot. But that might be only a reflection of the humid air pouring in through the porthole. "And what happens if we reach port without discovering why Annie was attacked and who was responsible?" I said softly. "The passengers will disperse and we'll never find answers."

He sighed. "You'll give your jewelry to the purser."

"Yes." I resumed my seat. "And Lin will sign a contract that I'll draw up."

"But that will mean accepting Wei Xi," Toru said. "The fact that she chose to hide her presence troubles me."

"My father advised me to know my adversaries. Only then could I sort fact from fiction, friend from foe."

"Sound advice," Phineas said.

"Following his reasoning, you'll understand why I've asked Lin and Xi to pack their belongings. Ah Jim found that the couple in the next cabin is willing to exchange theirs for Lin's—for a mover's fee, of course." I smiled. "But the shipping line will pay for the upgrade. The cabins are close enough to satisfy convention... at least, in a broad sense."

"If you're positive this is what you want," Phineas said.

"The alternatives are no better. And I confess I'll be glad to put some distance between me and Mr. Small. When I think of how he treated Annie—" I looked down. Unclenched my hands. My fingernails had left sharp grooves in the palms.

My guardians exchanged glances. Questions silently asked and answered.

"You have our approval," Phineas said. "But Toru will talk to the captain about keeping a guard on your door."

"And someone to taste my food?" I was only half joking.

"I will look into it." Toru's tone was grim.

"At present, I think we can hold off on the food-tasting," Phineas said. Then to me, "Is that it, my dear, or do you have other concerns?"

"I was hoping for news about the investigation."

"Dr. Doyle stopped by. He said the officers continue to interview witnesses. That's all we know. I expect we'll receive an update this evening, when the captain's had time to compile the information."

"I'd like to attend."

"Of course."

"Excellent. Um, I have a few questions on a related subject, Uncle P, if you aren't too tired."

"I can rest later. What is it?"

"How and when did you learn that Hsu Lin was on board?"

Toru answered for him. "Ah Hong, the cabin attendant for Hsu Lin's section, delivered a letter just after we left Yokohama harbor. It was from Lin's grandfather. It bore his seal."

"A formal letter, then."

"Most formal. It said that his granddaughter was sailing to meet her betrothed in San Francisco, and it asked if, as a friend of longstanding, I would—" He stopped. Looked at Phineas. "No, that is not correct. He asked *us* to make sure that Lin was comfortable and had everything she needed. Which I did, the first afternoon."

"So," I said, digesting this new information. "Her grandfather knew you both were aboard, and presumably, that I was with you. Did he mention my father?"

"He wrote that he was 'sorry to hear of the death of your friend and partner, Mr. Gawain Glendower Rees.'"

My father's full name wasn't known to many.

Phineas anticipated my question. "You would expect the full name to be used on official documents. Which this wasn't. It read as if he didn't know Glen, or wasn't used to dealing with foreigners. Neither of which is true."

Toru said, "The letter stated that he had heard the sad news from one of my brothers."

"Of course you can't check that for weeks," I said.

"I have no reason to doubt that he signed the letter," Toru said. "Our families correspond regularly and frequently. And the request was a natural one."

"Yet presented in an odd way," I said. "Did the letter mention my father in relation to Lin?"

"The letter noted that Rees had been an honorable man who had not shied away from his duties to educate his daughter, Hsu Lin, and to provide her a chance at a better life. For that, he said, he would forever be in your father's debt. Or words to that effect."

Phineas struggled to sit up. I stood and tucked an extra pillow behind his shoulders. "Does the grandfather speak English?" he asked Toru.

"Some. But he has scribes and translators for his business letters."

"In this case, I think Lin stepped in," Phineas said. "She might be laying the groundwork for a suit against the estate—if she can find a jurisdiction that recognizes an illegitimate child is entitled to inherit. Keri's right to be wary."

"I think my father would have told me if he'd formally acknowledged her."

"I've seen nothing among his papers that even hints at it," Phineas said.

"Nor have I. Which may be why she tried to steal his signet ring. I'm betting she has a duplicate of that letter bearing her grandfather's seal."

"I'll burn our copy," Phineas said.

"It won't matter," Toru said. "There are witnesses who will swear they delivered it."

"Though that won't prove what the letter actually contained."

It was time for the noon meal, and I had decisions to deliver. "You know, I'm not against providing Lin with a settlement from my father's estate. At least not on principle. But if Lin, her family, or Wei Xi had anything to do with Annie's disappearance..."

"Don't worry," Phineas said. "Lin won't get a penny unless we're satisfied she had nothing to do with that. Not even then, if we feel she's attempted to manipulate us."

"I agree. And given what happened this morning, I'd prefer to keep Lin and her watchdog as far away from our business affairs as possible."

"That goes without saying, my dear. Is that it?" Phineas' voice sounded stretched and tired.

"For now. Have a quiet dinner and a nap. I'll see you both at tea."

I opened the door and found the guard in the passageway. He fell in behind me as I headed for my cabin.

A room of my own for the next ten days. It sounded like bliss. Annie, wonderful as she was, had one flaw. She snored like a sailor after a night ashore.

Chapter 10

12:22 p.m.

I **STOPPED AT AH** Jim's station on my way to my cabin and asked that he take messages to the Smalls and to Hsu Lin that my guardians had approved the cabin exchange. I also asked him to have a light lunch delivered. I was hungry. The biscuits and tea I'd shared hadn't made up for the barely touched breakfast.

The new guard waited by my door. His name tag read "Robie." He formally relieved my morning guard, opened the door for me, and said, "I checked it out, Miss Rees. All seems to be in order."

"Thank you, Mr. Robie."

"Just Robie, miss, if you don't mind." The Scots accent was stronger than with my morning guard. "Out" was "oot," "don't" was "doona."

I nodded. "You're welcome to borrow a chair from my cabin, Robie. You can guard my door as easily sitting, as standing."

"Captain wouldn't like it, miss."

"As you wish." My words echoed Lin's of an hour ago, but without the edge.

He closed the door behind me. This morning's ensemble had been taken away, presumably to be cleaned and pressed. I checked the jewelry in the dish on the dresser and in the silk case I kept in a drawer. All there. I'd half-expected Lin to double back and liberate the pieces she'd tried to steal before. Maybe she hadn't had time.

Robie in tow, I took the jewelry to the purser to store in the vault, and then continued on to the library. I'd seen that Mr. Arnold sometimes worked there, although the purser told me he also had a desk on the bridge.

I was in luck. "Mr. Arnold, sir, might I have a word?"

The pen wavered above the inkwell, then stilled. He took the quill between thumbs and forefingers and laid it carefully in the slot at the top of the desk. The pen rocked softly. He stilled it with the lightest touch. Beautiful fingers, I noticed—long and slender and as liberally stained with ink as my father's had been. And my mother's. Arnold stood, tugged his jacket straight, and faced me. "How may I help you, Miss Rees?"

"Last night you had a logbook or ledger in which you'd entered the comments of all the interviews you conducted among the passengers. I'd like to review a couple of the entries."

Arnold considered this for a moment. The steward rose and opened the porthole. Humid, salty air wafted in carrying the scents of cologne, pomade, and tobacco. Around me, the furniture was arranged much as it had been last night. But in the interim, someone had shifted the armchairs. I itched to restore them to order and a more pleasing configuration. Had the steward not been there, I might have done so.

"I believe the captain would find it a reasonable request," I added. "But if you'd prefer that I submit a formal letter..."

"That won't be necessary." Arnold pulled the ledger from a drawer in the desk and waited.

"Miss Hsu Lin and her companion, Miss Wei Xi. I don't know their cabin number, but it's on the starboard side of the First Class deck."

He turned pages and employed his ruler until he found the entries.

"Did they say they'd seen anything last night?" I asked. "They keep to their cabin, I understand, but they might have been taking a turn on deck after dark."

He caught my drift. As the only Chinese and Eurasian passengers in First Class, and perhaps on the entire ship, they might not feel entirely comfortable socializing with the European and American contingent. After nightfall, they would encounter fewer people.

Arnold called the steward over. "You interviewed Misses Hsu and Wei last night, Turner."

"In a manner of speaking, Mr. Arnold. The young one, Miss Hsu, never opened the door, see. Said she wasn't dressed to receive visitors, and that anyway, as a betrothed woman, she couldn't receive a man late at night. I told her that a passenger was missing, so we needed to check all the cabins and ask if anyone had seen Miss Bonney. But Miss Hsu wouldn't budge. Said they was afraid to open the door at night, no matter who it was. Claimed they'd et in their cabin, per usual, and hadn't been out all night. I checked with the galley. Two full chicken dinners, extra rice and vegetables."

"This interview was at half-past eleven?" Arnold asked.

"Yessir."

"And you heard only the one voice?"

"Yessir. A soft voice. No accent to speak of. I wouldn't have knowed she were Chinese, just by that."

So Wei Xi might have been out all night, and no one the wiser.

"Thank you, Turner," Arnold said.

"Did you also interview the Smalls, Mr. Turner?" I asked.

His eager helpfulness dropped off. "No, miss. They was on the port side, see."

"I understand. You've been most helpful, and I thank you."

Arnold skimmed the list in the ledger. "Mr. Small was interviewed at 11:45 p.m.," he said. "You learned the gist of it last night, correct?"

"Yes. But I understood they both were going to the games room after they saw Annie at the deck door. Were they interviewed in their cabin or in the card room?"

"Mr. Small was in the games room... with Mr. Lamb." He looked up. "Who also dined with the captain last night."

I didn't think I imagined the note of dislike in Arnold's voice. But I couldn't tell whether it was based on some knowledge of Lamb's nefarious history or an instinctive reaction to the man.

"I recall Mr. Lamb." An understatement. "And his presence at the captain's table means Lamb can provide an alibi for Mr. Small only *after* our party dispersed."

"Precisely. But this is strange. Mrs. Small was interviewed at 11:05 in her *cabin*."

That was about the time I was coming around from my first fainting spell. I hadn't been aware of what was going on in the passageway or the cabin next door. I said, "A surprisingly short game of draughts or whist, wouldn't you say?"

"We'll check that. The Smalls weren't interviewed a second time this morning. We're still working through the Third-Class passengers."

The investigation was going at a slug's pace. Frustrating. But Arnold's answers had suggested new lines of inquiry. Lamb and Small were acquaintances, at the very least. Perhaps Toru could sit in on a game tonight and see whether the friendship was deep or shallow.

"Thank you, Mr. Arnold."

"My pleasure, Miss Rees. We wish to understand what happened as much as you do, so please let me know if you have more questions."

Wanting to mull over the new information and pose a question or two to my half-sister, I took the long route back to my cabin. The starboard passageway was a mirror image of my own port side. Interior cabins on the left, exterior on the right. At the end of the corridor, a man disappeared around the corner into a short connecting passageway. His height, build, and dress reminded me of Mr. Small or Mr. Lamb. The Smalls' effects were being transferred to the larger starboard cabin. I wondered where Lamb's cabin was.

I'd never seen Gideon Lamb coming or going, nor heard his distinctive nasal, upper-crust accent in the port passageway. He was, my father had learned, from Baton Rouge, Louisiana, the son of an actress who worked a stretch of the Mississippi. He had grown up on riverboats—under another name, no doubt. The New England accent was new.

Robie and I made our way aft along the starboard passageway. Halfway down, a steward stood in the entrance to Hsu Lin's cabin, a tray in his left hand.

Whether he was coming or going, I couldn't say. He said something in Chinese, stopping mid-sentence when he sensed our approach.

"Hold on there," Robie called, and he brushed by me. He was tall and long-legged and covered the distance in a few strides.

The steward bent his head, swiveled toward us, and flicked the tray and its contents neatly at Robie, who flinched from the flying teapot, cups, and plates. The smaller man lunged forward. Light from a wall lamp flashed on metal.

"Watch out!" I yelled.

Robie reared back, colliding with me. A blade slid along the side of his chest, catching for a moment in the uniform cloth before slicing free. In that second, I leaned away. My left shoulder hit the bulkhead and I felt a burning, like hot iron, on my forearm. Robie snapped his elbow down to trap the man's hand. A dagger clattered to the wood near my feet.

The steward pulled away and fled down the passageway. At the end, he turned the corner and disappeared.

Robie took off after him, but stopped at the corner and looked back. I'd slid down the bulkhead till I was sitting on my heels "Go," I said.

He shook his head. He couldn't leave me alone. I understood: The steward might circle around and finish what he'd started.

I heard the door to Lin's cabin click shut. She or Wei Xi had witnessed the altercation, yet hadn't shouted out. Perhaps there wasn't time. It had happened so very quickly, from one breath to the next.

"You're bleeding, Miss Rees," Robie said, kneeling beside me.

"So are you, Robie."

He looked down. Fingered the slice in his jacket. Saw the darkening stain. "Just a scratch."

I reached for the dagger that had narrowly missed my heart. Could this be the knife that had sliced my jacket that first night and pierced Annie last night?

Robie's hand beat mine to the blade. "I'll take this to

the captain after we visit Sick Bay. Don't worry, we'll scour the ship for the sonofa—" He caught himself.

"My sentiments, exactly, Robie. And thank you for saving my life."

It was dim in the passageway, but I could have sworn Robie blushed. He hurried me along the same path our attacker had taken, looking for the nearest sailor. Found a seaman swabbing the deck outside. He'd seen a steward run down the ladder, he said, but the man's destination was anyone's guess. Robie dispatched the sailor with a message alerting the captain of the incident and asking Stowall to meet us in Sick Bay.

The bright sunlight showed the spreading stain on Robie's side. He leaned against the ladder railing for a moment. Bloody footprints marred the freshly scrubbed deck. Robie's wound was worse than I'd thought. He was listing toward his injured side.

My own wound throbbed. A small red rivulet slid down my left arm and dripped from my fingers.

"Come," I said, taking his left arm with my undamaged right. People were converging on us. No reason to frighten the masses—or at least, not yet. I waved them away, said it was just a minor accident. The doctor was nearby. We'd be fine.

Robie gathered himself, and we accomplished the steps down to Sick Bay without incident. The room was empty but for the good doctor, who sat at his desk bringing his log up to date. Phineas had told me that Doyle preferred making cabin calls, leaving Sick Bay for emergencies. This qualified.

"What have we here, now?" His Irish brogue was comforting, reminding me of Tom and Mary Daly. And Annie.

Robie started to answer and then stopped, swaying. Blood drained from his face. Doyle jumped up and helped him sit on the nearest of the two narrow beds, where he promptly fell to the side in a faint.

Doyle felt his wrist for a pulse. "Shock. Happens to the best of 'em."

I reached for the little purse I wore at my waist. "I have vinegar—"

"No, Miss Rees. My work's easier with him out. But could you help me with his legs?"

We swung Robie's legs up and straightened him out. His feet hung over the end of the thin mattress. I'd dripped blood on the clean white sheet.

I started to explain, but Doyle said, "Wait." He walked across the passageway and opened a door without knocking. A medical supply room, I deduced, given the stocked shelves on the periphery.

"Sir?" said the burly orderly seated at his desk, working on what appeared to be an inventory.

"I need your assistance, Kidd. Bring dressings."

Doyle left the door open and returned to where I stood in the middle of the room, one eye on Robie, the other on the doctor. "Well?" Doyle said, as he began to unbutton Robie's jacket.

I kept it short and to the point. Explanations could await the captain. "Two knife wounds, Doctor. Mr. Robie bore the brunt of it, so his wound is graver than mine." I waggled my left arm, elevated, now, to slow the blood loss. "Captain Stowall has been alerted to meet us here."

"Please take the second bed, Miss Rees." Doyle pulled a carbolic acid wash from one cupboard, clean linen cloths and iodine from another. Kidd deposited dressing and stitching materials on a wheeled tray and unfolded a screen between the two beds. "Let's see what we've got, then, Mr. Kidd."

I heard them removing Robie's jacket and blouson, Doyle's voice commenting and directing. "My, my, what *have* you been up to, son?"

Robie didn't answer, not even a groan.

"Yes, wash it with the carbolic... See here? Slid right along the skin. Then he must have turned, 'cause the blade slipped clean between the ribs. No wonder he was bleeding like a stuck pig. Pass the iodine. Now hold the sides together, Mr. Kidd, and I'll show you how it's done."

The sound of footsteps approaching. That would be Stowall and company.

"Robie's out at the moment, Captain," Doyle said. "And a blessing that is. His wound should heal cleanly, but he'll need rest for a day, and light duty for another week.

We don't want him pulling these stitches."

"Understood. The girl?"

"In t'other bed. I'll deal with her next. But you can talk to her."

I had been stretched out, forearm still elevated, but now I hitched my torso up to lean against the bulkhead. I was cradling my arm when the captain and Mr. Arnold came around the screen.

"Mr. Robie stepped between me and our attacker, Captain. Probably saved my life. I hope you'll note that in the log."

He smiled and turned to Arnold, whose pencil scribbled away. "So noted, Captain."

"This wasn't an accident, then," Stowall said to me.

"More like desperation." I described the incident, my voice just loud enough to carry over the screen to the doctor. The captain didn't interrupt. As I finished, I heard the doctor washing his hands. Seconds later, he stood by my bed.

"Well, let's have a look, shall we? No, don't go, Captain. She can talk while I work."

My bloody fingers fumbled with the small buttons on the left sleeve.

"Let me, Miss Rees." Doyle's broad hands and short fingers were surprisingly dexterous. "I've dealt with my share of tiny buttons. I've four little girls at home in Galway."

"Then they're lucky girls," I said. "My father was a fine draftsman, but all thumbs when it came to buttons and bows." The memory triggered the threat of tears. I swallowed hard and bit the inside of my cheek until the pressure receded.

Doyle clucked over the scratch running down my forearm. It could just as easily have slipped between *my* ribs.

"It's not deep, Miss Rees. Should knit well. I'll just take a few stitches in the deepest part, then clean, dress, and bind it. Nature will do the rest. But you'll have a scar, I fear."

"I have others. I lived in mining camps, and my parents felt it was best not to coddle me."

Kidd wheeled around the tray with a clean basin of water, the carbolic acid, iodine, and sterile dressings. Robie's cut clothes were tucked under his arm. Kidd said, with a smile, that he'd go find a clean uniform for the local hero.

The little bay where I lay was crowded, the temperature rising, the odors of sweating bodies and blood strong, pervasive. Doyle soaked a cloth in dilute carbolic acid and began cleaning the blood from my hand and arm, working toward the wound. "This'll sting a bit."

The flash of pain made me gasp, and for a moment I felt light-headed. But if I should faint, at least they wouldn't have to pick me up off the deck.

The moment passed. The pain receded slightly, then flared again as he dabbed iodine along the cut. He held the sides of the wound together and put in ten neat stitches. "There, that's the worst of it, Miss Rees."

My stomach muscles unclenched. I breathed again and wiped my eyes with the cloth square the doctor proffered. Next door, I heard Kidd return.

While Doyle set about bandaging and wrapping, I asked, "Captain, would you get word to my guardians, please? And put another guard on my cabin? I'd hate to escape this man twice, only to find him awaiting my return."

"I presume the knife—Where is the weapon?"

"I have it, sir," called Mr. Kidd. I heard rustling, then Kidd handed over the dagger, wrapped in cloth.

"Used the first night, and today. Thrice if our inference is correct, and Annie..." The tears were back. I bit the other cheek.

"Take your time, Miss Rees," Stowall said.

I nodded. Breathed deeply. Started again. "It seems likely that the man who stabbed Robie and me did the same to Annie last night. Before he pushed her overboard." I blew my nose on the cotton square. "He seemed to be aiming for my heart just now. Next time he might not miss."

The captain examined the dagger. "Nothing distinctive here. I've seen a thousand like it hawked in Pacific ports." He wrapped the dagger again and handed it to Mr. Arnold. "Are you up to answering some questions, Miss Rees?"

I nodded. Dr. Doyle attached one last knot to the dressing, patted my hand, then returned around the curtain to Robie.

"Could you describe your attacker?" Stowall asked.

"He was the size and build of my cabin steward, Ah Jim, but his queue was longer and his face narrower, with a pointed chin. One eyebrow, the left, was scarred or had been singed." I pulled my drawing pad and pencil from my pocket, grateful that the wound was on my left arm. "It's easier if I draw him."

Stowall and Arnold were quiet as I sketched.

"I think I might have glimpsed him before." I studied the drawing. Made a slight correction to the eyes and eyebrows. Couldn't put my finger on what seemed familiar.

I tore off the sheet and handed it to Stowall. "The man was dressed in a cabin steward's uniform."

"Do you recognize him, Arnold?"

"No, sir."

The captain made a *hrummphing* sound. "The attack occurred at the door to Miss Hsu's cabin. That was your destination, Miss Rees?"

"Yes."

"Did you have an appointment with Miss Hsu or Miss Wei Xi?"

"Not exactly. I met with them this morning to discuss Miss Hsu acting as my companion. Mr. Quade and Dr. Nakagawa approved the plan, and I'd sent my cabin steward to notify Miss Hsu of that decision. But a subsequent conversation raised a few concerns I wanted to discuss with them."

"Are you willing to share those concerns, Miss Rees?"

I glanced at Mr. Arnold, who had looked up from his note-taking. I had no desire to put his job at risk by revealing that his ledger entry had triggered my reservations. He winked. I thought for a moment I was mistaken, until I saw a slight smile touch his mouth.

"Yes, Miss Rees. Arnold reported your meeting."

"Good. It was something Mr. Arnold related about the

information gained in the interviews with Miss Hsu and the Smalls. Apparently, Miss Hsu didn't open her cabin door when the searchers came. She told them she was afraid to open the door that late at night. Moreover, she felt that it was improper to open the door to a man, given her betrothed state. Since the searchers spoke only to Miss Hsu, I wished to ask her if she was alone in the cabin last night. And if not, whether Miss Wei had been there the entire evening. I wanted to watch their reactions."

"I'd like answers to the same questions," Stowall said. "And to one more, given that Miss Hsu opened her door to our mystery steward not an hour ago."

"You wish to know whether the man who stabbed us was hiding in their room last night," I said. "And perhaps for the voyage thus far?"

The captain *hrummphed* again. "If he's a stowaway, that might explain why Mr. Arnold failed to recognize the man from your drawing." Stowall turned to Arnold. "Please commence a more thorough search of the ship. Every cabin and closet. Immediately."

Arnold handed his notebook and pencil to the captain and left us.

The captain took a moment to marshal his thoughts. "Your attacker was standing at or in the cabin doorway, holding a tray?"

"Yes. He said something in a conversational tone, in Chinese, so I got the impression the door was open."

"Do you know what roused Robie's suspicions of the man?"

"No. Mr. Robie just called out to the man and brushed by me."

"And you don't know whether the man was coming or going?"

"No. Wait. The teapot was empty, or nearly so, and the cups had been used. Three cups," I said, before he could ask.

"He wouldn't be delivering a used tray of tea, so he must have just collected it."

"Or have been stopped after collecting the tray from another cabin. Or—" I stopped, not wanting to state the third option.

"Or have been in the room overnight," Stowall finished the thought. "Quite so, Miss Rees. If the latter, he might have felt it was safe to leave while most passengers were at their mid-day meal."

In silence we explored the ramifications of a murderer running free on a ship carrying more than a thousand souls.

"Captain?" I said.

"Yes?"

"When you talk to Miss Hsu, you might ask her why she closed her door after the altercation in the passageway. One would think the normal response would be to offer assistance."

"In Britain or the Americas, perhaps, but that doesn't hold true for Asia, where it's sometimes wiser not to get involved."

An excellent point. "If you were to summon her and Miss Wei Xi to a meeting, it would be natural for you to ask for their input concerning the activity outside their door. My guardians would have questions, too."

"My thoughts exactly. We'll meet in my dining alcove after luncheon—" Stowall looked at his watch. "Which I'm afraid we've missed."

"I'd already requested a tray in my room."

"I suspect the tea will be cold. No matter. I'll arrange an early tea to accompany our meeting. Say half past two? You'll need time to change."

A noise at the Sick Bay door. The sound of Toru's voice. And Uncle P's more muffled tones. I called out that I was behind the screen.

"Your ward is fine," Dr. Doyle said when they crowded into the space. "Just a scratch, though she'll have to come back next week to have the stitches removed."

My guardians didn't seem convinced. No doubt it was the mention of stitches.

"He's telling the truth," I said. "I'll explain on the way back to my cabin. That is, if you'll escort me. You'll have to be my protectors until the captain assigns someone else. Mr. Robie's wounds were more severe than my own."

"He'll recover?" Phineas asked.

"Won't be down for long," said Doyle. "He's young.

And tough as elephant hide."

Captain Stowall closed Arnold's notebook. "Miss Rees and I have agreed to meet with Miss Hsu and her companion at 1430 hours for an early tea," he said to my guardians. "I presume you can join us?"

"Of course," Phineas said. He looked at Toru, then at me. I nodded. Our business meeting, set for four o'clock, might have to be postponed. "You have alerted Miss Hsu, Captain?"

"I'll ask Mr. Arnold to relay the message." He turned to go.

"Do you speak French, Captain?" I asked.

He paused. "Of course, Miss Rees. As does Mr. Arnold."

"Then may we conduct our meeting in that language, please? Hsu Lin said that her companion doesn't speak or understand it."

"And you trust her?"

"Not at all. But we can test it. My guardians read people much better than I do."

"Shoes," came Robie's voice from the other side of the screen. It sounded like he was saying Hsu Lin's name.

A rustling, and then the orderly folded back the screen.

"Welcome back, Robie," Stowall said to the sheet-shrouded man. "Miss Rees has been singing your praises."

Color infused Robie's face. "Did I hear aright, Captain? You wanted to know what set me off? It was the blighter's shoes, sir. He was out of uniform. Wore black cloth slippers, he did."

Chapter 11

1:40 p.m.

CAPTAIN **S**TOWALL, **FOR ONLY** the second time since I'd met him, seemed at a loss for words. As were my guardians. While I was trying to remember exactly what footwear my own cabin steward wore.

I prided myself on noticing details of the world around me, but could picture no more than the tips of shiny black shoes peeking out from under Ah Jim's uniform.

Robie broke the silence. "Them black slippers wasn't regulation, sir, and the soles was white. 'Twas the edges of the soles I noticed, y'see."

I did see. The soles of uniform-issue shoes were black.

"Quick thinking, Robie," Stowall said. "Now get some rest. Once you're feeling up to it, we'll put you back on watch."

"Light duty for a few days, Captain," Doyle reminded him. "Don't want him fainting and hitting his head."

"No, no, Doyle, that wouldn't do. I was thinking he could help keep an eye on Miss Rees. His reflexes might be a bit slow at the moment, but his keen instincts more than make up for it. And we'll give him a chair for a day or two."

"Suits me, Captain," Robie said. "As long as Miss Rees don't mind a gimpy guard in the rotation. I can recover my strength as easily there as in my bunk."

"Ever shot a revolver, Mr. Robie?" I asked.

This time he didn't correct my use of a title. "Just target practice, miss."

"Well, if Captain Stowall allows you to carry one, I think it will more than make up for your temporary lack of mobility."

"Agreed," said Stowall. "If Arnold can't find a sidearm among our munitions, I'll loan Robie mine."

* * *

A new guard, short and stocky, stepped forward to block entry to my cabin. "Coleman" his tag read.

"I'm Keridec Rees." I gestured to my companions. "Dr. Nakagawa and Mr. Quade are my guardians."

Coleman didn't move except to ring a small bell hanging from his belt. "I'll just confirm with the cabin steward."

Ah Jim trotted down the passageway, confirmed our identities, and unlocked the cabin.

"For the moment, no one else is allowed entry without our permission or Captain Stowall's," I told Coleman. "Ah Jim, has the Smalls' cabin been vacated and cleaned?"

"Yes, missy."

"How about Miss Hsu's cabin? Is it ready for the Smalls?"

"All done." He nodded toward the cabin just aft of mine. I could hear something being dragged across the deck.

"Good. Thank you for your help. My guardians will take care of any charges accruing from the exchange."

Ah Jim beamed and bowed and retreated to his station.

"See you in thirty minutes, Keri," Phineas said. He patted my shoulder, and Toru pressed my hand before heading to their cabins.

"Mr. Coleman?" I said.

"Yes, miss?"

"You heard what happened to Mr. Robie and me?" I held up my arm with its smooth white bandage.

"The whole ship knows, Miss Rees. Robie's all right?"

"Back on duty in no time. But it was a close thing. Please stay alert."

"Don't worry, miss. No one'll get by me."

"Thank you. Things will get a bit more complicated this afternoon. You saw Miss Hsu and Miss Wei move in?

Yes, well, Miss Hsu will be my companion for the remainder of the journey. We'll have to figure out a system, so you'll know when to admit her."

"Our orders are to guard *you*, miss. So, the simplest plan would be to allow her into your cabin only when you're here."

"That suits me. Thank you, Mr. Coleman."

I closed the door and leaned against it. Thirty minutes, Phineas had said. Not much time.

I filled the sink with warm water and sponged the dried blood from my hands, arms, and torso. The violated dermis beneath its dressing alternately throbbed and burned. How much worse must poor Robie be feeling? Our assailant had a lot to answer for.

I wondered who he was. Robie hadn't recognized the man, yet he must have come aboard either at Shanghai or Yokohama. But what was his relationship with Hsu Lin and Wei Xi?

East and West seemed to be colliding near the International Date Line, established only last year. I felt as if I were always playing the black chess pieces, always on the defensive. But how to end one game and begin another, this time playing white?

I sank down before the dressing table, left arm in my lap, right arm supporting my forehead. Closed my eyes. The darkness soothed me and allowed my mind to breathe. I suspected the answers lay with Hsu Lin. I wanted to trust her, but right out of the gate she'd tried to steal from me. And then a steward who'd been standing in her cabin doorway tried to kill me. Not an auspicious beginning to our relationship.

We needed to start over if we were to spend time together. But how? I refused to give her what she'd attempted to steal, my father's signet ring. I thought of all the reasons that ring could be important to her. The presumed authority it carried, identifying her as his daughter. The emotional meaning of owning something tangible of her father's. The monetary value of the gold.

Another avenue of possibilities opened up. Hsu Lin would be bringing a dowry with her, but she would have little or no funds of her own. On the journey, Wei Xi would control the purse strings. In the future, Lin's husband would control her life. Her fate had been ordained by her family and the husband they'd chosen for her. In San Francisco she would have status, but it would be circumscribed within a closed society under increasing attacks from the white population. She'd be left with only memories of a wider world. How would she react?

I didn't know her well enough to say. But if, like me, she craved the freedom to explore our world, then perhaps *that* was the impetus behind her pocketing the ring and necklace. Jewelry could be sold or bartered anywhere.

I pondered independence and how, given the circumstances, a woman went about achieving it. At that moment, my own application for legal emancipation was wending its way through the California court system. My father had wanted me to be free to sign contracts and decide my own destiny. My guardians supported the plan. Only my grandmother would fight it—once she knew my father was dead. She would want to control my inheritance from both parents. Constance, Countess de Keridec had fought for a larger share of my mother's bequest to me. And lost. But then I'd had Father to help make the case for my receiving that inheritance, a trivial amount compared to my parents' large and complex estate.

I put aside my own problems. Was there anything I could do to help Lin achieve at least some measure of independence? If I could promise her a small nest egg by the end of the voyage, I could more readily trust that she'd help protect me. My guardians and I had yet to execute a contract for her services, a contract similar to or identical with the one I had with Annie. We hadn't discussed Lin's salary or how the money would be paid. Yet, if I guessed correctly, Wei Xi would insist on holding any money Lin earned. Lin was underage. She would see none of it.

Solutions arose like scenes in a shadow play cast upon a wall. I discarded one after another until only one remained: I could and would establish an account with the purser in Lin's name. I would add to the sum each day, increasing the amount as we got closer to San Francisco. And if I reached port alive, then my guardians and I would quietly, and without Xi's notice, add a cash wedding present to the sum, a dowry from Lin's father. She and I were the only offspring of Glen Rees, as far as I knew. In his name I owed her that much.

Unless she'd had something to do with Annie's disappearance, or the attack on me this morning.

I shook my head. I had no control over what would happen once Lin and I parted company. She would have to solve those problems. But before I made any move to help her, I must determine if I could trust her with my life for even an hour. She had questions to answer. Let the inquisition begin.

I refocused on the matter at hand. Of the new frocks made in Tokyo as I waited for my father to heal, only two, in addition to my traveling costume, were relatively easy to put on and remove without the aid of a maid. Of those, one was caked in blood, my own and Robie's, and had a slit on the sleeve. I'd left the buttons of the sleeve undone after my visit to Sick Bay. Now, I fumbled with the buttons on the right cuff and shoulder. I threw the stained linen dress over the top of the screen. Held up a black muslin frock. Skirt full enough to allow breezes to cool my legs as I walked. Bell-shaped sleeves that wouldn't irritate the dressing. No buttons, just a contrasting bone-white sash that wrapped several times about my waist, tying in the back. I slipped the finely pleated bodice over my head. I left the bustle and corset in the closet, making do with a slimmer silhouette—more girl than woman.

My hair had held, but I covered the braids with a hat made to match the dress. I rang for Ah Jim and opened the door at his knock. He collected the untouched lunch he'd delivered eons ago, promised that my soiled dress would be cleaned, repaired, and pressed, then went to summon my guardians.

While I waited, I riffled through Annie's papers until I found her copy of the contract. I penciled in some changes. I would ask my guardians to review the changes before submitting the contract to the shipboard scribes.

I moved on to the questions I wanted to ask Hsu Lin and Wei Xi at the meeting. I was jotting them down when I heard the sound of my guardians' voices outside in the passageway.

The players were assembling for Act II. Time to raise the curtain.

Chapter 12

2:25 p.m.

PHINEAS, **T**ORU, **AND** *I* had a whispered conversation before we knocked on Lin's cabin door. I handed Toru the list of questions I'd made, and said I preferred that he ask them for me. Remaining in the background now would make establishing a relationship with Lin less awkward later.

In silence we escorted Lin and Wei Xi to the dining salon. Captain Stowall, Mr. Arnold, and a stranger met us at the alcove and trailed us inside. Stowall took his usual seat at the head of the table, adding a sense of déjà vu to the proceedings. Arnold set his ledger in front of the place to Stowall's left, then stepped back. Once he and Toru seated Lin and her companion, Arnold moved to stand beside a buffet table where snowy damask cloths covered odd geometric shapes. The hidden objects injected tension into an already edgy atmosphere.

I chose a chair in the corner behind Stowall's right shoulder. The stranger sat at the opposite end of the table from the captain. I could see Lin's and Xi's faces, but not Stowall's, except in profile. I took out my sketchpad and tried to capture the scene in a few strokes, beginning with the stranger's face and upper torso. He was the one unknown in the room.

The man was of middle age, with ruddy skin and abundant ginger hair. Mutton-chop whiskers, a thick mustache, and bushy eyebrows obscured the lines and planes of his face. But eyes of a startling blue—like chips of ice and just as piercing—found mine for a moment. I sensed he'd read my entire history in that glance. A strange experience, uncomfortable, as if my soul had been laid bare.

I watched Phineas take his measure and then caught the gleam of recognition that touched Uncle P's eyes. Whether it was the man he knew or just the type, I wasn't sure. I'd winkle it out of him later. Toru, by contrast, seemed to be memorizing the stranger's features so that he could recognize him the next time they met.

Once everyone was seated, a server delivered tea, setting mine on a side table next to me. It had been so long since I'd eaten that my stomach was convinced that my throat had been cut, as Annie used to say. The seaman, correctly interpreting my beseeching look, filled a plate with finger sandwiches and biscuits, and with a slight smile set the plate beside my teacup. I tugged off my lace gloves and nibbled as daintily as possible, thankful I wouldn't have to stand and raid the main table for sustenance.

Captain Stowall introduced the stranger as George Mayweather. Stowall gave no reason for Mayweather's presence. Xi's face tightened around the eyes and mouth as she stole looks at Mayweather, Arnold, the buffet table, and the captain. She lifted her teacup, and sipped. The cup clattered against the saucer when she set it down.

Lin, face composed, ignored Honorable Aunt Xi. Lin had allowed herself one sidelong glance at Mayweather before focusing on the teacup lying untouched before her. Her hands remained on her lap. If this was a trial, her erect bearing declared, she would refuse to participate.

When the white-gloved seaman had poured me a second cup of tea and replenished my plate of finger food, Stowall dismissed him. Arnold moved to the front of the buffet table. Turning his back to the room, he flicked off the cloth that covered approximately three quarters of the table and pulled a board from under the table. He leaned the board against the bulkhead behind the tabletop. Then he stepped aside again so we could see.

Affixed to the board were my drawings of Annie, the stern deck where she was last seen, her hatpin, and the face of the man who had attacked Robie and me. The drawings told a story for Lin and Wei Xi. Lin's glance touched each object in turn. Xi's gaze remained on the picture of the knife-wielder.

I half-rose from my chair to get a better view of the table. Saw Annie's hat and my mother's bloody hatpin. Stood completely to watch Arnold remove the serviette covering the remaining objects. There, catching the light, were the dagger that had cut me a few hours before... and a small black slipper, cotton or silk, with a woven sole of bleached straw or bamboo.

Where had Arnold found it?

And then I knew. Clever man, Mr. Arnold. He need only borrow one from his cabin steward. The shoes were as common among the Chinese crew as were the shaved foreheads and queues they still wore to demonstrate fealty to their Manchurian conquerors two centuries before. As soon as the passengers disembarked in San Francisco, the Chinese crew would doff their uniforms and don their apparel for shore leave in Chinatown.

Chinatown. Where Lin's fiancé resided. Where she and Wei Xi would live.

Wei Xi's stunned look said the shoe had meaning for her and she hadn't guessed it was a hoax.

And Lin? I saw a flash of pain about the eyes before she closed them and bent her head, shutting out the table, the people, the room.

I picked up my tablet and sketched the looks I'd just seen. Yet a look was not the story, and I would uncover every last detail. Annie deserved nothing less.

A single tear dropped onto the paper, and I rubbed it absently, thinking Robie, too, deserved no less.

The captain broke the silence. "You understand why we're here, Miss Hsu?" He spoke French with a Québécois accent and phrasing.

"I do, Captain Stowall," Lin replied in Parisian French, formal and precise.

A frown wrinkled Wei Xi's forehead. Lin's advice had been correct—Xi could not follow rapid French.

Lin said something in Chinese. Mayweather adjusted his posture slightly, as if to look in Toru's direction. But I wondered if he might favor his right ear, now turned toward Lin and Xi, and if he'd been asked to sit in on the interview as an independent translator, someone to confirm what was said. His hands were hidden in his lap, but I'd seen him remove a notebook from his pocket as he sat. He must be taking notes blindly, below the level of the tabletop. Quite a feat.

"Then let us proceed," Stowall said, launching into a summary of what we knew so far about Annie's disappearance. The second search had produced no sign of her, nor had anyone other than the deckhand admitted seeing her walk to the stern. We were left with the hat, hatpin, and blood on the railing.

"My conclusion, for the record," the captain said, "will be 'Lost at sea subsequent to altercation with unknown person or persons.'"

Stowall must have heard or sensed my sharp intake of breath. "A tragedy for all concerned, but especially for Miss Rees." He turned his torso so he could see me. "Our sincerest condolences for your loss, Miss Rees."

"Thank you, Captain. And please thank the crew for their diligent search. It could not have been easy."

"I shall, of course." Stowall closed the logbook from which he'd read, steepled his fingers, and fixed his gaze on Lin, who was translating the findings for Wei Xi. Was that a note of relief that crossed Xi's face, or satisfaction?

I felt anger flare in the pit of my stomach. I banked it down, trusting there would be an opportunity later to express outrage.

"But now we must move into the next phase of our investigation—finding the perpetrator or perpetrators of the inferred altercation." He signaled to Arnold, who removed the tacks holding up my drawing of the man who'd stabbed Robie. Arnold set the drawing on the table between Lin and Wei Xi. Lin made no move to pick it up. Xi turned her head and stared at the captain.

"This man, dressed as a steward, was seen leaving your cabin late this morning, Miss Hsu and Miss Wei," Stowall said. "He attacked and tried to kill Miss Rees and her guard, Seaman Robie. Do you know this man?"

Stowall waited while Lin translated. Xi shook her head vehemently, underlining the movements with Chinese negatives. Arnold had taken his seat and was recording the questions and responses.

Lin looked at me, then at the door, as if wishing she

were anywhere but in this room. I leaned forward, perching on the edge of my seat. Her answer was everything—knowledge and culpability, or innocence.

She didn't nod or shake her head, just said very softly, almost diffidently, "*Oui, Monsieur. C'est mon frère.*"

Her *brother?* I overbalanced and slid forward onto my knees. Toru helped me up. "Are you hurt?" he asked as he retrieved my sketchbook and pencil.

Mortified, I felt the blood rush to my face. "I'm fine." I brushed off my dress.

He laughed softly. "Quite the exclamation point, my dear Keri."

Mayweather's notebook was on the table. He extricated the pencil point from a hole in the paper and jotted another note.

"Are your stitches intact?" asked Captain Stowall, ever practical.

I examined my bandages. No blood stains, although the cut screamed. "Still in order, Captain. I apologize for the disruption. But Hsu Lin's statement raises any number of questions. May I?"

"It's irregular, but everything about this case is irregular. Please proceed."

I stood. The words stuck in my throat. I had to try twice. "I had heard your mother died in childbirth, or shortly thereafter. Is this an older brother?"

"By three minutes, according to Aunt Xi."

The world began to spin. I found the chair with my hand and sat. Closing my eyes, I allowed my mind to sweep the chess pieces from the board and reset it for a new game. My half-brother had tried to kill me. And he'd most likely murdered Annie.

I smelled brandy. Phineas stood before me with a tiny goblet of amber liquid. "Drink it."

I drank. And choked, of course. He patted my back. I thought a smile touched Lin's mouth. Wei Xi was speaking, demanding, in a high-pitched voice, quite unlike her normal tones. Lin ignored her.

"More tea would be nice," I said. Arnold went out to find the steward and get a fresh pot. "Again, I apologize, Captain. The news is, er, unexpected."

"To us all. After the attack this morning, Dr. Nakagawa informed us that Miss Hsu is your half-sister. He thought your drawing of the attacker showed a slight resemblance to Miss Hsu. But her confirmation of his identity complicates our search for a motive in the case of Miss Bonney."

My eyes fell on the drawing, still lying on the table between Lin and Wei Xi. I understood now why I'd sensed a niggling familiarity in my attacker's features. The shape of the face was Lin's, although heavier. But not much. And like her, the young man moved gracefully, as if it were integral to his sinew and skeleton.

Arnold returned with a pot of tea and poured me a cup before circling the table to refresh the other cups. When he was seated and had picked up his pen, I said, "Miss Hsu, my sister, did you know this man, or know *of* him, before you embarked on this voyage?"

She shook her head. "I have learned that he was given into the care of our mother's owner shortly after birth. He and I were impure, you see, a stain upon my mother's family. But he was male, and therefore useful. As a tool, if nothing more. You know the rest of my tale."

"But I don't," said Stowall.

Lin's hand hovered over the picture of her brother. One finger descended, a moth's touch. "Our mother's owner gave me to my grandmother, to be exposed on a hillside, as both he and my grandfather wished. It was midwinter, and I would not have lasted an hour, much less a night. But my grandmother could not do it. She delivered me to the Eurasian orphanage and informed my mother. Later that night, our mother freed herself from slavery in the only way she could."

Wei Xi tugged at Lin's sleeve, demanding a translation. Lin shook her off.

"What is your brother's name?" Stowall asked.

"He has no family name," Lin said, "as befits a mixed-breed bastard. Aunt Xi raised him, apparently. She calls him '*Hun d'un*.'"

The French words made no sense. Had she switched from French to Mandarin when she'd reached his name?

Lin repeated the word, then gave a longer phrase in

Chinese. In French, she said, "*Chaos*, for short. More precisely, *Chaos-Contained-in-Box.* Or in a trunk."

I sent Toru a beseeching look. He took a card from his pocket, jotted a note on it and passed it to Phineas, who passed it to me.

It said, *Hundun. Or Hézi lǐ de hùndùn.*

I had a half-brother named Chaos-in-a-Box.

Chapter 13

I STARED AT LIN. We all stared. "I had the same reaction," Lin said to me, ignoring the others. "Wei Xi explained that when he was a baby she used a box as his bassinette. The boxes became bigger as he grew. She had her own, private wing in her brother's house. Only her brother, our mother's owner, knew. They trained Hundun as a tool to collect information. And as a weapon. He speaks and reads several languages. Wei Xi smuggled him into places in a specially made trunk. He is small and agile, as you saw."

This last was said with ironic humor. But she brushed away a tear at the horror of his life.

"Hundun received training in languages so he could understand what he overheard," I said.

"The Wei family traffics in information," Lin said. "Hundun's their secret weapon."

Stowall, face an angry red, found his voice. "Your brother lived in a *trunk?*"

She nodded. "Hundun was kept a secret from the rest of the household, even from the other retainers, and taught from babyhood to live silently. He told me that Wei Xi rewarded him with food, and with time in the sunlight. He worked mostly at night."

"When, exactly, were you introduced to your brother?" Toru asked.

"Last night, as the men searched for Miss Bonney."

"So, he was in your cabin when the searchers arrived," I said.

She studied her hands while weighing her response.

"What would you have had me do, Keri? I had just learned I had a brother, a twin. I was hearing his history, what had happened to him in the intervening years. He was wearing a steward's uniform, so I thought he worked

103

on the ship and would lose his job if I opened the door. I did not know, then, that I had a half-sister named Keridec Rees who had a maidservant named Anne Bonney. Nor did I know what had happened to Miss Bonney." She looked at the drawings and the hat, hatpin, dagger, and shoe. "All I knew was that I did not want my new brother discovered in our cabin. And for my own sake, I did not want the crew to discover me alone with a man. What I told them was true. That it would destroy my reputation."

"Miss Wei was no longer in the cabin?" Stowall asked.

"That is correct, Captain. She answered the door when he knocked, introduced us, waited for the shock to subside, then put on her cloak and went out. I did not ask where."

"Lin," I said, keeping my voice soft and even so that she didn't know how important her response would be. "Can you remember what time Hundun arrived?"

Her face revealed the mental process as her memory arranged and rearranged the puzzle pieces of time and place until a coherent picture emerged. A quick mind, like mine. Like our brother's, no doubt, despite his wretched upbringing.

"The cabin steward always makes a final check at ten, to turn down the beds and ask if we need anything before we retire. Soon after he left last night, I heard voices and footsteps in the passageway. Two men, one asking for a carafe of water. He said he'd broken his." She smiled. "I heard the second man hunt up a carafe, fill it with water at the station, and deliver it to the man's cabin before knocking on our door. His service and uniform were the reasons why I surmised my brother was employed on the ship. He and I had been talking for less than an hour when the searchers asked me to open the door."

"When Miss Wei admitted your brother to your cabin," I said, "was he carrying anything?" I gave her no hints. I didn't want to place a memory where there wasn't one—or condemn our brother out of hand.

"Only a little bag he had found. In the passageway, he said. A woman's purse. Silk. Grayish purple."

"Mauve?"

"Yes. Did you lose one? No? Well, I looked inside to

see if it had identification of some kind, but there were only the usual things women carry—handkerchief, coins, smelling salts, a folding comb in a tortoiseshell holder. That is all."

"What happened to the bag?"

"Aunt Xi said she would take it to the purser's desk. That's why she left immediately after introducing me to my brother."

I had my answers—the who and the where, the when and the how, if not the all-important why. The bag had never reached the purser. I suspected Wei Xi had tossed it overboard, or perhaps hidden it to give to whomever had ordered my death. And when she learned that the wrong person had died, Wei Xi might have retrieved and disposed of the purse in the dead of night. No evidence to link her, Lin, or Hundun to the crime.

I sat back. Looked at the sketchbook in my hand. Rubbed my thumb over the cover. A little pocket I'd sewn into the leather contained my mother's letter calling my father back to San Francisco. She'd finally agreed to marry him. I carried it like a talisman, a piece of home.

I felt Mayweather's piercing gaze. As if he knew the pattern of my thoughts. But how could he? We'd never met. I'd never heard his name before this afternoon.

Stowall returned to an issue that rankled. "Can you tell us how and where your brother came aboard my ship?" he asked Lin.

"This morning, Aunt Xi told me that he came aboard in one of her trunks. In Shanghai. She insisted on unpacking our things, saying she did not trust the steward. This seemed in keeping with her personality, so I thought nothing of it. She sent me on an errand to the purser, and released my brother while I was out. He left the cabin and found a hiding place on the ship. She has been taking him food."

"Just what is the relationship between you and Miss Wei?" Stowall asked.

"Aunt Xi has two brothers. One is my betrothed in San Francisco. The other is the man in Shanghai who owned my mother and my brother. Wei Xi will be my sister-in-law."

"It sounds as if Miss Wei is an integral part of their family business," Toru said.

"That is my understanding. I had met her only once before we embarked. Much of what I am telling you I learned from my brother last night. She is a partner, and merchants are excluded from the Chinese Immigration Act. For now. But my brother has no such exclusion. Aunt Xi told me my betrothed wishes to use Hundun's services in California, and so he had to be smuggled across the ocean."

I thought of the letter Toru had received from Lin's grandfather after the ship sailed. I shifted in my seat to attract my guardians' notice. They looked at the captain, then back to me. Stowall sighed. "Yes, Miss Rees?"

I turned to Lin. "But how did Wei Xi and her brothers find out about *me*? About my father's death? About my being aboard this ship, heading home? Did your grandfather find out somehow and tell them? Did you?"

The shutters went down on Lin's eyes. She was only prepared to go so far.

I pressed her. "Because before you met your brother last night, he'd attempted to kill me twice—once the first night out of Yokohama. That he mistook Anne Bonney for me is clear. But who directed his actions? And why?"

"I don't have the answers you seek," she said.

I tried one last question, more for the record than in expectation of an answer. "Why did you close the door instead of calling for help when Mr. Robie and I were being attacked outside your cabin? The normal thing to do would be to offer assistance."

She turned the drawing of Hundun over on the table, folded her hands in her lap, and stared down, lips pressed together in a firm line.

Silence descended on the alcove. Then Phineas and Captain Stowall spoke at once. Both stopped. Phineas gestured to Stowall to continue.

"Miss Hsu, why don't you bring Miss Wei up to date, as she's become a central player in this rather Shakespearean drama." Stowall's effort to diffuse the tension fell flat.

Lin turned to Xi and commenced translating. I could

hear the staff setting up for afternoon tea in the main dining room. Clink of porcelain, rumble of tables being shifted, snap of clean tablecloths, murmur of voices. Someone laughed.

No one in the alcove seemed to be finding their thoughts remotely humorous, with the possible exception of Mayweather, who was smiling openly. Easy for him to smile. His life wasn't in danger.

Mayweather, the odd man out, sensed the direction of my attention, and sketched me a half salute with his left hand. But his pencil never left the paper. He was writing down everything Lin and Xi said in some form of shorthand.

Toru and Phineas caught Mayweather's gesture. A quiet side conversation ensued. I could guess their focus. My father had left illegitimate children behind, and one of them had been fashioned into a weapon.

The evil that men do lives after them. Father's legacy would have impressed even the Bard.

Wei Xi loosed a flood of words. Lin didn't attempt to staunch the flow. Mayweather's pencil flew over the paper. The captain, in English, tried to quiet Wei Xi. She either didn't understand or didn't care. And then everyone, except Arnold and me, began talking at once. At least three languages. Voices rising.

Arnold tapped a spoon against his teacup. No response. No one could hear it.

I stood and said in French, loudly enough to be heard at the far side of the dining room, "Lin, please ask your aunt where my brother is now."

The noise level rose, overwhelming my senses. I sat down in my corner. Put my hands over my ears. Leaned forward until my forehead touched my knees. I felt a hand on the top of my head. Toru. I recognized the scent of his pomade.

"Hold on," he said. "Phineas will take care of it."

I heard a *thwack* as someone applied a cane to the slats of a chair. The noise eased slightly. Another *thwack*, even louder, made me wince. The noise level abated. My jangled nerves followed suit. Slowly. I sat up and put my hands in my lap.

"Captain," Phineas said, "Dr. Nakagawa and I have decided to revise our original arrangements for Miss Rees."

"In what respects, Mr. Quade?"

"Given that Miss Wei appears to have been complicit in smuggling aboard Miss Hsu's brother and supplying him with food, Miss Wei seems to be compromised. She must be prevented from having further contact with Miss Rees. This is true whether or not Miss Wei actively participated in later events such as the death of Miss Bonney."

"What do you propose?"

"That Miss Wei be confined, under guard, for the remainder of the voyage—or, at the very least, until you have apprehended Miss Hsu's brother, confirmed his identity, and determined his guilt or innocence."

"We have a storage room below decks we can use. Anything else?"

"Miss Rees requires a companion. Miss Hsu is still the most likely candidate, as she's given evidence against her brother and her future sister-in-law. And she's already moved into the cabin next door. But her actions last night and this morning raise questions about her motivations. We'd prefer to finish questioning her now, but we have an important meeting. It might be prudent to confine Miss Hsu to her cabin in the interim."

"Agreed. Mr. Arnold and I will continue *our* interview with Miss Hsu and Miss Wei, and then deliver them to their respective quarters. Mr. Arnold will report the substance of what we learn later."

"Captain?" I said.

"Yes, Miss Rees?"

"Would you be so kind as to send a couple of sailors ahead to my cabin? Please ask them to check under the berth and examine the trunk that's stored there. I'd prefer to avoid midnight surprises."

"As would I, Miss Rees. As would I."

I nodded to Lin as I left the alcove. A smile touched her lips for a moment, though I might have imagined it. We both knew I was abandoning her—as she'd been abandoned by her mother and her family.

Phineas and Toru, trailed by a guard, escorted me back to my cabin. In our passageway, we met the sailors Captain Stowall had sent ahead to check the cabin. I felt like I was four again, imagining a *chupacabra* hiding under the bed. *There be monsters.*

"The trunk was pulled out, Miss Rees," said one of the seamen. "Was that how you left it?"

I looked at his name tag. "No, Mr. Biggs."

"Thought not. Looks like someone crawled in behind it at some point. May have dropped this." Biggs held out his hand.

"This" was a small square of rice paper with writing on it. Chinese or Japanese. I handed the paper to Toru, who skimmed it, frowned, and said, "It's a name and address on Dupont Street in San Francisco."

"Chinatown," Phineas said.

Toru nodded. "The name is Chinese."

"If that's all, miss?" The sailors took a step, as if to go.

"Almost. When you looked under the bunk, did you happen to see a brass urn in the corner?"

"No, miss. Just the paper."

Hundun had taken the urn with our father's ashes. Whatever could he want with it?

I said, "How did he get into my cabin with a guard outside the door? And how did he manage to leave, carrying a ginger jar?"

"The guard wasn't there when we arrived."

"Did you look behind the screen in my room?"

"No. Just under the berth, like we was ordered."

Toru walked back to Ah Jim's station. They had a murmured conversation. The steward trotted down the passageway to unlock my cabin again. I watched Biggs go inside to check behind the screen.

Toru, Phineas, and I followed more slowly. Phineas said, "Did Ah Jim see what happened to the guard?"

"No," Toru said. "But Ah Jim wasn't at his station the entire time. He answered calls in a couple of the cabins. He hasn't seen the guard for at least an hour."

Biggs came out and shrugged. No guard. But I was sure he wouldn't have left his post. The captain ran a tight ship.

I asked Ah Jim to unlock Lin's cabin next door. He hesitated. Biggs told him to go ahead, that we weren't going to rob the place, just check it.

Inside Lin's cabin, on the deck, lay the guard, unconscious, with a knot the size of a lemon on the back of his head.

Phineas sent Biggs to report to the captain and request Dr. Doyle, then said to the other seaman, "Check Miss Wei's trunk, please."

Ah Jim and the sailor pulled out two trunks and opened them. Both held a few clothes. Behind the screen, I found another trunk, standing on end in the corner. It was of varnished teak, with cushioned insides and air holes spaced like the design of twisting wind.

Chaos.

* * *

I locked my cabin door behind me. Two guards outside. Secure. My jangled nerves began to ease.

Phineas and Toru had sent a note to Mrs. Hartfield postponing our meeting. Supper was four hours away. Yet food held no attraction. All I wanted was to dissolve into sleep. But the aberrant cooler temperatures of last night had dissipated. Now, heat and humidity were like living things.

My arm throbbed. I hadn't noticed it during the inquiry or the cabin search. Distractions kept my pain in abeyance. There were none in my silent room. I heard only the background noises of a floating city at tea time.

I stripped off my clothes, sponged my sticky skin for the third time that day, and donned a simple silk shift the color of cherry blossoms. Sighing, I eased my body down on the mattress.

But sometimes one is too tired to sleep. My father taught me that. The mind roils, worrying a problem, personal or circumstantial.

I used to go looking for one of my parents when my mind wouldn't quiet. More often than not, I would find my father working at his desk. In mining camps, the desk would be makeshift—planks laid atop sawhorses or stumps. In his San Francisco office, a simple heavy

Mission-style piece. In his university office in Lima, a carved Spanish writing desk transported by some long-ago colonist. When I would sneak in, sometimes he would close what he was doing and put it away in the safe. Other times he would let me sit on his lap and we would look at a mining plan he was drafting or student exercise he was grading. The mining school in Lima was only a few years old, and he was hoping to establish it as one of the best in the Western Hemisphere. But that was before my mother died, before he returned to roaming the world, daughter in tow, seeking new prospects for the company.

I often wondered what was in those papers he hid away in his safe. When he thought he was going to die, he'd had me take his papers from the safe at Toru's family estate and bring them to the hospital. I sat by his bed as he went through them, and then found my way to the hospital furnace to destroy those pages he entrusted to me. The rest went back in the leather portfolio that, along with his maps and field notebooks, he entrusted to Phineas. I had never asked Phineas about them. I felt he would tell me when he judged I was ready. Until then, my father's secrets would be a burden too heavy for me to bear.

Still, I wondered if my father's work could have caused someone to hire Wei Xi and her brothers. Or had something much more prosaic—greed, jealousy, pride, or lust for power—have triggered the murders?

I wasn't sure I'd ever know the answer to those questions. But now, as I lay on my berth, something else bothered me. Why had Chaos taken the brass urn with our father's ashes?

Part III

On board the O&OL Oceanic, northern Pacific Ocean
Wednesday, August 5, 1885

"Yield not you to your troubles, but march more boldly to
meet them, in the path your fortune shall permit you."
— Virgil, The Aeneid VI (translated by James Lonsdale
and Samuel Lee, 1871)

Chapter 14

3:45 a.m.

I WOKE AS THE stars were blinking out. I'd been dreaming I was in a box and Wei Xi was lowering the lid.

Knowing that my half-brother was at large and planning his next attack infused the morning with tension. But I shook it off. Today they would find him and lock him in a different kind of box. This evening, if I could arrange it, we would have a memorial for Annie.

I couldn't ask my guardians to walk with me so early, and Lin was confined to her cabin, as far as I knew, so I opted for a leisurely bath and an early breakfast.

The night steward brought my cleaned and mended frock and took my order. Breakfast arrived as I was pinning up my hair. Enough food for two. Good. I hadn't roused for dinner last night.

As I feasted on fruit compote, three slices of toast, and two boiled eggs, I listed the remaining questions I wanted to ask Wei Xi. At the bottom of the list, I added the translation Toru had provided of the name and address on the note left under my berth. I made a second list of questions for my coming interview with Hsu Lin, and copied both lists for my guardians.

When the teapot was half down, I thought to offer the guard a share of what was left. He refused, saying it was against regulations, thank you very kindly. He couldn't protect me with his hands occupied with a teacup.

This conversation was conducted sotto voce, so as not to wake nearby passengers. I said I understood, and changed the subject. "How is Mr. Robie?"

"Coming along, miss. Coming along. You can see for yourself, soon. He'll be on at oh-five-hundred when we double up again."

The clock showed four forty-five.

"Mr. Arnold didn't think you'd be up this early, Miss Rees, or he'd have sent Robie by now."

Down the hall, Phineas emerged from his cabin. Using hand signals, I asked if I could join him on his morning perambulation. He nodded.

Robie arrived three minutes later, looking rested, but walking as if he favored his right side. He must have been waiting in the wings. We both smiled, acknowledging silently that it was good to have survived yesterday's attack.

He had a pistol tucked in his belt. I brought out a chair, saying it was doctor's orders. Robie hesitated. I insisted. He sat. If he stood as soon as I was out of sight, well, one could only do so much.

I grabbed my sketchpad and the lists. The night guard accompanied me. We found Phineas on deck, by the rail, face lifted to the lightening sky. It would be another scorching day, but blessed coolness infused the morning air.

Toru joined us after the first lap around the deck. He brought up the delayed business meeting.

"Did you and Mrs. Hartfield set a new time to meet?" I asked. Her presence would solve several problems for me. She could answer legal questions, draw up my will, and serve as the mature female presence required by convention.

"She will be available at midmorning," Toru said.

"Perhaps we could use the captain's dining alcove again," I said. "More private. I don't think one of our cabins would do at all."

That settled, I asked how they'd spent their evenings, and if they'd learned anything new about our culprit.

"I retired to my cabin for the rest of the day," Phineas said. "Dr. Doyle came after dinner for a game of draughts. He said he'd heard nothing about Hundun other than that he is still at large, despite an exhaustive search. Doyle also said that Wei Xi is confined, under guard, below decks. And she has gone silent."

"Well, there's no reason we can't submit questions to

Mr. Arnold for his next round with her," I said. I handed Phineas the lists I'd made and asked if they'd had an opportunity to question Hsu Lin further.

Toru shook his head. Phineas jotted down a couple of additional questions and handed the page to Toru. We had discovered a rhythm that worked for us—everyone seeking answers to the same suite of questions, and then meeting to discuss the results.

"I'll arrange a meeting with Hsu Lin," I said. "I've composed a contract I think will do."

Toru folded my list of questions and tucked it into the pocket of his dove-gray silk vest. He wore it over a white shirt with sleeves turned up so that a passing breeze could cool his wrists. No coat. He looked like what he was: a geologist comfortable with the greater world, not a slave to the strictures of dress.

They walked me to my door. Robie stood as I approached and gave me a broad smile. My guardians waited while I retrieved the draft contract. "Make any amendments you wish," I said. "I'd like to have a scribe draft it before our meeting with Mrs. Hartfield."

"If there are no problems, I will take it to the scribe myself," Toru said.

I kissed their cheeks. "Then I shall see you later this morning, gentlemen. *À bientôt.*"

Chapter 15

6:25 a.m.

H*SU LIN MUST HAVE* heard me moving around. She
knocked on the adjoining wall, and we both
poked our heads out into the corridor. I waved for her to
join me. Might as well begin the inquisition now.

She'd ordered breakfast so asked that it be
redirected to my cabin. I requested a carafe of coffee. We
sat at the small table. I wondered what they were serving
Wei Xi, and if she'd had a restful night.

Lin seemed to have slept well. No bloodshot eyes. No
circles below. And when the food came, she did not pick
at it as she had yesterday. Perhaps she welcomed the
absence of less-than-honorable Aunt Xi.

When Lin pushed her plate to the side and refilled
her cup, I said, "Do you mind sharing with me what you
know of your mother? And how she met Father?"

She tipped her head to the side like a bird on a
branch studying a worm below, then straightened her
neck and met my eyes. "I will tell you what I have learned
about Wing-Li from various people over the years. Some
of them hated or despised her. But they all agreed that
she was beautiful. And reckless.

"She was born in the year of the horse, as Hundun
and I were. She was passionate, stubborn, and contrary
by nature. Hated having her feet bound. Fought to be
taught reading and writing and healing with herbs. She
lost those battles. And others.

"Her father, my grandfather, owed a favor to a
government official in Shanghai Province. My mother's
brother and a Japanese merchant had fought over a
woman. The Japanese man died of his wounds. If my
uncle's part in it were revealed, the family would lose

status, power, and our Japanese market. So, in exchange for the official's silence, Grandfather offered him a share in the business."

The more Lin spoke, the more colloquial her English became. Almost no accent or struggle to find the right word. She looked down at her cup or at the sky outside the porthole, but not at me. It was as if she was talking to herself.

"But the official," she continued, "who was an old family friend, asked instead for my mother. Not in marriage or as a concubine, either of which would have been honorable positions. Rather, she would be installed as the man's mistress in a separate dwelling with its own staff. And though he might use her when he wished, her main purpose, and what she was eventually trained for, was spying. He made her available as an escort for visiting dignitaries and businessmen. She learned their secrets and relayed them to her owner. And because she was quick, and because he agreed to educate her, she became very skilled in her profession."

"This official... Was he Wei Xi's brother?"

"Her father."

"And how old was your mother when the man took her?"

Lin sighed and found my eyes. "Eleven."

She told me Wing-Li had been twenty-three when the provincial official introduced her to our father. She was offered as companion and translator for as long as Father was in Shanghai. She induced him to talk about his work, even sailed upriver with him to explore mining properties.

I had trouble believing my father would have been taken in by a beautiful body and an inquisitive mind. He'd been playing the business game for several years by then.

"I assume she had previously avoided bearing children," I said. "What happened?"

"Grandmother told me Wing-Li hoped that if she were with child, her owner would stop watching her so closely."

"She wanted to escape, and she thought Father could help?"

"Yes. But he left before she confirmed she was with child."

The letter I carried in my sketchbook cover was Sabine de Keridec's acceptance of my father's oft-repeated marriage proposal. She said she would set sail from Calais on the morning tide. Destination: San Francisco. My father had packed his bags and boarded the first ship heading east.

If he'd known that the woman he'd left behind in Shanghai was carrying his children, would it have changed things? I doubted it. Once he'd been apprised of Hsu Lin's existence, he'd paid to have his daughter educated, in hopes she might have a better life than her mother. But beyond that he hadn't been willing to go.

I stood and walked to the dresser. Picked up the signet ring and took it back to the table. "You recognized this belonged to Father?"

She hesitated, then gave a slight nod. "He was wearing it when he visited me last winter. I wanted something that was his. I have a wedding tiara that was my grandmother's, but nothing owned by my parents."

"But that doesn't explain the necklace. Did you imagine I would just let it go?"

"What right had *you* to a jade Chinese dragon?" The words stabbed the space between us. "It should have been mine."

I held her gaze. "Would it make any difference if I told you it was a gift from Phineas and Toru last Christmas?"

"I thought—"

"They bought it in the Philippines." I let her dwell on that for a moment. "But I think there's another reason why you stole from me so overtly."

Her posture stilled.

"To take my measure. Was I a simple schoolgirl, naïve, innocent, perhaps so self-centered I wouldn't notice? Would I stand up to you?"

Her continued silence told me more than words.

"Together, Hsu Lin, you and I could make a formidable unit. But set in opposition? The battle would result, at best, in a Pyrrhic victory for one of us. Ergo, I suggest a truce."

I took a small, cloth-wrapped parcel from the pocket of my skirt and slid the package across the table. She didn't move.

"Go ahead. It won't bite."

She opened the scarlet silk to reveal a pair of hair pins, long as knitting needles, topped with golden plum blossoms, each petal carefully crafted. "They're from a little shop in Tokyo. I believe they're quite old. They suit your coloring."

My voice stumbled on the last word. I couldn't tell her that Father had been saving them for my sixteenth birthday.

I rose, went to the sink, and cooled my face with a damp cloth. Instead of returning to the table, I stood by the porthole. Parting the curtains, I watched the ship's huge shadow glide over sapphire swells. On the deck, three tow-headed girls crooned to their dolls in German.

"Keri." When I turned, she was refolding the material into a package. "It is too much."

I leaned down and wrapped her fingers around the silk. "Would you refuse a gift from your father? I found them among his effects. For all I know, they were intended for you." As lies go, it was a minor infraction, especially if it aided the *rapprochement* of estranged sisters.

I felt her fingers weighing the costs of accepting the gift. She blinked twice, slowly, but I saw no other signs of emotion as I removed my hands. *Baby steps, Keri.*

Lin met my eyes. Hers were shadowed, but dry. She stood. The package disappeared into her pocket as she turned toward the door.

"Wait, please, Lin."

She halted, her back to me.

I spoke just loud enough for her to hear. "I've taken the liberty of drawing up a contract, modeled on the one I had with Annie. My guardians are reviewing it." I outlined the terms. "The salary will be paid into an account with the purser, to which only you will have access."

"Why would you help me when my brother and Wei Xi hurt you so. And when I failed to help you yesterday?"

"Because you've been hurt, too. And because I sense

this marriage is not of your choosing."

Finally, she turned. She scanned my face.

"As it is, neither of us is free," I said. "We're both underage. But as long as I have guards assigned to me, and guardians to act as escorts, we can get away with flaunting convention. At least a little."

"The other passengers expect me to act strangely because I'm of mixed blood."

"Truly?"

She smiled then, and the smile became a laugh. "It helps when I pretend that I cannot speak their language. You'll simply have to follow suit when I suddenly switch to French."

It was my turn to laugh, something I hadn't done in days. I said, "In addition to the funds, if you wish, we can tailor Annie's clothes to fit you. You are shorter, so it would be a matter of taking in the seams and hemming the skirts. Do you sew? I'm capable of fashioning clothes and doing minor repairs, but I'm not a seamstress."

"I was taught fine work by the nuns. The trade is listed on my passport."

We shook on it. And I felt my spirits lift, as if Annie were giving her blessing.

"Will you come with me to the library?" I asked.

"Yes. Let us begin our new journey surrounded by books. I love books."

Chapter 16

HSU **LIN AND I** left Robie to guard my cabin. The second guard followed us to the library, where Mr. Arnold sat at his usual desk. I suspected he worked there to make it easier to serve as courier between passengers and captain, or perhaps to collect information from overheard conversations and pass it up the line.

This time, Arnold was not alone. The widow Pomfrew and her daughter sat on the sofa, sharing a post-breakfast pot of coffee.

I said good morning and moved to the bookshelves near the steward's desk. Chose a book at random—travel stories by Mrs. Isabella Bird on a trip across the United States—and stood as if immersed in the narrative. Lin, perceiving my wish for a more private conversation with the captain's secretary, took a seat in an armchair across from the women, nodded hello, and picked up a copy of *Century Magazine* from the coffee table.

The Pomfrew conversation came to an abrupt halt. I saw a look of dismay cross the elder woman's face, which I interpreted as her reluctance to share close quarters with my Eurasian sister. Mrs. Pomfrew tut-tutted, hoping, I guessed, to drive us away. When that didn't work, she made a faux search of the space around her person. "Oh, dear, Penelope, I seem to have left my music in the cabin."

Her daughter sighed. "Do you want me to fetch it for you, Mother?"

"Why don't we go together? I should freshen up before the rehearsal."

Penelope pulled a small watch from her pocket. Diamonds winked in the light from the portholes. "We have—"

"Not much time. I know, dear." Mrs. Pomfrew stood and pulled Penelope to her feet.

"But—"

"If we hurry, we'll just make it. And, did I tell you? Mr. Lamb said last night that he'd attend."

The words magically erased Penelope's resistance. "Why didn't you say so right off, Mother?"

I mouthed a thank you to Lin, returned the book to the shelf, noted the grin the steward was trying to suppress, and edged close to where Arnold was updating his logbook.

"Nicely done, Miss Rees," he said, without looking up.

"Miss Hsu deserves the credit, Mr. Arnold."

"Admittedly. I suppose you want the results of our interviews with Miss Wei and with Mrs. Edward Small?"

"By all means."

Arnold found the correct page in the logbook. "I re-interviewed Mrs. Small." He studied the entry as if composing a summary.

"I don't suppose your notes include her Christian name?" It always irritated me when wives were referred to by their husband's name, as if they had no life or personality outside the bubble of marriage. Hundreds of times I'd heard my mother ask the same question.

"Felicity Tigard Small."

"Thank you, Mr. Arnold."

"Mrs. Small said that when she and her husband were speaking to Miss Bonney, he made an ungentle-manly comment about your companion."

"That makes the third such incident with Mr. Small."

"So I understand." Arnold's even tone was tinged with distaste. "This one resulted in a tiff between the Smalls that lasted all the way to the games parlor. Mrs. Small abandoned her plan to play cards and insisted he walk her back to their cabin before he joined his own game."

"Did Felicity Small tell you what her husband said to Annie?"

Arnold hesitated, then ran a finger around his neck, under his collar, as if the material had shrunk in the wash. "It was not so much what Mr. Small said as where he was gazing while he spoke. When I pressed Mrs. Small, she said her husband had had too much wine and brandy with dinner, on top of several glasses of whiskey prior to the meal."

This mirrored Annie's earlier interactions with him. She'd told me his language had been bold and suggestive, and he'd smelled of spirits. She said the hair rose on her neck whenever their paths crossed.

"I take it the newlywed Felicity Small had not before experienced this side of Mr. Small."

"Suffice it to say, Mrs. Small was much put out that her husband, when inebriated, found his remark humorous. She didn't. Her vexation has not yet dissipated."

An understatement. I pressed him. "Given that scenario, could you share Mr. Small's comment?"

I'm not sure why Arnold decided to tell me, but he read directly from his notes, not meeting my eyes. "Mrs. Small claims he said, referring to Miss Bonney: 'Too much woman for a one-armed man.' But Mrs. Small understood that her husband was quoting an observation someone else had made."

"Did you ask her from whom the comment originated?"

"I did. It was made by Mr. Gideon Lamb, she thought, although there were five men at the card table Sunday evening."

"Thank you, Mr. Arnold. It seems a pattern was developing in the way Mr. Small treated Annie. But the quote you shared demonstrates that at least five men, including Mr. Small and Mr. Lamb were aware that Michael McGinn was courting Annie. What we don't know is whether the gossip or the sentiment behind it had any bearing on her disappearance.

"Moreover, there's the question of Mr. Small's alibi that night. Mr. Lamb was dining with the captain when Annie disappeared, so Lamb can't supply an alibi for anyone outside the alcove. And he would have joined their card game when it was already in progress. Which leads us to other questions: Who else was at the card table? When did each of them arrive? And, were any of them on deck a few minutes before ten o'clock?"

"I've already sent men to follow up with Mr. Lamb, and to re-interview the other men at the card table."

I hesitated, unsure how to broach the next topic.

"Something else, Miss Rees?"

I lowered my soft tones even further. "My question concerns Mr. Mayweather, who sat in on the interview with Miss Hsu and Miss Wei."

He did look up then, a wariness in his eyes. "Go on," he said and returned to his smooth, neat writing. He was recording our conversation.

"In short, Mr. Arnold, who is Mr. Mayweather, this British man who speaks fluent French and Mandarin?"

The quill pen stopped scratching. "We've known Mr. Mayweather for many years. But I'll have to check with Captain Stowall before I answer any questions about him."

"Yes, please confer with the captain about what, if anything, you can share with me." I didn't tell him that, in the meantime, I'd see what I could find out myself.

"As you wish, Miss Rees."

"Were you able to extract any more information about Hundun from Miss Wei? My guardians and I are concerned he will make another attempt on my life."

"Miss Wei refused to speak any further. She is also refusing food. If this continues, we may ask Miss Hsu to visit her and encourage her to eat."

We looked over at Lin. She nodded.

"It's settled then." Arnold made a note. "Is that all?"

I set an envelope by his pen hand. "A list of questions my guardians and I think pertinent."

"May I?" His fingers touched the flap, which I'd left open.

I nodded.

He pulled out the sheet of ship's stationery and unfolded it. I'd memorized the questions.

1. Where did Miss Wei go after Hundun visited her cabin the night Annie disappeared?

2. Related to question 1: Did Miss Wei reveal

what she'd done with Annie's purse? Wei Xi said she was going to give it to the purser. Did she? Or did she empty it of anything of value and then throw it overboard? Or did she give it to someone else on board?

3. Did the crew see Wei Xi talking to anyone on deck the night Annie disappeared? A Chinese crew member, perhaps (although Wei Xi also understands and speaks at least rudimentary English)? A passenger?

4. Did Miss Wei reveal where Hundun had been hiding since being smuggled aboard in Shanghai? Where did she leave food for him?

5. Has the search revealed any trace of Hundun?

"I'll take these to Captain Stowall directly," Arnold said. "Where will you be, if you're not in your cabin?"

The Pomfrews entered the library again, this time with Felicity Small. Strength in numbers. They were hoping, no doubt, that Lin and I had vacated the room.

"I'll be in a business meeting, and then..." I shrugged.

"I have a suggestion." Arnold's words couldn't have carried more than a few feet.

I replied just as softly. "Any place that would give Lin a bit of respite from the rudeness of her fellow passengers."

"We have a small chapel. It might be a refuge for you both. And anytime you wish, we can ask the chaplain to stop by. Mr. Quade sent the captain a note this morning, asking about arranging a memorial service for Miss Bonney, given that..."

"Given that the evidence supports a finding of 'lost at sea.'"

My heart felt squeezed in a vise. I'd awakened that morning knowing I'd have to organize a memorial service. But I'd been avoiding taking the first step. Phineas had taken it for me.

"Whoever is on duty will send word to Chaplain

Colins." Arnold gestured toward the faithful shadow who'd been standing just inside the door and watching every person who entered. "When you're ready, Miss Rees."

"And Mr. McGinn?" If I was having a hard time dealing with Annie's loss, how much worse must Michael be suffering? I felt guilty that I'd made no effort to contact him yesterday, to at least attempt to console him.

"Of course."

"Thank you, Mr. Arnold."

I collected my other shadow, Hsu Lin, and offered a brisk good morning to the Pomfrews and Felicity Small as we swept by.

Chapter 17

8:45 a.m.

I *PARTED WITH HSU* Lin, promising to see her at lunch. I needed privacy to consider Annie's memorial service. And I needed to prepare for the ten o'clock business meeting.

The cabin had been cleaned, soiled clothes taken to the laundry, and Lin's breakfast tray removed. When they'd made up my berth, Ah Jim had found my sketchpad among the sheets. The book and pencil now resided on the night table. Next to the book was a small, green glass cylinder chased with silver. It held two gardenias, just starting to yellow. The color contrasted with the stark white paper wrapped around the vase and tied with a twist of hemp. A small bronze Chinese coin had been threaded through the hemp.

The paper sleeve hadn't been there yesterday when I'd returned from having my wound dressed by the doctor. I remembered lifting the vase to smell the flowers, my mother's favorite scent, before going to the meeting in the alcove. I'd been so distracted or tired ever since that I couldn't say when the paper was added. But I was on edge enough to be concerned about any unexplained changes in my environment. Besides, I preferred the green glass to a paper sleeve.

I sat on the berth, slid the vase toward me, and untied the hemp bow. The paper sprang open. Two pages from one of my sketchbooks, covered in tiny script. Idiomatic English. A letter, hidden in plain sight.

Sister—

You were an assignment. I knew where and when, but I did not know why. I was trained not to ask why. In my profession, reasons are unimportant. And where I go soon, there will be no why—and no more Chaos, either within or without a box.

Men were ordered to kill a man named Rees on the sacred mountain. When their efforts failed and it appeared Rees would recover, I was brought in. The man's name meant nothing to me then. He was simply a man in a hospital bed. I poisoned his water carafe late one night as he slept. But hours later, someone used the carafe as a vase for flowers. In the end, Wei Xi fulfilled the contract.

Blades do not question the smith who made them. I knew from the mirror and my training that I was a bastard, a mongrel, but I did not know until last night which parent was Asian—or that I had tried and failed to kill my father. Nor was I told that the target aboard the ship is my half-sister.

I am sorry for killing your friend. It was an error—the third error I have made since I began working. The second error was missing you that first night aboard. The fourth and final error was missing your heart this morning. I am not sorry I failed to kill you. Had I been successful, only one of our father's children would have been left. Two is better than one. I am glad I had the chance to meet both of you.

The address I left under your berth is where you will find the person who ordered that your life and our father's life be taken. That person is an intermediary, hired for the purpose. Wei Xi told me that the one who paid is from your country. I would have helped you find him, but I realize I was never meant to reach port. I am disposable.

You must know that you are still a target—although not my target. Despite that pressure and concern, please do what you can to help our sister avoid my fate. She also, I suspect, is considered disposable by the person who engaged Wei Xi and her brothers.

I listened to your conversation this morning from a hiding place above the after deck. I like the quickness of your mind, its energy and facility, the surprising way you puzzle things out. I think we might have got on well together if the river of life had flowed in a different direction.

The signature was a whirlwind above an open box. The note had been written yesterday and secreted in my cabin.

It was possible the note was a ruse to entice me to let down my guard. It was possible that Hundun had no plans to end his life. But I believed the truth and sincerity of his words. For I was the one who had put flowers in Father's water carafe very early one morning. I couldn't understand then why they were wilted by evening. Hundun's note confirmed what I'd suspected—that my father had been murdered.

I felt cold, empty, as if I'd been orphaned twice.

I roused myself. I could mourn later. There were decisions to make. First and foremost, what to do with the new information? If I found a way to stop Hundun, he'd still face the gibbet in some British port. I didn't believe our father would have wanted the gallows for his only son, but Annie would have demanded Hundun atone for his sins. Both were right. Yet, wasn't Hundun atoning by choosing to end his life as his mother had done?

I let the paper curl closed. The letter changed everything. We no longer needed to know Mr. Small's alibi for the time of Annie's death, or check the alibis of the other men at the poker game. Hundun had confessed to killing Annie by mistake. The unknowns now were who had hired the Wei family to kill my father and me— and why.

The answers to those questions might have to wait till we were in San Francisco, unless I was right about Wei Xi delivering Annie's purse or its contents to someone on board as proof the deed was done. Right now I must show the note to my guardians and send the original to the captain. And I must keep the contents from Hsu Lin, at least until she had visited Wei Xi and encouraged her to answer our questions. Once Lin learned that Hundun had been ordered by the Wei family to kill our father, I doubted she would be able to hide her anger and disgust.

I made two copies of the note. I folded one and put it in the leather cover of my sketchbook, next to my mother's letter. The original I retied into a scroll for the captain. I then composed messages to Chaplain Colins and Michael, suggesting we meet at one thirty.

A knock broke the silence. That would be my guardians. I picked up the second copy and the notes and opened the door.

Chapter 18

ROBIE WAS REGALING **PHINEAS** and Toru with his version of Hundun's attack. "Oh, didn't see you there, Miss Rees. All set?"

"Yes, thank you, Robie. Will you accompany us, please?" I thanked our other guard for staying behind to watch over my cabin, and tucked my hand through Toru's arm. "Could we stop by the purser's station, please?"

Phineas led off, as there wasn't room for us to walk three abreast. I asked, "Will Mrs. Hartfield be meeting us there?"

"Her plans changed," Toru said. "She's in the middle of a draughts tournament."

"And she's winning?"

"I think she will play Mr. Lamb in the final pairing. She said she'd be happy to work with us anytime after that match concludes."

She must be clever, imaginative, and competitive. Boded well for our relationship, whether short or long. "Well, I know who I'm rooting for."

"Indeed," Toru said.

I handed the messages and scroll over to a courier standing by the purser's desk, requesting that he place the scroll directly into either Mr. Arnold's hands or the captain's.

At the alcove door, Toru asked Robie if he'd like a chair while he waited outside. "Yes, thank you, sir. But don't you worry none. Won't no one get by me." He showed us his pistol. "You go ahead and have your meeting. I'll make sure you won't be disturbed."

"Mr. Robie, you are truly a knight in shining armor," I said.

He blushed, as I knew he would. "Just Robie, miss."

"We'll see you in an hour, then, Just Robie."

Phineas smiled behind his burgundy-colored neckerchief. Toru, shaking his head, closed the door behind us. "You will be a deadly flirt in another couple of years, Keri."

"It might be a useful tool to learn, gentlemen," I said. "Portable and nonlethal."

"Not always," Phineas said. "Men are unpredictable creatures."

"But I'll have you two to guide me, won't I?"

I sat at the end of the table. Phineas sighed as he claimed the chair on my right, opened his attaché case, and removed a file and a pencil. Being my guardian was not an easy job.

Toru set his hat on the table, took the chair on my left, and crossed one elegant leg over another. He smoothed the wrinkles out of pale gray pants and folded his hands. "Shall we begin?"

From past experience I knew that Toru would remember, word for word, what was discussed and decided. He was an extraordinarily aural learner, spoke five or six languages fluently, and understood several more. Had he decided on espionage as a career, instead of geology, his talents would have made him a formidable asset for any country. Or adversary.

I pulled my sketchbook from my pocket and handed Phineas the copy of Hundun's note I'd made for them. I gave my copy to Toru.

"What's this, then?" Phineas asked.

"Hundun left this in my room. I found it this morning. I've sent the original to the captain."

Phineas skimmed the letter. "So, he's confessing to killing Miss Bonney, knowing who attacked Glen on Fujiyama, and attempting to poison Glen in the hospital. But not to killing him. We have Miss Wei to thank for that." He cleared his throat, but speech was beyond him. His best friend and colleague had been murdered. He gestured to Toru to take over.

Toru's dark gaze was hard as schorl, as if the anger and helplessness of that day on Mount Fuji hadn't faded with time. "I gather your half-brother does not expect to reach America alive. If I have the opportunity, I will make sure he does not."

"Toru, no," I said. "I couldn't bear to lose you, too."

His eyes softened as he touched my hand. "I will be careful. And you… are you coping?"

I'd locked away my emotional response to my father's murder. The anger, tears, and fears now resided in a corner of my mind. There they would stay until we were safely on shore and I had the breathing space to mourn properly. My parents had taught me how to cope with horrors during our escape from South America.

I patted Toru's cheek. "Physically, I am well. But the threat is still out there, and we're no closer to identifying the person or persons pulling the strings. He or she or they may be on the ship, or waiting to strike when we reach port. Or both. And we still don't know why."

"But we have one assassin under guard, and one who is assuring you that he will not attempt to injure you again. In addition, we have a little over a week's reprieve before we reach shore. That gives us time to narrow down the field of possible perpetrators."

"How do we do that without knowing the motive?"

"By exploring who would benefit most by Glen's death," Phineas said. "And yours."

"It would help to know more about my father's past. The answers may lie there."

"More than likely." Phineas passed Toru the file he'd taken from his attaché case. I recognized it as one I'd created while my father was in hospital. "Company assets might hold some clues, if the attacks are business-related."

Toru skimmed the file, then closed it and looked at me. "Having worked with your father both in the office and in the field, you are familiar with the mining exploration and engineering sides of the business."

I nodded. My father had found me boy's clothes and taken me down into the mines to show me how he made the measurements and maps that directed the development of the mining properties. I'd seen gold, silver, copper, lead, mercury, and tin mines, subsurface and open-pit. Each operation and situation was unique.

"I recommend we focus on the few updates Phineas and I received by letter in the days after Glen died," Toru continued. "It would save time."

I began taking notes.

"We suggest putting the Philippines project on hold," Phineas said to me. "The prospects will require too much capital. The technology to develop the claims will need to be created before we can proceed. You and Toru can discuss the potential with Rep once we reach San Francisco."

"Rep" was Rhoderic Evans Perry, a young mining engineer and geologist. Another Welshman my father had fostered and brought to America to assist in the field and lab work and to draft reports. He'd been educated in England and the United States, including summer field seasons with various geological surveys of the West. I'd known him for four years.

"Agreed," I said. "Next?"

"The Sonora and Durango mines," Toru said. "We will be starting Phase II on the former and Phase IV on the latter by year's end."

And so it continued for our mines and prospects in Peru, Mexico, California, Nevada, Arizona, New Mexico, Colorado, and Idaho. Our company had been set up to find properties, stake and file claims, determine their economic potential, create mining plans, and bring mines into production. My father's genius had lain in finding properties and assessing potential, although he could handle any phase of planning and production.

Toru's interests lay in deposits associated with old volcanic terrains, as one would expect from someone born in Japan. However, he was a very good negotiator, and he excelled at training young geologists. He had spent the last year and a half teaching at the new University of Tokyo. He wanted his country to produce as many qualified geologists as possible within one generation. With that aim in mind, he and his students had spent six months of his tenure in the field, prospecting for viable deposits with my father and Phineas.

Phineas, who had studied and trained alongside my father in Europe and the western States, developed the properties and oversaw the staff we put in place to manage the mines and claims. His talents lay in sensing when things were amiss—when the price of the ores had fluctuated to the point where it was not profitable to continue mining, for example, or when someone was trying to move in on our properties—and coming up with solutions to the problems. In addition to bringing properties into production, it was his job to shut down a mine, inform the miners and site geologists, and provide severance pay.

My guardians and I went through the list quickly until we reached the projects at risk. Someone, or some company, was trying to usurp our properties in California. This was always a problem, and had been since men had jumped mines and prospects at the beginning of the mining boom in the West.

We three were quiet for a moment, each waiting for another to speak. Finally I said, "We'll have to replace my father, won't we." Not a question. "You two have other strengths, or other specializations. That's why the triumvirate worked so well for so long."

"Glen was talented and had the energy of three men," Phineas said. "As a geologist, he'll be difficult to replace."

"What about Clarence King?"

King had led the geologic exploration of the 40th Parallel, a transect across the West. He'd brought together the best young geologists and cartographers, and a photographer to help document their work. The publication was still one of the most comprehensive and beautifully presented geologic studies I'd ever seen. Six years ago, King had convinced Congress of the need for a United States Geological Survey to continue the topographical and geological exploration of the western territories and to help open the West to exploitation of the natural resources. On top of that, he'd saved investors from fraud by exposing a diamond and gemstone hoax. He was also an accomplished writer.

"He has the same sort of brilliance as your father," Phineas said. "And a similar charisma. But..." He looked at

Toru, who gave a slight shake of the head. "But he has other demands on his time, including a mine in Mexico. Plus, I don't think he'd be willing to relocate from the East Coast to San Francisco."

"Samuel Emmons?" I said.

Samuel Franklin Emmons had trained at the mining schools in Paris and Freiburg with Phineas and my father. He'd introduced my father to my mother in Paris. Toru had met him on the slopes of an Italian volcano. They'd all been good friends, and that bond had lasted. I'd met "Mr. Em," as he suggested I call him, at our home in San Francisco when I was a toddler. I don't think Emmons had children, though I remembered my mother mentioning a wife. He'd dined with us whenever his geology path crossed my father's over the years.

Emmons had worked with Clarence King on the 40th Parallel Survey. Six years ago, King had tasked him with heading up the Rocky Mountain Division of the U.S. Geological Survey, headquartered in Denver. Emmons and his crew had mapped the Leadville ore deposits and studied how they'd formed. That paper, with accompanying maps, was due to be published next year.

The summer I turned ten, my family joined the boomtown throng at Leadville. Around the Survey campfire, Emmons told me stories of his adventures mapping in the West. When he discovered I had advanced drafting skills and was careful in my work, he'd given me small drafting jobs to do while my parents were out exploring the rocks and plants. The camp cook had kept an eye on me, and he let me help with meal preparation. It had been one of the best summers of my life.

"It is a good suggestion, Keri," Toru said.

"I don't think he'd leave the Survey, but he might explore for us on a contract basis," Phineas said, his voice little more than a croak. He was tiring. "Perhaps as a favor, to fill in while we find someone else. But he's never been interested in the nuts and bolts of bringing a mine from concept to production. He prefers making geologic maps and figuring out how the deposits originated. That said, he might suggest a mining engineer we can hire on a trial basis to see if he fits." The effort of speech sent him into a coughing fit.

"Is Rep ready to bring on as a partner?" I asked. "He's been holding the fort while we've been overseas. Any problems?"

Toru and Phineas looked at each other. "Glen and I weren't much older than Rep when we started the company," Phineas said. "And Glen was grooming him to join the firm. Perhaps it's time."

"Can you estimate the net worth of the company?" I asked.

Toru quoted a figure off the top of his head. I stared. He said, "You tended to see only the financial statements for the project your father was working on at the time, instead of the whole picture. Depending on economic fluctuations, the total might be off by as much as ten per cent."

"Does Grand-mère know?"

Constance de Keridec refused to manage her spending. My grandfather had left her comfortably well off, and my mother's bequest had added a stipend, but my grandmother continued to live beyond her means.

"I'd hate to have my parents' legacy disappear down the rabbit hole," I said.

"Umm," Phineas began.

"What's wrong? What haven't you told me?"

"The picture is more complicated, from your standpoint, than you realize." Toru looked disconcerted as he struggled with how to deliver the, presumably bad, news.

"Whatever it is, it can't be worse than discovering that I have an assassin for a half-brother, that both my father and Annie were murdered, and that someone's determined to prevent me from reaching port."

Toru straightened the crease in his pant leg, brushed off a piece of imaginary lint, uncrossed his legs, crossed them the other way, and took a deep breath. "Have you ever read, or did your parents ever discuss with you, the incorporation of our company?"

"I know it's a privately held company, not traded on the stock exchange. That the only partners are you two and my father. And all of you own equal shares."

"That is nearly correct. But the difference is important."

Oh, dear. "Go on."

"We three do not own equal shares. The articles of incorporation gave equal shares to the original three partners." He paused. I wanted to kick him. "The original three partners were your father, your mother, who put up her inheritance from her paternal grandmother's estate, and Phineas. When I was brought into the company, I bought three percent from each of the partners. Your mother was good enough to allow me to purchase another ten percent from her share."

My mouth fell open, closed, opened, closed. I must have resembled a carp feeding on the bottom of a pond.

I did rapid mental calculations. "My father would have inherited my mother's share, which means I will own fifty and two-thirds percent of the company, once the will is probated. You, Phineas, own thirty and a third percent." I looked at Toru. "And you own nineteen percent."

He nodded.

"So, not equal partners, then."

Phineas smiled. "Not nearly." His voice had faded to a whisper.

"Do you resent that inequity, now that my father is no longer here to pull his weight?"

"Life is a toss of the dice," Phineas said. "We all knew that going in. And look what happened. First your mother, then your father, and now—"

"No, Uncle P!" I flung myself out of my chair and knelt beside him. "We will fight this illness. People heal. I've heard stories."

Toru had risen when I moved. He put a hand under my chin, lifting it so I would look at him. "But you can see what looms on the horizon once the vultures discover your father is dead and Phineas is ill."

I rose and reclaimed my chair. "I suspect the word is already out, at least on this ship. And if the murders were orchestrated to make our company and/or my inheritance ripe for the plunder, then we've got our work cut out for us, don't we?"

Both men grunted assent.

"The first order of business is to keep me alive so that my grandmother doesn't inherit a majority stake in the company. The second is to fight like the devil to get the courts to grant my emancipation. Then any document or contract I sign will be inviolate."

Nods this time, so I kept going. "The third order of business is to keep this a secret from my half-siblings, who could tie things up in court and prevent the company from doing business as usual. And the fourth—" I thought about the final imperative, "—the fourth order of business is to hire working replacements for my father as quickly as possible. If it takes three men to replace him, then we'll find three good men. Apart from Rep, they won't be partners. They'll be employees. But in future, anything's possible. Now, what have I left out?"

"Rep's shares," Toru said.

"Does he have the wherewithal to purchase shares from us?"

"His mother died a year ago, I think. His father, when Rep was at university. Rep was the only heir. I expect the will has been probated by now."

"I'll put up ten and one-third of my father's shares," I said.

"I'll offer eight of mine," Phineas croaked, then coughed.

Toru handed him a pill and went to the door to request a glass of water. I heard him murmur to Robie. Too late, now, to wonder if some of the conversation had been overheard. Toward the end, I'd forgotten to keep my voice down.

When Phineas had taken the tablet, drained the glass, and replaced the burgundy neckerchief, he said, "And if I give Toru three and one-third shares..." His voice failed.

"You do not have to do this," Toru said.

"Yes, he does," I said. "This way, if anything happens to Phineas and to me, you and Rep will have enough shares between you to block someone's takeover of the company, even while Uncle P's will is in probate."

Pain darkened Toru's eyes. "I understand. But then

you and I, Phineas, must also revise our wills." When Phineas nodded, Toru added, "Ten and a third of mine will go back to Keri, twelve to you, or to Rep, as the case may be."

I understood at once that this would strengthen our positions in the company. "Uncle T, will you hunt up Mrs. Hartfield for us? I think we'd better execute those wills today, if she's amenable."

"I will reach her."

"Keri, my dear, there's one last thing." Phineas looked pale and drawn. Purple half-moons lay under his eyes.

"What did I forget?"

"Only that it must have occurred to you that if you remake your will as you outlined, then Toru, Rep, and I would benefit most should your life be short."

I stood, knocking over my chair with a clatter. I faced my protectors, my guardians, and felt the banked-down anger flare up, engulfing me. "How could you, Uncle P? How could you put that thought in my head?"

The door opened and Robie stuck his head in. "Everything as it should be, Miss Rees?"

I glared at my uncles, who seemed taken aback and unable to respond. They hadn't seen me overcome with anger since I was little, when my fingers weren't as fast as my brain. Before I learned to deal with the frustrations that plagued my days.

I calmed myself enough to say, "No, Mr. Robie. Everything's not as it should be. Please escort me back to my cabin."

I stalked out on uncoordinated limbs. Whatever grace of movement I'd gained through the years, abandoned me. The possibility my guardians or Rep might act out of self-interest shook my foundations.

I passed staff and passengers as Robie and I traversed the dining room and passageways. But the figures were faceless, nameless, lacking individuality, like sea lions crowding a rock amid a cacophony of barking noise.

When we reached my cabin, I said, "I need to shoot at something, Mr. Robie. Preferably not a person. But if you don't have any bottles or clay birds, I'll settle for winging someone you despise."

"You have a gun? If not, I'll loan you the captain's."

"I have my father's revolvers. And I know how to use them."

"Ammunition, miss?"

"Enough."

"Once I've seen you to your cabin, and I've, um, checked with the captain, I'll send Ah Jim for some bottles."

Chapter 19

ROBIE WAS AS GOOD as his word. No doubt he reported to Captain Stowall that all had not gone well at the Requna Mining and Development Company business meeting. I didn't care. As long as the captain granted me permission to shoot, I wasn't fussy about the environs. Or the target.

Stowall gave us the after deck, the place where, if Chaplain Colins concurred, he would lead a memorial service for Annie. Well, I was going to give Annie a two-gun send off right now. Twenty-one guns would be better, offering a louder salute to her short life. Two would have to do. And, unfortunately, I'd have to use them alternately. My brain hadn't yet mastered aiming and shooting two pistols at once, although I was ambidextrous enough to shoot accurately with either hand. Perhaps by the time we left the ship, I would be expert at shooting two simultaneously. It depended on the availability of bottles.

I changed into my traveling costume, wishing I could just wear trousers and have done with it, as I used to do in the hinterlands. My father had drawn me a picture of how the women who worked in the mines in Wales and England had dressed: trousers under skirts, with the skirts drawn up so they wouldn't get caught in the machinery. They would have done away with the skirts entirely if men hadn't passed laws that said women could be jailed for wearing "men's" clothes. My father thought it a stupid law. As did my mother. My delicate, feminine grandmother took the opposite view. How was I going to survive living with her?

I took out my father's revolvers in their hand-tooled leather holsters. I'd shot at targets before. Bows and arrows. Various guns. Whatever was to hand. My parents felt I should become comfortable with firearms and lose my aversion to the noise they produced. I was hypersensitive to loud sounds, so they'd turned my training into sporting competitions. I used cotton plugs in my ears to reduce the noise, and was taught to ignore sound and concentrate solely on the target. It worked. The precision of focusing, sighting, shooting, and competing suited my temperament.

A scene drifted into my mind—a memory of the first sea journey after my mother's death. I'd turned in upon myself, like a paper folded again and again until it was a small, dense, dodecahedron, a pale imitation of a garnet crystal. My father had handed me his brace of pistols and a box of ammunition, and we'd gone to the after deck of the ship. The seas were rolling in even, predictable swells. He'd rounded up assorted glass bottles—paid dearly for them, no doubt, as the ship would have returned them for refilling when we reached port.

That was the first time I'd aimed from the deck of a moving ship. An hour later, I'd released much of my aggression, my mind had cleared, and I was able to face the future.

I heard a knock on my cabin door. Hsu Lin. Toru stood behind her. He held up his hands, palms out. "I come in peace."

I stepped aside to allow them to enter. Lin, dressed in a black tunic and pants of heavy silk, crossed to the small table and took the chair with the best view of the room. Toru remained standing by the open door. "Mr. Arnold sent word that you will be shooting," he said. "Anything in particular?"

"Bottles, clay tiles, chipped dishes. Whatever Mr. Robie can find."

"Ah. Well, the captain thought one or both of your guardians should be present."

"To keep me in line, or to serve as targets?"

"I think he has given up on the former." Toru smiled. "And he would rather not have more dead bodies turn up on his watch."

"I see you've brought Miss Hsu to guarantee

circumspect behavior."

"That would be putting too much burden on her young shoulders."

I sighed. "You don't have to worry. I'll behave."

"Phineas and I are counting on it. You have your father's pistols?"

I pointed to where the holstered guns rested on my berth. "Would you like to shoot with me?"

"Perhaps. I will bring mine, in the event."

"And bring Uncle P if he's feeling up to it."

Toru's face lightened. "He would not miss it. We met, you know, at a shooting contest."

"Truly? In England?"

"France. Near Versailles. To settle an argument."

I grinned. "A duel at dawn."

"Nothing quite so dramatic. The competitor lost, but kept his life."

"So, if you and Phineas hadn't triumphed that day, I'd never have met you."

"Most likely not—although the pool of geologists is relatively small."

"Then I'm very glad you went to Versailles that day."

"As am I, my dear ward." He gave a formal bow. "I shall collect my pistols and return directly."

I thought Lin moved, though when I closed the door after Toru and turned back into the cabin, she still sat at the table, fingers toying with the green glass vase.

She met my eyes and said, "Toru is, er—"

"Unavailable? Quite."

"Ah. *Quel dommage.*"

"I'll tell him you said that."

"Please, no. You would not embarrass me."

I laughed, without promising. "Have you ever shot a gun?"

"The nuns did not approve of guns. Or perhaps they did not think it wise to expose their students to temptation."

I wondered how rough the discipline had been at her boarding school, and how much resentment she carried.

"Then perhaps it's time you learned."

Chapter 20

11:00 a.m.

A **SHIP IS A** moving island on which all things are magnified. The endless horizon of the northern Pacific throws into bas-relief those personal habits that can be ignored on land. Stories told once too often. Loud laughter amplified. Overbearing, condescending men, chattering women, and screaming children become irritants in close quarters. There is no escape. Hence, outdoor distractions and passing entertainment draw crowds like rats to a block of cheese.

Somehow, word of my target shooting had spread. By the time Toru, Lin, Robie, and I reached the stern, we had to push our way through a noisy throng. Lin tugged on my sleeve and said, "Too many people, Keri. I will return to my cabin." And before I could respond or insist she take a guard with her, she had slipped away.

The captain had posted additional guards, some looking down from above. Everyone would be distracted, and Stowall didn't want another death or accident aboard his ship.

The big ship pitched up and down with each swell. The helmsman headed into them at a slight angle, perhaps fifteen degrees, and my body swayed in time. If conditions maintained, I should be able to aim and fire true.

"Is this a private party, or can anyone join in?"

Gideon Lamb was at my elbow. He must have been drawn by the commotion. He was not in a happy frame of mind. Something had happened. Anger radiated from him in waves, a match to my own underlying edginess. Toru's peace overture in my cabin had done little to mollify me.

"I'm in no mood for company, Mr. Lamb."

"Then how about a competition?"

Toru, continuing to brave my antipathy, stood beside me. I couldn't see Phineas.

I threw caution to the Pacific winds. "You want to shoot against me, Mr. Lamb?"

"Why not?"

I could think of no good reason that wouldn't sound churlish, and I was striving to bring credit to my guardians. Yet I hesitated. Pondered. Behind us the natives were growing restless.

I hit upon a tactic that would put Lamb off. With all apparent innocence, I said, "I thought you were competing in the draughts tournament with Mrs. Hartfield. Is it over so quickly, then?"

Under the brim of his pale straw hat, a blotchy red infused his face. The skin around his eyes tightened. "It's over."

So, he'd lost—and to a woman.

"Fancy a small wager on the outcome, Miss Rees?"

"I haven't agreed to compete, Mr. Lamb. Besides, my father taught me never to gamble except on a sure thing. And even then, it's unwise. The competition might be rigged."

"A wager on a sure thing is no gamble."

"I expect that was the point of his sermon."

"We wouldn't bet money. But perhaps, if I win, you'd dine with me tonight?"

It sounded innocent enough, but alarm bells started clanging in my mind. "Why would you want to dine with a girl who's wet behind the ears, and in mourning? My companion and I wouldn't be good company."

"You have a new companion, then."

He hadn't bothered to offer his condolences on Annie's loss. He had a purpose and a plan and was single-minded in his pursuit of the goal.

"Miss Hsu."

I doubted he'd want to be seen dining with a half-Chinese woman, but he didn't follow that thread. He said, "That was quickly done."

"She was available and qualified. Now, about the

shooting—I daresay we haven't enough bottles for a competition."

"I have several boxes of clay tiles that I brought with me from China. Enough for our sport, I daresay."

If he'd brought tiles and guns, then he would be an accomplished marksman. I supposed he'd planned to compete with other men during the voyage, wagering on the results. So why waste the tiles on me?

It came to me, then, that he must know about the inheritance. Or was theorizing based upon what he'd learned at that captain's dinner about the deaths of my parents. As an only child, of course I'd inherit. And perhaps it didn't even matter how much. He'd known my father and Toru before, knew they were in business together. Might even have heard before we left Yokohama of what had befallen my father there. Could he be behind the events of Japan and aboard the ship?

"Why don't you ask Miss Pomfrew to shoot with you?" I asked.

His smile showed that he took my question for subtle interest in him, not what I'd intended at all. I'd meant only to jibe him about that night at the captain's table.

Toru cleared his throat. The bottles were ready.

"I will compete with you on one condition, Mr. Lamb." I spoke loudly enough for the crew and passengers to hear.

"Name it."

"That the winner donates twenty-five new books to the Merchant Seaman's Library in San Francisco. The donation will be in the name of Anne Bonney."

"The *winner* donates?"

"That is the condition."

"And the loser gives nothing?"

"If I lose, I will acknowledge that a better marksman won the day. If you lose, the same." *But you will have been beaten by a girl in her early teens in front of witnesses.*

His lips clenched below the neat mustache. This was a wager he couldn't win. He understood, then, that he had underestimated me.

"I would not play draughts with young Keri," Toru said. "I haven't won a game since she was six."

So Toru had heard about Lamb's loss to Mrs. Hartfield. My guardian was subtly turning the knife in the wound, and perhaps goading Lamb for his own purposes.

"Mother used to say that the most satisfying games were ones in which we tried to perfect our skills, that we weren't playing the other person or team, only playing against ourselves. Whether we won or lost was unimportant."

Toru smiled at me. He'd been there when my mother had said those words. "A wise woman."

"Not my philosophy at all," Lamb said. "I play to win."

What he meant was that he played for money or power. Nothing else. "Fine," I said. "You accept my conditions?"

"It seems I must, since I broached the subject."

I held out my hand. "Twenty-five new books, all different titles, to the Seaman's Library. Let's shake on it."

We shook. I squinted up to where the captain stood on a small platform jutting out from below the bridge. "Captain Stowall, which of your seamen on deck has the best vision?"

He conferred with Mr. Arnold, who was standing next to him. "That would be Robie, Miss Rees."

"Excellent. Mr. Robie, will you call the shots for us, hit or miss?"

"Aye, miss."

"And Captain, who has the best throwing arm in your crew?"

This time he didn't have to check with his mate. "That would be Mr. Arnold. He pitches for a cricket team."

"Mr. Arnold, will you come down and toss the targets?"

Arnold was already on his way down. I turned to Lamb. "I assume the captain's choices, impartial as they are, will be acceptable to you."

Lamb's gaze shifted to a seaman who was holding a box in his hands. The tiles, I presumed. A finely-tooled leather gun case rested atop the wooden box. I guessed Gideon Lamb had planned to have his own seaman toss the tiles, giving Lamb an edge.

Lamb's nostrils flared, then he shrugged. "It seems

the decision's been made."

I saw Priscilla Pomfrew at the edge of the gathering crowd. She'd overheard his churlish reply. I wondered if it would dampen her enthusiasm.

"We each have two pistols, six shots per pistol," I said. "Shall we do one round of twelve each? Might as well not waste ammunition."

"Fine."

"Alternate shots, or each shoots twelve in succession?"

"Succession. Ladies first, of course."

"I'm only a girl. Let's flip for it."

Arnold had joined us. He fished a coin out of a jacket pocket. An American penny. "Call it."

"Heads," I said.

Lamb didn't speak.

"You're tails, Mr. Lamb." Arnold flipped, caught, and slapped on the back of his hand. "Heads."

"I'd like to go second," I said.

Only one decision remained. Because we hadn't enough bottles, I suggested each starting with six bottles and ending with six tiles.

Lamb shrugged again and picked up his first pistol from the green velvet bed in the ornate box. He raised his left arm to just below shoulder level, crooked his arm, set the gun on that platform, and said, "Ready!"

Arnold tossed high and clean. The brown bottle flew end over end. As it started to fall, Lamb fired.

"Hit!" Robie called.

One by one, Lamb struck cleanly. I could feel the tension in the air. We were facing northwest off the stern railing, the sun high overhead. I was standing near where Annie had gone over the side. The voices behind me faded. The world narrowed to glinting brown, green, blue, and clear bottles, to dull tiles.

The ninth throw, a tile, was launched, and a shot fired. I watched the tile land whole, with a little splash, and sink quickly into the wake. "Miss!" Robie called.

"I can see that," said Lamb.

I sensed or heard the intakes of breath that accompanied the next three pitches, only released at the sound of breaking tile.

"Eleven hits for Mr. Lamb."

Toru touched my shoulder. Met my eye. Slipped his hand into his pocket where his derringer lay. I got the message. Lamb might try to distract me as I shot. Or worse. He was, at the moment, reloading. Perhaps he thought there would be a shoot-off. Toru would watch my back, but he was warning me to beware.

The first three bottles were clean hits. I was in the rhythm of the sport when I sensed Lamb edging closer to my left side with each subsequent shot. By the time I slipped my father's pearl handled revolver into its empty holster and drew the matching Colt .45, Lamb was less than a meter away.

He'd removed his hat, and the wind blew the red-gold hair, fine and straight as spider's silk, over the crown of his head and onto his forehead, erasing the neat central part he favored. His pomade was no match for the stiff wind, and I saw smuts from the smokestack settle on the gold, giving it a speckled appearance. I expect he planned to lurch into me at one of the next two shots, or clear his throat loudly, or call out to distract me. Something.

"Uncle T," I said to the man on my right. "The boat is pitching, and I'd rather not follow Annie into the drink while I'm focusing on the tiles. Would you mind hooking a finger through my belt as a counterweight?"

"*Je comprends*," he said and moved around my back so that he could put his left hand on the rail and his right hand at the back of my gun belt. This forced Lamb to take a few steps back, and gave me a bit of a buffer. Toru's body would block any object Lamb threw at me, and prevent him from sticking me with a needle or hatpin. That Lamb was angry enough to try any of those tricks, I didn't doubt.

"*Fermez votres oreilles*," Toru whispered. He always used the formal "you" with me, as did Phineas. They felt it was proper, under the circumstances. Guardians had power given by law, rather than by birth. I might refer to them using the familiar form, but they didn't reciprocate, though I'd known them all my life.

I closed my ears, as Toru requested, but not my eyes, and said, "Ready, Mr. Arnold."

The gun was heavy, and I shot as I'd been taught six years ago: left hand pulled back the pin, right hand held the gun and pulled the trigger. Sixth shot. Clean. Seventh... I flinched as grit hit my eyes, but I'd seen the tile's arc and squeezed off a shot that caught the tile as it fell. I rubbed my eyes with the sleeve of my cotton tunic.

"Mr. Lamb, would you mind stepping closer to Mr. Robie, please. I'm feeling a bit crowded. Thank you."

He grunted and moved back a few steps. I lowered the veil on my hat, and tied it in place around my neck. It would keep any grit out.

I saw Lamb smile. He assumed I couldn't see as well now. But the fine silk net wasn't an impediment. I shot by judging angle, arc, and speed, and I could see perfectly well for those.

"Shall we finish it off, Mr. Arnold?"

In rapid succession I called, he threw, I fired. If Lamb tried to distract me, I didn't notice. As I untied and lifted my veil, I heard applause, but Lamb wasn't clapping. If he could have killed me right then, he would have.

I thanked Arnold and Robie, curtsied to Captain Stowall, then held out my hand to Lamb. "Tough about that ninth shot," I said. "But it's all for a good cause." I gave him what I thought was a nice smile, not at all triumphant.

He took my hand, leaned in, and said, "Miss Bonney is wrapped in the arms of Davy Jones. Perhaps you'll make it a *ménage à trois*, hmm?"

Startled, I pulled my hand away and lurched backwards into Toru and Robie, who had resumed his guard duty. A glance at Lamb's face showed a crooked smile. He tipped his hat and said loudly enough for the audience to hear, "Well played, Miss Rees."

My stomach heaved as if I'd been struck with *le mal de mer*. I stumbled to the rail, leaned over, and lost whatever food remained undigested. I felt Toru's hand on my back, the calm strength of him flowing in to quiet my mind and center my emotions. Robie stood stalwartly on the left, and someone posted himself on my right flank—

Arnold, I realized, when ink-stained fingers proffered a pristine white serviette. The three men were like a folding screen, blocking me from the sight of the curious.

I stayed there, hunched over, watching the wake point the way to the horizon. A cloud passed over the sun, turning the sea from slate blue to a deep teal green. Smutty smoke from the stack drifted backwards, to be torn to shreds by the rising wind. For a moment the direction changed and I smelled clean salt-laden air, heard the flap of the sails again, where before my ears had been shut to anything by my own misery.

An object, oblong and richly carved, flew end over end before it landed with a small splash in the center of the wake. Lamb's gun box, though whether the guns were inside, I couldn't tell. When I straightened and turned, he was disappearing down the port deck, his valet with the box of remaining tiles scurrying behind him.

Looking once more at the following sea, I saw the box still bobbing on the wake. Perhaps it would be swept on a current all the way to the coast of North America.

"What did Mr. Lamb say to you?" Arnold asked.

I felt a flush rising in my cheeks. Robie quoted Lamb's comment exactly, but in a low voice that wouldn't carry to the passengers still lingering in the shade of the bulkhead.

"If you're up to it, Miss Rees and Dr. Nakagawa," Arnold said, "I think a short summary meeting is in order. While things are fresh in your minds. I have answers to the questions you left with me this morning. I'll make sure tea and brandy are available."

My throat was raw from retching. I looked at Toru, who gave one of his slight shrugs, leaving it up to me. After the way I'd left him and Phineas earlier, I understood his reluctance to speak for me.

"Thank you, Mr. Arnold. I agree that a sharing of information is in order. But I'd like to have lunch and meet with the chaplain first, if that's acceptable. I'm hoping he'll agree to have Annie's memorial this evening."

"Of course. What time are you meeting him?"

"One thirty, I thought. If he's available."

"Then I'll send a message to Mr. McGinn, in case he wishes to attend. As for your meeting with Captain Stowall, would 1500 hours in the captain's dining alcove be acceptable?"

"Perfectly."

Arnold left us, moving quickly toward the ladder leading to the bridge. Robie fell in behind Toru and me. The satisfaction I'd felt at shooting successfully was gone, squashed by Lamb's suggestion and his abysmal sportsmanship. He'd been a minor annoyance before. Now he'd revealed himself as a very nasty foe. But that didn't mean he was *the* Foe, the force behind the attempts on my life, the dark wind that had directed Wei Xi's and Hundun's attacks on my family.

"Uncle T," I said, as we walked quickly toward my cabin, "why did Phineas say I had to consider that you and he might be behind the attacks on my father, Annie, and me?"

"Because you will hear that from others, who do not comprehend our longstanding relationship. Those others, outside our circle, will see only the fact that if you and your father were dead, Phineas, Rep, and I would have the most to gain from the business."

"But that's not even true! If I die before my majority, my grandmother inherits everything of mine. She would be the controlling partner. Worse, if she marries, her husband would be the controlling partner. It's only after I achieve my majority—or my minority will is validated— that you would stand to gain."

"Others will not see the fine details. They will only look at the broad strokes on the canvas. They will say that we, as your guardians, exerted undue influence on you. I'm sure your grandmother, once she learns of your father's death and our appointments as guardians, will apply to the courts to dismiss us. What we told you at the end of the meeting will be the basis for her court case. And she may yet win."

"Then we'll be keeping Mrs. Hartfield busy in the next few days. She said she'd be available after her last match. If that was with Mr. Lamb, she should be free now. But I'd rather wait until tea time, if it's all right with you and Phineas. After I see the chaplain and we meet with the captain."

"I will check with Phineas and Mrs. Hartfield."

"I've had enough of crowds and noise," I said, apropos of nothing.

"Entertaining our shipmates might not have figured into your shooting plans, but you have now made your presence known. You and Miss Hsu do not fit any of society's artificial categories. You might as well embrace your differences and begin as you mean to go on. If you take part in a selected few activities, the other passengers will soon become accustomed to you—as they have to me."

Toru was right. Freedom for us lay in charting our own paths through the wilderness of others' expectations.

We paused outside my cabin door. Toru said, "Would you and Miss Hsu care to lunch with me in the main dining room?"

"I'm sure she'd enjoy the company. May I have a few minutes to freshen up?"

"Ten minutes enough?"

"Barely."

"Good. I will send Miss Hsu a note."

As I closed the door, I heard Robie relating the events on the aft deck to the second guard. I felt as if two people—one logical and rational, the other overcome with fear and indecision—warred throughout my brain and nervous system. I couldn't seem to pull the cotton tunic over my head. Lamb's attack, his emotional evisceration, was something new, something personal, something for which my parents, tutors, nurses, and companions hadn't prepared me.

I'd dealt with fear and confusion before, when I'd lost my parents. When I'd lost Annie. But I couldn't seem to focus on the next step. It was a kind of paralysis. I wanted to curl up on my bunk, pull the covers over my head, and sleep till we reached San Francisco.

I finally found the way out of the maze of my clothes and tossed them over the screen. I quickly rinsed the smuts from my face and hands, then changed into a freshly-laundered, black cotton frock with lace bodice and sleeves. Only three buttons, at the back of the high neck. I left them undone for the present and opened the door.

Mr. Robie and the second guard had been replaced. I asked one guard to summon Lin for me. She was there in a moment, dressed in a black skirt of European cut and fitted gold-embroidered black jacket. She wrinkled her nose. "You smell like gunpowder."

"I haven't time to wash my hair. Sorry. Can't be helped."

"You feel better?" she asked, as she did up my buttons, rewrapped my braids, and set the hat with the veil on top.

"I fought a dragon and defeated him. For now."

"Mr. Lamb is an unpredictable foe. We might need another guard."

She didn't know the half of it. "I was thinking of requesting a phalanx."

Stepping over to a vase on the table, she took one of the flowers and tucked it into the band of my hat. We smiled at each other in the mirror—one tall, one small and slender. Unlike in all except for wavy dark hair, a dusting of freckles, a small hump on our noses, and our smiles. All compliments of our father.

Someone tapped on the door. "'Once more unto the breach'?" I said.

"*Encore une fois.*"

Chapter 21

12:10 p.m.

TORU SELECTED A TABLE in a corner of the dining salon. He seated Lin with her back to the room so that she wouldn't see the curious glances sent our way.

I told Toru about the service I was organizing. "Have you thought of flowers?" Lin asked.

"Not yet. But I have an idea."

The server arrived to take our order. I asked him when the flowers on the tables would be changed. "Today, after luncheon," he said.

"Will you ask the chief steward if I may have the discarded flowers?"

Toru followed my question with an explanation in Japanese. The server nodded several times and replied in the same language, then headed for the kitchen.

"They are very sorry for your loss," Toru said. "They will send the freshest of the blooms to your cabin, along with some ribbon."

"You're a marvel, Uncle T. Thank you."

"It is a little thing." He took a sip from his water glass. "Phineas saw Dr. Doyle this morning. He said you were to report to Sick Bay this afternoon, after our meeting with Mrs. Hartfield."

Mr. Mayweather entered the salon, the first time I'd seen him outside of the interview room yesterday. He made straight for our table and asked if he could take the empty chair.

Toru looked at us. Lin gave a slight nod. I said, "Of course, Mr. Mayweather. Please join us. I'm sure Hsu Lin might like to converse in her native language for a spell, and give her English and French a break."

Lin flashed me a look from under lowered lashes. She

wanted no such thing.

The soup course arrived, a delicate chicken broth enclosing a few vegetables. I picked up my spoon and asked, "When did you come aboard, Mr. Mayweather?"

"In Shanghai."

"You were there for business or for pleasure?"

"It's always a pleasure to visit Shanghai."

I tried again. "You understand Chinese as if you were born there. And French."

"Missionary parents. Learned Wu and Mandarin from the cradle." His face lightened, as if he'd reached safe ground. "Picked up French from a tutor, and majored in languages and Oriental history at Edinburgh. Seemed a good fit."

"And are you a missionary like your parents, Mr. Mayweather?" Lin asked.

He laughed, a deep, rumbling sound that seemed to start in his toes. "Didn't have the calling, Miss Hsu."

"Your facility with languages must be useful in your employment," I said.

"I'm a civil servant, if that's what you're driving at, Miss Rees. Just doing my duty to God and country, by more practical means than my parents." And in a murmur that wouldn't carry beyond my ears, added, "Much like your father."

My spoon clattered against the porcelain bowl.

"Yes, I met him twenty years ago. But he was only with us for three years, at least officially. I was his contact in Shanghai and a few other places. I was with him when he got the letter from your mother calling him to San Francisco."

Lin heard this last part. Color stained her cheeks. After my mother's death, my father had folded that letter into a silk scapular, which he wore over his heart. I had inherited the letter and everything else of his. Hsu Lin (and her twin) had received nothing.

Toru engaged Mayweather. Lin and I ate in silence. Family history had descended like a pall over the table. I made our excuses and left after the third course with my sister and our shadow guard.

"I must meet with Chaplain Colins to discuss Annie's

memorial," I said as we walked. "Would you like to accompany me to the chapel?"

"I think a peaceful chapel is exactly what I need right now."

I made a decision in that moment. Pulling my sketchbook from my pocket, I removed the copy of Hundun's letter and handed it to her. "This was left in my room at some point. I only discovered it this morning."

Tears gathered in her eyes as she read the letter. When she finished, I said, "I'll make you a copy, if you wish."

"No, possessing it would be too dangerous for me once I reach land. But thank you, Keri, for trusting me."

Chapter 22

1:15 p.m.

L IN AND *I* WERE fifteen minutes early for my meeting with Reverend Colins. The guard checked the chapel. Empty. He retreated outside to give Lin and me privacy.

I smelled candle wax, incense, and… chicken broth, soy, rice, and wine. The wine was understandable, given the purpose of the room. But this wasn't sacramental wine. More like rice wine. As if the Chinese crew gathered in the quiet chapel to break bread—or as if Hundun had been hiding here. If the latter, then someone other than Wei Xi had brought him food. Wei Xi had been incarcerated in the hold since tea time yesterday.

I realized there was another option. Hundun might have foraged around the ship late at night. An unsettling thought.

Lin took a seat just inside the double doors, folded her hands, and closed her eyes. If she smelled the aromas of cooked food, she gave nothing away. But then, I had an acute olfactory sense to match my acute aural sense. Perhaps she didn't share those traits.

I followed my nose toward the sacristy. The smell was stronger in the small side chamber. There, vestments draped a waist-high cabinet with shallow drawers, awaiting the next service. Beside the vestments were a *Book of Common Prayer*, a St. James Bible, and a hymnal. All familiar sights.

The desk on which Chaplain Colins wrote his sermons hugged one bulkhead. In the corner were a tall cabinet and a bookcase with various editions of the Bible, Old Testament and New, and English and Hebrew editions of the Torah, though no scroll that I could see.

Dictionaries abounded—all the European languages, as well as Japanese, Greek, Latin, Hebrew, and Chinese. I might pick the chaplain's brain during the remainder of the voyage, if he'd let me. He could test me on my Latin and Greek translations, and perhaps a few other areas, as well.

On a high shelf perched the complete works of William Shakespeare, Herman Melville's *Moby Dick*, the poems of Samuel Taylor Coleridge, Keats, and Shelley, a book of maps, and Charles Darwin's *Voyage of the Beagle* and *On the Origin of Species*. And under glass on the chaplain's desktop was a colored map of the world, so he could plot his voyages.

Chaplain Colins was a man after my own heart. I suspected I'd find journals with interesting observations in the drawers of the large desk.

I looked for a place where a small man might hide. I checked the tall closet. Bottles of holy water occupied one shelf. Some were empty. *Well, why not?* A man confined will stay hydrated with holy water, and be grateful for it. I wondered if my brother refilled them with unblessed water during his nightly jaunts.

I closed the closet door and checked the remaining bulkheads. The main door stood ajar, prevented from opening fully by a low sea chest, longer than standard issue, covered with stamps from various ports around the globe. Probably the chaplain's or his predecessor's personal trunk. Navy issue. No padlocks. Fasteners unlatched. But someone had punched the familiar whirlwind design in the top and near the handle.

I caught my breath. If my brother was in there, I couldn't face opening the lid, couldn't face seeing him in a box. It would give me nightmares.

I turned to leave. A final glance at the bulkhead opposite revealed a handle set into the meter-wide space between the bookcase and the tall closet. Looking more closely, I found the outlines of a door. Of course. The chaplain's office would have an attached water closet. It would do double duty as a changing room and for fainting attendees during services.

The air in the room was hot and close. My heartbeat

raced as I touched the handle. Turned it. Felt resistance.

"Thank you for leaving me the letter," I whispered. "But know they continue searching the ship for you. They will find you."

The resistance eased, and the door opened enough that I could see the face of the man who had tried to kill me.

"I understand." His English was clear, but came not as easily to his tongue as it did to Lin's.

"We haven't time for a conversation. The chaplain's coming. But I have one question: Do you know anything about our father's work in Shanghai, back when he met your mother?"

"Only what Wei Xi told me. It may or may not be true."

I took my sketchbook from its leather cover. The pencil dangled from a string glued to the binding. The drawings that had revealed the murder scene and the murderer were missing now, tacked up on Mr. Arnold's board.

I slipped the book through the slot. "Please, will you write down what you know?"

He took it in two hands, as if it were a precious gift.

"Hsu Lin is in the chapel. Would you like to speak with her?"

"Only if she wishes it."

Grabbing a piece of paper from the stack on the chaplain's desk and a pencil from a weighted beer stein, I hurried back into the chapel and whispered to Lin. A look of shock crossed her face. She nodded and almost ran to the vestry door.

I paced across the back of the chapel. Indecision and confusion set a kaleidoscope of colors and patterns swirling in my brain. Annie's killer. My father's would-be killer. My brother. The man who'd accepted the job of killing me, had bungled it twice, then reconsidered.

Reconsidered. Changed course. Why?

Surely it wasn't anything Wei Xi had said. But meeting Lin, and then discovering he had not one, but *two* sisters, that he'd been manipulated and trained from birth while being given a false history. Was that the deciding factor? Did he, like me, consider lies the unforgivable breach of trust? Perhaps he'd tell me, if we had time.

But of one thing I was sure. For the first time when Hundun was able to move about freely and to choose to obey or not obey directives, when either choice meant he would be sacrificed for someone else's machinations, he had chosen to contact me and effectively lay down his arms. At least toward me. I understood he would not allow himself to be captured. He would not choose shackles, humiliation, and a noose, but instead a death how, where, and when he decided.

I felt torn between sorrow at the loss of Annie and guilt that she'd died in my place. I felt despair at the choices my brother had made and would make, and a growing anger at the Wei family and the person or persons who had set the murders in motion. Had I possessed my father's pistol at that moment, I might have sought out Wei Xi and ended her life. How ironic that I was pacing in this place of peace when that most un-Christian desire shook me.

Enough. My intellect couldn't function in a maelstrom. Also, I didn't want the chaplain to see my fractured state of mind. He might ask questions that would lead me to blurt out things I'd rather he not know, such as who was presently occupying the vestry water closet.

I sat, breathed deeply and regularly for a minute, and forced my mind to address the business of Annie's memorial. I owed her that. Taking a hymnal from a nearby table to use as a lap desk, I was scribbling an addendum to what I'd like the memorial service to include when the guard opened the door for the chaplain and Michael McGinn.

Annie's fiancé pulled the cap from his head. He looked as if he hadn't slept in two days. His eyes and nose were red. But he was freshly bathed and shaven, and his clothes were clean.

"Mr. McGinn." I set aside the hymnal, rose, and clasped his good hand in both of mine. "Thank you for coming."

"I realized on the way up that I canna do this now, Miss Keri." His voice rasped out the words. "Whatever you decide, it will suit me fine. Just send me word about time and place. Oh, and I'd like to recite a poem, if I may."

"Which one?" asked Colins.

"'Annabel Lee.' Annie loved it." Michael pulled on his cap, opened the door, and was gone.

I turned to the chaplain, held out my hand, and said, "Chaplain Colins, I'm Keridec Rees."

Colins was a man of my height with pale skin, pale blue eyes, wispy light brown hair, and a trim waistline. His uniform was crisp, despite the heat. The lapel held a small gold cross.

Colins wiped his nose with a damp handkerchief. "Sorry," he said. "Nose has been running all day. You're unaccompanied?"

"No, my new companion, Miss Hsu, was feeling a bit queasy. It's been a trying time these past thirty-six hours. I looked for you in the office, found the facilities, and I gave her some privacy while I waited for you."

He wiped his nose again, and I stopped worrying about him being able to smell the chicken and rice wine. I resumed my seat by the door, requiring Colins to stay at that end of the room. "She will be out in a minute," I said. "By that time, I shall have shared my notes with you."

"Religion?"

"Roman Catholic. Both Michael and Annie. Devout. But the Anglican words over the grave will do until I reach San Francisco and can have a mass said for the repose of her soul. And, as you'd not met her, I wouldn't expect a summary of her life. We'll all know why we're there."

"I would be happy to oblige, Miss Rees." After wiping his nose yet again, he took a small notebook from his pocket and jotted down my name and my request. "Had you thought of including any hymns? I play the organ."

"That's kind of you, Reverend. However, I'd prefer to have the service on the aft deck at the place she went into the sea. You know the story?"

"Everyone is aware of the circumstances, Miss Rees."

"Good. That saves time and—"

"Emotional distress?"

His sympathy undermined my defenses. Tears welled up. I nodded. "Annie was like a sister..." I paused. Stared at the deck. Words seemed to be deserting me.

Colins' voice seemed to come from far away. "I'm here for spiritual succor, Miss Rees."

I took another deep breath. Cleared my throat. "Thank you, sir. I need to get through this first."

"Understood. So, on the after deck, we'll have to sing a cappella, although I have a pitch pipe to get us started. And a harmonica, if you'd like accompaniment?"

"Yes to the harmonica. The song I'd like to use is not a hymn, if you don't mind. I'm a bit, er, unconventional. But the song was a favorite of hers."

I waited until he nodded for me to go on. Death is a very personal thing. He wasn't rigid, it seemed, about how spirits were sent on to the afterlife.

"'Bring Back My Bonnie to Me.'"

I waited. He contemplated, then said, "Apropos. And it has the added benefit that everyone will know the words. It's been very popular at our shipboard entertainment nights."

I breathed a sigh of relief.

Colins said, "Do you have any reservations about my opening with a psalm in addition to the formal words?"

"Which psalm?"

"Twenty-three."

As I was still walking in the shadow of death, the psalm seemed appropriate. "Yes, please lead with that, Reverend Colins. It will comfort me. And I'd like to have the service this evening at sunset. Is that possible?"

"I'm at your service, Miss Rees. I will meet you on the after deck at seven thirty."

The door to his office opened. Lin came out. She'd been crying again, I thought, and had covered up the stained cheeks with a light layer of rice powder. I introduced them, shook his hand, and we took our leave. Our faithful guard escorted us toward our cabins.

"You had a good visit?" I said softly.

"We overheard your plan. He has his own." Her voice caught on the last two words. She drew a long, calming breath. "Why did you not tell the chaplain about Hundun?"

"Because, initially, Mr. McGinn was there. He would have killed Hundun. And who could blame him? But Annie would not have wanted her Michael hanged for murder."

Lin looked at me from the side of her eyes, still disbelieving.

"And then it was too late to tell the chaplain," I said. "How would I explain your spending all that time with Hundun?"

I knew she wasn't satisfied with my reasons. Nor was I. But all she said was, "Thank you for facilitating our visit. It was a kindness I will not forget."

Chapter 23

M R. ARNOLD WAS TALKING to our guards when we arrived in the passageway outside our cabins.

"Would you consider accompanying me to the hold to visit Miss Wei?" he asked Lin. "She still refuses to speak or eat."

"Of course, Mr. Arnold. I will be with you in a moment."

I had forty-five minutes free before I needed to leave for the meeting with Captain Stowall. I went to Annie's trunk. Her name was stenciled on the lid. Her identification papers were in a side pocket. I studied them. She had become a naturalized citizen of the United States in San Francisco thirty months ago. She'd been so proud that day.

I removed all the odds and ends Annie had collected or worn over the past few years. She was an orphan, her only relatives my middle-aged housekeepers, Tom and Mary Daly. I would take home only a few of Annie's possessions—the daybooks covering the time she'd been my maid and companion, and a locket that had been her grandmother's.

On the table I put mementos to give to Michael. A small picture in an oval frame. A handkerchief embroidered with forget-me-nots. It smelled of lavender. Everything in the trunk smelled of lavender. Like Annie.

I fingered the cotton and linen garments hanging in the closet. Basic daywear, lightly worn. Annie, too, was returning home with a new wardrobe, augmented by clothes I'd outgrown. I pictured her sitting with me, tailoring the coat and one of the dresses for herself.

I heard Lin return from visiting Wei Xi. A short visit.

It must not have gone well. I left my cabin and knocked on Lin's door. She looked as if she'd been crying. "What is it?" I asked when she stepped aside to allow me to enter.

The room had a Spartan look. Every sign of Wei Xi had been erased. Yet Lin had confined her presence to only half of the space, as if that was all she was entitled to. Or as if she'd always shared a room, and respected the invisible borders set up by joint tenants.

"I took Aunt Xi some dried plums and almond biscuits," she said. "She refused them. She blames *me* for her incarceration."

"That's nonsensical."

Lin lifted one shoulder.

"She may change her mind as the days pass," I said.

"I hope so. I left the food. I will try again tonight or tomorrow." She sank onto a chair and stared out the porthole. "I will belong to her family once we reach San Francisco."

An idea, half-formed, began to blossom. I said, "I began sorting through Annie's things. It's time for you to choose any pieces you'd like to alter for yourself."

She jumped up. "Thank you. It will give me something to do."

I opened my cabin door to find the flowers had been delivered. Two trays were on the dressing table, the flowers covered by damp cloths to keep them fresh. Annie would have known exactly how to use them.

"I don't suppose you include flower arranging among your other talents," I said.

"The nuns considered it a required art. They invited a Japanese woman to teach us. I paid attention."

My own experience had been confined to plucking wildflowers from the tracksides, hillsides, and gardens of our far-flung lodgings, identifying them with my mother, placing them in water before drawing them, or pressing them for her collections. "Would you be able to create a wreath and select the best of the other blooms so each of us can toss one in the water?"

She peeked under one of the towels. "How many blooms?"

"A dozen or two should do it, I think."

"Easily done. Now to the clothes."

I pointed to the dresses and light coats hanging in Annie's closet. "Take whatever suits your fancy. Anything you can't use, I'll offer to women in steerage. Mr. McGinn might know of someone in need of clothes who is handy with a needle."

As I had done, Lin fingered the material of each item.

"Did you wear western dress at school?" I asked.

"Of a kind. Uniforms. Brown or gray cotton dresses, simply cut, with white pinafores. Nothing as nice as these."

She picked out a dress of cotton lawn with a pattern of tiny white flowers on a field of green. Annie had loved the way it brought out her eyes. Lin held it up in front of her, studying the effect in the mirror. Her face was subdued. "Aunt Xi says I will wear traditional Chinese clothes in America. And I will be confined to the home, except on the Chinese New Year and special occasions. She said I would not need Western dresses. I suspect I shall go mad."

"How good an actress are you, Lin?"

"We performed plays at school."

"Can you do an Irish brogue?"

"Of course."

"I have Annie's papers. With some funds, and outfitted in Western clothes, perhaps you could find a way to escape the destiny others set for you. But the transformation won't be easy."

"Nothing in my life has been easy."

Annie's description on her papers might be a problem. The height was close enough, if Lin wore shoes with heels. The weight could be fudged by adding padding around Lin's waist. Her black hair could be obscured with a hat and veil. But Annie's green eyes were nothing like Lin's darker ones. And we'd have to find a way to draw the fold of her upper eyelid into flatness. It was a risk. Would Lin be willing to take it?

"Perhaps I'll invite Michael to tea so you can tune your ear to his accent," I said.

The silence was palpable. When she turned from the mirror, her eyes held a question. "Why would you do this for me?"

"I, too, would go crazy very quickly if confined in a house." I grinned. "Are you waiting for an engraved invitation?"

"I will get my sewing basket."

She was back in a minute, holding a box covered in crimson silk. "Dr. Nakagawa is coming down the passageway."

I took a new sketchpad and pencil from my trunk, fitted the pad into the leather cover, and collected a file of my father's papers from the bedside table. "You're welcome to work here while I'm gone. We'll be about an hour."

When I closed the door, two of Annie's dresses lay on her berth. Lin's head was bent over a selection of threads.

Chapter 24

3:00 p.m.

TORU AND I WERE the first ones to arrive at the dining alcove. We left Robie outside and sat in silence, immersed in our respective thoughts. The exhibits board from yesterday was gone. I would have to ask Arnold if I might have my mother's hatpin back now. I saw no reason to wait.

The door opened. Mayweather came in.

"May I speak with you alone?" he asked me.

I shook my head. "I'm sorry. Dr. Nakagawa stays."

He gave a little grunt and pulled out the same chair at the end of the table that he had occupied yesterday. Took out his notebook. Searched his pockets for a pencil. Finally located the stub of one in his vest pocket. He said, "Miss Hsu wasn't at the target shooting. Since she is your new companion, I wondered why she abandoned you."

It was an odd way to start a conversation. "Lin said the crowds made her uneasy."

"Understandable, given the current anti-Chinese sentiment." He changed tack. "I was thinking of attending Miss Bonney's memorial service."

"You knew Annie, Mr. Mayweather? She never mentioned you."

"The purser introduced us our second day out. I joined the group at her breakfast table. You were still taking meals in your cabin, then."

I scented a subplot. I wondered how much he'd tell me. "You sought her out."

"Yes."

"As a way to reach me."

"Yes. You didn't know about my relationship with your father, but Glen and I still exchanged information when our paths crossed in Asian ports."

Beside me, Toru shifted slightly in his chair. "Tokyo?"

Mayweather nodded. "I sought Glen out shortly after your party arrived. I wanted to pass on a warning. For old times' sake." He turned his head at the sound of approaching footsteps. His voice sharpened, and he raced to get the words out. "I saw what happened at the shooting. Couldn't hear what Lamb said to you, but I saw your reaction. Don't trust him. He doesn't play by the Marquess of Queensberry rules."

Mayweather seemed to be hopping between topics. I said, "You warned my father about Mr. Lamb?"

The double doors opened. Mayweather scribbled something on his tablet, tore out the page, crumpled it, and tossed it up the table to me. I tucked the note in my pocket and removed my sketchpad and pencil, wondering what additional surprises this meeting would hold. It was disconcerting to realize that I hadn't known my father at all. And I didn't know how to interpret the warning about Lamb.

Phoebe Hartfield preceded Michael McGinn into the alcove. She had a slender frame, but not frail, and was dressed in a pale-gray, cotton dress trimmed with aubergine. A delicate amethyst pendant hung from a velvet ribbon by a bow of gold. Matching amethyst teardrops dangled from her lobes and flashed in the light. Fingerless lace gloves showed an absence of rings, not even the faint band of one recently removed from her left ring finger. A widow, then. Or a divorcée.

I stood to greet her, as did Toru and Mayweather. Mrs. Hartfield paused mid-stride, nodded to each of us, and waited for Toru to introduce and seat her.

I sketched Phoebe Hartfield while I listened to her rich contralto voice engage Mayweather. I wanted the same information, but calming my emotions and capturing Hartfield were more important. So, I let the words flow over and past me. I could always ask Toru or Mrs. Hartfield later.

Finished, I looked up. Toru had taken the chair to Mrs. Hartfield's left. Michael sat to her right, his face scored by lines of exhaustion. The last two days had taxed his reserves.

I said, "Mr. McGinn, I haven't had time to send a note with the particulars of Annie's memorial service. The chaplain and I decided on seven thirty this evening on the after deck."

Michael turned his attention from Mayweather to me. "I'll be there, Miss Rees."

Silence descended as we awaited the arrival of Captain Stowall. Mrs. Hartfield pulled the hatpin and removed her straw chapeau, revealing a high forehead and square face surrounded by a halo of frizzy hair the color of mesquite bark. Brows like a circumflex above each eye. Long nose. Firm broad lips. The hair was confined into one long plait wrapped in a tight figure eight over the crown and back of her head. No wisps escaped. No bangs or ringlets softened the profile. This was a woman who lived and breathed her intellect. All else was secondary.

She set the chapeau on the table in front of a notebook, perhaps seven inches by four and a half, and two sharpened pencils. When she opened the slick leather cover, I saw finely ruled vellum. I coveted paper, especially unique notebooks.

"Didn't I hear you won the draughts competition from Mr. Lamb?" I asked her. "Well done."

"And the same to you, Miss Rees. This has not been Mr. Lamb's day, I fear."

"How did he respond?"

"There was a crowd watching. He wished to change the rules to the best two games out of three, but when I demurred, he, er, conceded."

Mayweather gave a little grunt. "Lamb doesn't relish losing to anyone. But to a woman? I wager he won't get over it soon. No, our Mr. Lamb holds grudges."

Phoebe Hartfield turned to him. "You know this for a fact?"

"I've had opportunities to observe him in action," Mayweather said. "Lamb attacks through friends or relatives, if he can't get at you directly."

Mrs. Hartfield asked, "Exactly what role do you play in the unfolding drama that has brought us here, Mr.

Mayweather, if you don't mind my asking?"

Mayweather was saved from answering by the arrival of Captain Stowall and Mr. Arnold. Stowall apologized for their tardiness. He greeted Phoebe Hartfield by name and with a wary little bow. I suspected she had been invited to the captain's table and had raised subjects or expressed opinions that hadn't set well. Stowall might deal easily with a precocious girl, but an opinionated woman? *C'est une autre paire de manches,* as my mother used to say. A different pair of sleeves, a different situation entirely.

"Which of you has retained legal counsel?" Stowall asked to the room in general.

"Dr. Nakagawa, Mr. Quade, and I have," I said. "There are forces at work wishing to prevent my reaching my majority. I wish to protect our company and my parents' legacy."

Stowall gave a stiff nod. Mayweather looked thoughtful. Phoebe Hartfield jotted down something followed by a question mark.

While the newcomers took their seats, I asked Hartfield about her tablet. She ran a hand over the paper and smiled. "I designed this and found a company that would produce them in bulk. Schmidt Label and Lithograph Company on Main Street in San Francisco."

I smiled back. "Thank you. I'll visit them at the first opportunity."

Stowall had claimed his place at the head of the table. Arnold sat next to me, ledger, quill pen, and inkwell at the ready. Robie slipped in, closed the door, and stood with his back to it. Eight of us today, counting our trusty guard.

"Mr. Arnold requested this meeting so that we could share what we've learned since yesterday," Stowall said.

"Thank you," Toru said. "As Mr. Quade found it necessary to rest before the memorial service, I am representing him, as well."

Arnold summarized quickly and succinctly. Their search hadn't turned up Annie's assailant. Wei Xi still wasn't answering questions or eating. The crew would remain on alert until Hundun was found.

Michael frowned, appeared confused and, finally,

astonished. He hadn't heard of Hundun, Wei Xi, or their significance to Annie's disappearance.

"Captain Stowall," Michael said, "I came today not only to learn how the investigation was advancing, but because I wished to offer evidence in this matter."

"Evidence? Please proceed, Mr. McGinn."

"Well, sir, it's this: I saw a small woman having a whispered conversation with a man outside my quarters two nights ago. It was very late, but it was too hot to sleep—and I was worried about why Annie hadn't come to meet me. So I made my way to the promenade deck. I was filling my pipe in the dark, when I overheard the argument. They were whispering in Chinese, but I heard Annie's name."

"You're sure?" I asked.

"For seven years I worked on ships with Chinese and Japanese crew members, Miss Keri. I learned a few words of Mandarin, enough to get what I needed on shore leave." He gave a lopsided twist of the lips. "That night I recognized the lilt of the language. It's a different kind of music than European languages. Or Japanese, Hindi, or a host of others."

"Why didn't you mention this that night, Michael?"

"I'm sorry. I couldn't think straight that night. I only remembered later, after I calmed down."

"The deck and cabin crews are Chinese, but there are only two Chinese or Eurasian passengers in First Class," Stowall said. "Miss Hsu and Miss Wei."

"I only caught a glimpse, but Miss Hsu is taller and slimmer than the woman I saw."

"Could you identify the man?" Stowall asked. "I know it was dark—"

"That's him, there at the end of the table. Dr. Nakagawa introduced him as Mr. George Mayweather."

In unison, all heads swiveled to look at Mayweather. He tapped the end of his pencil on his open notebook, dropped the pencil, and raised his hands as if in surrender. "You've got me dead to rights, Mr. McGinn."

"Put down your hands, Mayweather," Stowall said. The man complied. "I trust you have an explanation?"

"I do, Captain." Mayweather leaned back in his chair,

posture relaxed, seemingly not the least bit sheepish or uncomfortable at the turn of events. "I confronted Miss Wei that night because I wished to discover if she'd had anything to do with Miss Bonney's disappearance. That's the reason McGinn overheard Miss Bonney's name."

"But your meeting was *before* we learned of Hundun's existence," Toru said. "Or his relationship to Miss Hsu and Miss Rees. What prompted you to question Miss Wei?"

Mayweather's gaze left Stowall and settled on Toru. "The good captain knows less about the background of some of the passengers than I do. I've followed Miss Wei's activities for many years. Suffice it to say that her presence has been noted in the vicinity of several disappearances, all prominent individuals. The same can be said for the premature and sudden demise of other personages. I discovered the pattern five years ago, and supplied the information to the relevant authorities. Nothing came of it. She's too careful for that."

My mind wrestled with the ramifications. Mayweather could see the pattern of the web, yes, but only the broad outlines of the weaver. Or weavers. Wei Xi's use of Hundun as a tool had protected her from discovery. Worse, the spinning had been going on for a long time. Five years ago, Hundun would have been only twelve.

"Am I correct in thinking you are on board to observe Wei Xi and Hsu Lin?" I asked Mayweather.

"You are correct," Stowall said. "Mr. Mayweather informed me of his intentions before we sailed. None of the previous affairs occurred on ocean voyages, he told me, though some took place on river journeys. This trans-Pacific crossing might be innocent, or there might be a target on board. Personally, I thought that unlikely. I was wrong. And for that, I am most heartily sorry, Mr. McGinn and Miss Rees."

I acknowledged the captain's apology, but focused on Mayweather. "So, you were suspicious that Wei Xi might be on board for a nefarious purpose. You knew that Annie was missing, and your mind immediately leaped to Wei Xi?"

"In a nutshell." Mayweather's elbows were on the table, hands clasped under his chin.

"Why would Wei Xi agree to meet you alone in the middle of the night?"

He sat back. "That wasn't the way it happened, Miss Rees. Not at all." His voice softened, easing the tension. "I thought if Wei Xi were planning to harm a passenger, the woman might be working with at least one partner. I watched. I listened. Miss Hsu never left the cabin, but Wei Xi did. I heard her return in the wee hours the first two nights. So, on the night Mr. McGinn mentions, after I learned of the search for Miss Bonney, I waited for Wei Xi to leave. She slipped out not long after the cabin steward came to her room."

"That would be Hundun dressed as a steward?"

"Indeed, although I didn't know it then. I literally ran into Miss Wei on the promenade deck. Must be losing my touch. She'd stopped to throw something over the side. I couldn't see what. But it was light enough not to make a splash."

Annie's purse. "And did you learn anything of value?"

He thought for a moment, as if deciding how much to tell us. "I learned nothing directly, Miss Rees. She denied knowing Miss Bonney or anything about her whereabouts."

"You said you learned nothing *directly* from Wei Xi," I said. "But you implied that you learned something indirectly."

He paused. The only sounds were Arnold's quill and Miss Hartfield's pencil scratching notes.

"I hid, then followed her again. I wanted to see if she'd go back to her cabin, or perhaps meet someone." Another pause. "Wei Xi and her brothers are paid to provide a service. I figured if she was on board to work, and my questions had upset her, she might report our conversation to an associate or contact. It was a long shot, I'll admit."

"And did she?" Stowall asked. "Report to anyone?"

"She entered the kitchen through an outer door. I knew the dining room was closed, so I circled around to the games room. She stayed in the kitchen, but one of the cooks came out and handed something like a domino tile to Gideon Lamb. He took a break from the card game. I saw Lamb and Miss Wei meet a cabin steward in the shadows on the stern deck."

"She would have needed someone like Hundun or Ah Jim to translate for her," Toru said. "Mr. Lamb doesn't speak Chinese, and Wei Xi doesn't speak much English. Did you overhear any of their conversation, Mayweather?"

"Couldn't get close enough."

"Why didn't you mention this before?" Toru asked. "You've had plenty of opportunities."

"I told Captain Stowall."

Stowall harrumphed like a character in *H.M.S Pinafore.* "Circumstantial. Can't accuse Lamb without solid evidence he's committed a crime. Otherwise he could accuse me of slander. Besides, I knew Lamb had an alibi for the time Miss Bonney disappeared. He was dining with me."

"That doesn't preclude his being involved," I said. "Mr. Lamb certainly revealed his true colors at the shoot this afternoon. He threatened to send me to the bottom of the ocean."

"*What?*" Stowall's voice thundered in the small room.

"It's true, Captain. Unfortunately, Lamb was careful to speak so that only Seaman Robie and I could hear."

"So *that's* why you fed your breakfast to the fish," Arnold said. "I thought it was a reaction to the competition."

"Mr. Lamb is a monster," said Hartfield.

Mayweather grinned. "You'll get no argument from me. Perhaps you and I can put our heads together and come up with a way to stop him."

"Let me know if you need help," Michael said. "I've only one good arm, but my brain still works."

Arnold stuck his pen into a holder, closed his logbook, and stood. "Double the guard on Miss Rees for the duration of the journey, Captain?"

"Agreed."

I would have a mini-phalanx. I hoped it would be enough.

The meeting broke up. While Toru stayed behind for a word with Mayweather, Stowall, and Arnold, I accompanied Robie, Michael, and Phoebe into the main dining room.

"Well," Hartfield said, "Dr. Nakagawa and Mr. Quade were right to seek me out, Miss Rees. There's a lot I still don't know, and you're facing a determined, violent adversary. Or adversaries. But I can help you shore up your legal defenses."

"Mrs. Hartfield, are you free to have tea in my cabin, say, in half an hour? That way, my guardians and I could discuss the details of what we need from you without being disturbed."

"An excellent idea, Miss Rees." She took one of her special notebooks from her purse and handed it to me. "I saw that you admired my tablet. You can start filling this one with notes at our meeting."

"It's lovely. Thank you." I ran a hand over the leather cover, resenting the limitations that gloves placed on my sense of touch. When I looked up, Toru was by my side, Michael had disappeared, and Phoebe Hartfield was striding away. A strong, capable, confident woman. I felt better knowing she'd be working with me.

I pulled from my pocket the crumpled note that Mayweather had tossed me earlier. It said: *Three months ago, Lamb managed an introduction to your grandmother.*

I handed the note to Toru. He skimmed it, grimaced, tucked the slip in his pocket, and offered me his arm. We didn't discuss it as we walked. No need. We both knew what Mayweather meant. My grandmother was the queen in Lamb's chess game. All hell would break loose when we reached port and my grandmother learned not only that my father was dead, but that he'd left her nothing in his will.

Or did she already know? Had Lamb managed to send word about Father's death via an earlier ship?

Impossible. Ships had left Yokohama in the days before the *Oceanic* departed, but they could not have reached San Francisco yet.

Unless she'd somehow learned that my father had been injured three months ago and had made sure that he never left the hospital. In that case, she'd presume his death was a fait accompli. And she could have arranged, via Lamb, that I never reached San Francisco.

Like my dear Annie, I would be "wrapped in the arms of Davy Jones."

Chapter 25

TORU AND I STOPPED at Sick Bay so Dr. Doyle could clean and dress my arm. A ten-minute operation. No sign of infection. My shooting escapade hadn't disturbed the stitches.

We encountered Phoebe Hartfield waiting at Ah Jim's station in the passageway near my cabin. "I've asked your steward to bring another table and tea for four," she said. "Is that right? Or do you want Miss Hsu to join us?"

"Not this time," Toru said. "Please excuse me while I fetch some papers from my cabin."

"And Uncle P?" I said.

"Of course." He set off down the hall as I opened my cabin door.

I smelled a faint mix of flower scents. The water pitcher on the dressing table held two dozen carnations, red and white. Beside the pitcher was a tray covered by a damp towel that hid an intricate wreath woven from the remaining flowers and accented by bows of white grosgrain ribbon. The effect was sweetly sentimental, yet it captured Annie's vibrant personality. I smiled. She would have loved it.

"Beautiful work—as good as any I've seen in San Francisco," said Hartfield from behind me. I'd forgotten she was there. "Did you make it?"

"Miss Hsu did. For tonight's service." I gently replaced the towel. Lin had never met Annie, as far as I knew, so this gesture was for me.

As if she'd read my thoughts, Hartfield said, "A memory to treasure."

Toru and Phineas were at the door, both carrying lap desks. Behind them, Ah Jim and another steward transported a table and chairs. "It seemed easiest to borrow mine," Toru said.

The cabin was transformed in moments. Tea arrived as I pulled my own portable desk from the closet. While I'd been in meetings, scribes had been creating clean drafts of three new wills.

We spent the next two hours reviewing the drafts, my emancipation case file, and the proposed changes to our company share structure with Phoebe Hartfield. She initially opposed my contributing the bulk of the shares we would offer to Rhoderic Perry. But when she saw I was adamant, she suggested we require that Rep, in addition to buying shares, bring mining prospects with him when he joined the firm. It's what Toru had done. The motion carried.

When Hartfield left with the various draft forms at the end of the meeting, I looked at Phineas and Toru. They nodded in unison. Phoebe Hartfield was capable, sharp, would fight to protect my interests, and was compatible with my guardians. I wasn't sure how far Mr. Sutherland, our company lawyer, had taken my emancipation case while I'd been away, but my guardians and I would ask Hartfield to take over the case when we reached San Francisco.

For the first time in days, perhaps unwisely, I began to relax.

* * *

Annie's memorial was held on the stern as the sun set that evening, timed so that most passengers would be at their aperitifs.

We gathered in a semicircle facing the direction from which we'd come. Phineas and Toru stood on either side of Michael McGinn and me; Hsu Lin, Phoebe Hartfield, and Mayweather right behind us. Captain Stowall, Arnold, Robie, and Dr. Doyle rounded out the company. Chaplain Colins faced us, his back to the wake of the ship, uniform hat tucked under his arm.

I had wanted a private ceremony—just those who knew her. But I saw Gideon Lamb and the Smalls slip into the shadows on the port side. Felicity's mouth was a grim line, as if her husband's comments about Annie still rankled. Edward Small's gaze found and fixed on the one-armed man who had captured Annie's heart. I wondered which Small had made the odd decision to attend, and why.

Michael, for his part, had donned his Sunday best. Black suit of light wool, white collarless shirt, green scarf at the neck, dark tweed cap. The scarf was for their birth country. I heard Annie's voice in my head wondering who had done up the buttons on his shirt. I almost laughed, hearing the jealous tone flavoring the words. But I didn't. No one, except perhaps Phineas, who shared my irreverent sense of humor, would have understood.

Colins read the Anglican eulogy for the dead. Michael and I sang "Bring Back My Bonnie to Me," and Michael read an excerpt from "Annabel Lee" that I'd written down for him. He had a natural rhythm and a carrying voice, and the meter of the poem fell to matching the wash of the waves against the hull like a sonorous music.

Through tear-blinded eyes, Michael and I tied his green scarf—symbol of a homeland neither would see again—around the wreath. Together we tossed the wreath into the waves and watched it splash and float away.

After I'd reclaimed some sort of composure, I turned back to the mourners and thanked them for attending the memorial. Lin handed me the flowers we'd kept out from the wreath, and I passed among the audience handing them out. One by one they tossed their flowers into the air and let the wind carry them back and away, a lighter farewell than the clods of earth tossed on my mother's wooden coffin. One by one they shook my hand and Michael's, and began to depart. The first to go were the Smalls, but Lamb lingered.

Only then did a form detach itself from the shadow thrown by a mast and sail on a shelf above the deck. A crouched form, misshapen, almost grotesque, I thought, until it resolved itself as my brother, holding our father's urn under his left arm.

I felt my sharp intake of breath. Lin must have heard it, for she turned to follow my stare. I heard her hiss some words in Chinese as Hundun dangled from the shelf by his right hand and dropped lightly to the deck.

Michael, Toru, Phineas, Stowall, Arnold, and Robie turned and surged forward, but even Toru was not fast enough to stop the intruder, who ran not away from them, but toward me.

I stood there, still as an obelisk, the perfect target. At that moment, I didn't care if he took me as he had Annie. That's what grief does.

I felt a tug on my skirt as he brushed by me to climb the stern railing, perching there like a falcon, bare feet curved for balance, the brass ginger jar still tucked under his left arm, a dagger in his right hand. Waiting. Below him the massive screws churned the water.

Hsu Lin moved forward till she stood shoulder to shoulder with me. Hundun's face lit up with a smile. He looked… happy.

I knew then that this dagger was only to keep us back. He meant to follow Annie's wreath into the waves.

As if reading my thoughts, he said, "This is my second truly free decision."

Second? "You mean after the notes you left for me?"

He nodded.

"We can't change your mind?"

He gestured with the arm holding the knife, a motion encompassing the whole world. "'It must follow, as the night the day.'"

Hamlet. Polonius' advice to Laertes. I finished the quote: "'Thou canst not then be false to any man.'"

"Not anymore."

"You would have liked our father," I said. "You inherited his smile."

"Did I?"

"And his freckles."

I didn't ask him not to jump. I didn't ask him to leave me the urn of ashes. He had as much right to them as I. And perhaps, had my father known of the son he'd left behind in Shanghai, he would have been at peace with a resting place in the center of the ocean, halfway between the continents of his children's births.

My brother said, "You had our father in life. He and I will spend eternity together."

"May he bring you comfort in whatever lies ahead." I

searched my pockets for a handkerchief. Found only the hard rectangularity of my sketchbook and what felt like a small bottle. No handkerchief. Toru gave me his—pure white, pressed, and ample enough to hide my face. I wiped my eyes so I could continue to see my brother.

Tears that Annie's service hadn't triggered now welled in Hsu Lin's eyes and slid silently down her cheeks. She held out her hand and took another step forward. As if she wanted to go with him.

He shook his head and said something to her in Chinese.

She replied.

Eyes fixed on us he smiled once more, tossed the dagger at my feet, and launched himself backwards into space. My sister and I did not rush to the rail to see him go under. I picked up the dagger, sank to the deck, crossed my legs like a child, and curled forward until my forehead felt the warmth of the deck. The metal of the knife was hot against my skin. Above and around me all was noise and chatter, subdued, hushed. In the distance I heard Dr. Doyle's voice, then Phineas saying, "Let her be."

Lin, too, had sunk to the deck. She took my left hand and held it in both of hers. My sister, comforting me, when I should be comforting her. We stayed that way until the sun finished setting.

I sat up, breathed deeply for a minute, saw that all but Robie, Michael, Phineas, and Toru had gone. Michael knelt at the rail, staring out at the limitless ocean. My guardians helped Lin and me stand. I went to Michael, touched his shoulder. "I'd like to talk with you again, Michael. Perhaps tomorrow?"

He didn't answer. I wondered if, for him, there would be a tomorrow.

The rest of us walked along the deck toward the cooler interior of the ship. The remaining light burnished Lin's skin and made her eyes glow. I realized how beautiful she was.

"What did your twin say, at the end?" I asked her softly, so no one else could hear.

She hesitated, warring with herself, perhaps, about whether to share his words or hold them close.

Eventually, as we reached the hatch, she made a decision. "He told me I must stay. That I still have work to do."

"Then I will help you if I can."

Back at my cabin, I invited her in for a few minutes. I set the dagger on the dressing table. I'd been carrying it, without thinking, since I'd picked it up on the deck. I still felt my brother's hand on the ivory handle.

Without speaking, we sat at the little breakfast table. Ah Jim had removed Toru's table and chairs and freshened the room, removing all signs of Lin's wreath-making. But the scent of carnations lingered.

As I poured glasses of water for each of us, I sensed Hsu Lin closing like a scallop, turning a hard calcareous shell toward me. She was hurting, though she had not known about her brother two days ago.

"You think I should have been the one to die, rather than Hundun," I said. "That it's all my fault he leapt from the deck."

"It isn't rational, I know. But yes. If it hadn't been for you, he'd still be alive."

"To go on working for his owners. No choice. What life would that be?"

I stood and crossed to the dressing table. Picked up the dagger. Offered it to her, ivory handle first. "Go ahead," I said. "Finish what your brother set out to do. Then, you will be the only one left of our father's line."

She took the knife, let her hand absorb its form and weight. She turned it this way and that, making figure eights in the air. She had, I decided, a healthy familiarity with knives. Something to remember. She held it out to me. "Perhaps later."

I refused to take the knife. "It's yours. A gift from your twin. You may have need of a weapon, even if it's not to kill your sister."

She studied me, then slid the knife into her pocket.

From my own pocket I took the sketchbook Hundun had left there as he brushed by me on the stern. Opening it, I saw words and pictures that went on, page after page. I didn't show them to Lin. I wanted to read them first.

My pocket also yielded a small bottle. It had the cross on the front symbolizing the holy nature of the water within—or the water that had once lain within. It now held a gray powder. He'd opened the urn and removed some of our father's ashes. I could release them wherever I chose. It was a kindness I hadn't anticipated.

I set the bottle and the sketchbook gently on the table. Crossed my arms beside them. Lowered my head. The tears came in earnest.

Perhaps ten minutes passed before the sobs stopped and I could breathe with only the occasional hiccup. I sat up and employed the fresh handkerchief Lin had placed within reach.

"At the end," Lin said, "as Hundun waited on the rail, you displayed no anger. Sorrow, yes. Pain, yes. But not hate or anger." She gestured to the sketchbook. On the first page was my copy of the note he'd left on the glass vase and the address he'd left under the berth. "Is this the reason you could not hate him? Because he had confessed his actions?"

"I suppose so."

"And my Honorable Aunt Xi?"

"My compassion does not yet extend to her. I'm not sure it ever will, because of what she did to him. She and her brothers formed and directed Hundun."

Lin stood and picked up the dagger. "When I find the shadow person who hired the Wei family, I will kill him."

"Or her?" I said. Lin had not been at the meeting in the dining alcove. She didn't know that Mayweather had seen Wei Xi with Gideon Lamb. And I hadn't shown her Mayweather's note about Lamb's introduction to my grandmother.

She nodded. "Or her. I will do this for our brother and father, and for my mother."

"I'd be satisfied with seeing the ghost captured and confined in prison."

Lin was at the door. "That, my sister, is the difference between us."

The cabin seemed strangely empty when she was gone. I didn't move for the longest time. Dr. Doyle stopped by to check on me. I told him I didn't need or want a sleeping draught. I preferred to be alone with my grief.

I'd lied. I desperately wanted to lose myself in sleep. But my mind refused to slow down. It was fixated on finding justice for Annie, for my father, even for my brother.

I stripped off my clothes, washed my body, cleaned my teeth, and donned a silk chemise. I sat for a time in the dark, feeling as if a fierce desert wind had hollowed me out, taking with it the last vestiges of childhood.

Denied sleep, that panacea for all nature's ills, eventually I lit a lamp, picked up *The Aeneid,* and opened to the place I'd left off reading:

"Twofold are the gates of Sleep; whereof the one is said to be of horn, by which an easy exit is granted to the visions of truth; the other glittering with the polished whiteness of ivory: but false the dreams the Powers below send to the world above."

I dearly hoped that wasn't an omen.

Part IV

O&OL Oceanic, Thursday, August 6 to Thursday, August 13, 1885

"Hail, you that at last have finished the dread dangers of the sea! But more grievous perils on land remain."
— Virgil, The Aeneid VI (translated by James Lonsdale and Samuel Lee, 1871)

Chapter 26

Thursday, 4:00 a.m.

I **WOKE FROM A** nightmare in the predawn hours. A shadowy figure was chasing me along deserted decks, through empty salons and passageways. I knocked on cabin doors as I passed. No response. It was a ghost ship.

These were the last days of freedom and privacy. Soon I would enter the home my grandmother had treated as her own for the past two years. The housekeepers, Tom and Mary Daly, would help protect me. My guardians' attention, however, would be divided. They owned a house on Russian Hill, but Phineas would be in hospital. Toru would be focused on Phineas and on the myriad details of running our business. I could help him with both, if he'd let me. But I no longer had Annie to accompany me around the city, and I could not trust anyone my grandmother found to replace Annie.

It would take time for my legal emancipation case to be heard by the court. I needed protection in the meantime—or a way to hide from my enemies. I would broach these subjects as I walked the deck with Phineas and Toru. Perhaps they'd have solutions I hadn't imagined.

I wrote a quick a message to Phineas, then rang for the night steward. When I opened my cabin door at his knock, the guard was gone.

My brother, Annie's murderer, had followed her into the deep. Wei Xi was locked in some space below decks with a guard nearby. The captain had been angered by Gideon Lamb's remarks to me, but had refused to take his threat seriously. It seemed the captain had canceled my protection detail.

I watched the night steward trot down the passageway to Phineas' cabin and knock softly. Phineas stepped out into the passageway and waved to me, then held up five fingers. Twice. He'd pick me up in ten minutes.

I pointed to Hsu Lin's cabin and shook my head. I didn't want to disturb her. She'd be feeling the loss of her twin more acutely than I felt the loss of a half-brother. Though she had only known him a short time, any opportunity that they might have had to become close had perished with Hundun off the stern deck.

The night steward, duty done, was back at his station. Or so I thought. He'd walked past me, but must have continued on to the head, or on some other errand. The huge screw throbbed like a heartbeat. The flapping of sails overhead provided a staccato counterpoint. As I turned back to my cabin I heard stumbling footsteps. Smelled whiskey. A hand clamped down on my right shoulder.

The man shoved me into the cabin. I stumbled, caught myself and turned in a crouch, and butted him in the groin with my shoulder. He doubled over. The odor of spirits seemed to come from everywhere—his mouth, his mustache and beard, his skin, even his clothes, making me gag. I couldn't scream.

I rose, slid around his bulk, and kicked the back of his knees. He went down. I reached for the door handle. Heard the rip of my travel costume. Looked down to see the blade barely miss my Achilles tendon. I leaped forward and was out the door and running down the passageway. I bumped the bulkhead of Lin's cabin in passing, but continued running to the safety of my guardians, pounding first on Toru's door, then Phineas'.

Toru opened first. "Small," I grunted. "In my cabin. He has a knife."

Phineas came through the connecting door into Toru's cabin in time to hear my words. "Stay here," he said. "Lock yourself in."

Toru grabbed a walking staff that did double duty for measuring thicknesses of rock. Lightweight, but deadly when used as a fighting stick. As I entered Toru's cabin,

Lin stepped out of hers.

Small must have been waiting for just such a diversion. He lumbered into the passageway, grabbed Lin from behind with an arm across her torso, and held a knife to her neck. We all paused, mid-motion. Behind Small I saw movement. Ah Jim, coming on duty. But he wouldn't dare do anything that might result in harm to Lin.

"You have nowhere to go, Mr. Small," said Phineas. "Let the girl go."

"I have nothing to lose at this point." Small slurred the words. He pulled Lin into her cabin. I heard the *snick* of the lock.

I retrieved one of my Colts from the cabin and fed bullets into the chamber, my fingers shaking. This wouldn't be target practice. I took one calming breath, left my cabin, and closed the door behind me.

Ah Jim had disappeared, no doubt gone to alert the officer on duty. I handed my revolver to Phineas. He checked the load and handed the gun back, saying, "You're the best shot. If you think you can do it."

"We'll soon find out," I said.

The passageway was filling with people in various states of dress—formal wear, nightwear, morning robes. Toru stayed by Lin's door to explain the situation and prevent Small escaping. Phineas and I threaded our way through the crowd, passing Gideon Lamb, still in evening dress, at the door to the deck. Dark blond stubble covered his cheeks and chin. He smiled. "What's all the excitement?"

We didn't answer.

The night lanterns and the predawn grayness illuminated the way on deck. Lin's porthole was open. I could hear her struggling with Small, but then all was quiet inside. An ominous sign.

I grasped the curtains and tugged the left drape aside an inch or two. Lin's cabin was lit only by a single lamp, turned low. It took my eyes a moment to grow accustomed to the dimness. I rested the Colt on the sill and waited.

The room was the mirror image of mine. It was as

uncluttered and nearly bare of personal objects as it had been the previous morning. Clothes stowed out of sight in the wardrobe, not tossed over the top of the screen, as I was wont to do. Nothing left out on the table or dressing table except a hairbrush and the two hairpins I'd given Lin. Was it only last evening that she'd worn the set to the memorial service?

The shadows of two people, one large, one small, merged by the cabin door. I could hear Small's harsh breathing.

Someone pounded on the door. Small let Lin go, picked up a chair and wedged it under the door handle. "I'll kill the girl if you break in!" he shouted. But his voice shook.

Lin moved swiftly to the gas lamp on the outer bulkhead, turned it up, then took a seat on the stool before the dressing table, her back to the mirror. Looking composed, lips set in a firm line, she began gathering her long hair, twisting it up on top of her head.

"Stop." Small stepped forward, half-blocking my view of Lin. If he moved as I fired, I'd hit her. "Leave it down."

"It is in my face, Mr. Small. A distraction."

"Proceed, then."

She reached back to take something from the dresser. A hairpin, long and sharp as a stiletto. Its golden top, shaped like a plum blossom, gleamed in the soft light as Lin slid the pin into her hair. She picked up the second. Small swayed, watching her, mesmerized.

I lifted the revolver, hoping that he would shift enough to lose his balance and step aside. My movement must have caught her eye. She leaned to her left slightly, glanced past him at the porthole, and nodded as she slipped the second hairpin into place.

Her hands dropped to her lap. "You have done nothing yet that cannot be undone, Mr. Small."

"I have. You don't—" He shook his head, as if trying to clear it. "But it's over now. She knows. There's only one way—"

"She knows what?"

He leaned forward and plucked a pin from her hair. The mass of hair tilted, but the other pin held.

Renewed pounding on the cabin door. The captain's voice this time, muffled but recognizable, asking for entry. Small turned and shouted his threat again. The pounding subsided.

"Think of your wife," Lin said, drawing his attention back to her. "You cannot do this to Mrs. Small."

"It's too late." The mirror over the dressing table reflected his expression. He was looking at the knife and hairpin as if he didn't know how they had found their way into his hands. He tossed the pin on the dressing table. I heard it roll.

Move, Small. Move away from my sister.

"Surely—" Lin began.

"You dance with the devil that brought you." Small raised the knife.

"Mr. Small," I called loudly, pushing aside the other curtain. Startled, he stepped back, searching for the source of the voice. "You forgot to close the porthole."

He lunged for the opening. My shot took him in the left shoulder. He stumbled back a step. The knife hand came up to the wound as he fell forward, landing with a thud. Lin was standing behind him, her hands empty.

She bent and pulled the hairpin from Small's side, where it had sunk all the way to the plum petals. She wiped it on his pant leg, spit on his unconscious face, and then looked up at me.

"He fell back against the hairpin when he was shot," she said, just loudly enough to be heard above the banging on the door. Having stated her position, she turned, removed the chair from under the handle, and opened the door. Sailors rushed in.

Chapter 27

TORU TOOK THE REVOLVER from my hand, which had dropped to my side. He passed the gun to Phineas and said, "I'll see to Hsu Lin, and tell Captain Stowall where you are."

I nodded. "Thank you. Please tell her I'll be with her in her cabin as soon as the hallway clears."

My legs were shaky as aspic. I sank down on the nearest deck chair and stared blindly out to sea. *I just shot a man. And Lin stabbed him with a hairpin my father bought for me.*

I must have spoken aloud, for Phineas said from the chair next to me, "If fortune smiles, you killed the bloke."

"Uncle P!"

"Whatever possessed him to attack you and your sister?" Behind the raised neckerchief his lips tightened.

"I don't know," I said. "He was drunk, but he said nothing to me. And when I foiled his attack, he took Lin. It was as if he felt compelled to kill *someone*. But why us?"

"If he survives, I'll see what I can find out. His choice of words worries me."

"That part about dancing with the devil?"

"Yes. Who's the devil?"

"And why would he have made a Faustian bargain in the first place?" I considered what I knew about Mr. Small. "Do me a favor, Uncle P?"

"Anything."

"Both Mr. Small and Mr. Lamb were still wearing evening clothes. They hadn't been to bed yet. Will you please find out if they gambled tonight? And if Mr. Small lost everything but his shirt?"

"Now?"

"No. I don't want to be alone right now."

Phineas took my hand in his. His eyes had the grim

look I'd last seen when he learned of the knife wound on my arm.

I'd forgotten all about the wound. But it throbbed again, as if I'd broken the stitches. I pulled up my sleeve and checked. There was enough light now to see that no red stain darkened the bandage. Dr. Doyle did good work.

"Your parents would be proud of you," Phineas said. "Toru and I are proud of you."

I squeezed his hand. What would I do when they were no longer a few cabin doors away?

We sat in silence. The sky was a rare shade of turquoise more typical of desert evenings, the clouds were streaks of coral. Cool air currents tugged at my hair until it streamed out behind me. I'd left my hair unbraided, holding the thick mass away from my face with a wide grosgrain ribbon. This was what freedom felt like.

People strolled past, but I couldn't have identified if they were friend or foe. I was looking inward. I'd witnessed war and death and tragedy in so many different forms. I'd honed my shooting skills on bottles and cans, scarecrows, and clay pigeons. But this was the first time I'd aimed at and felled a human being.

And then Toru and Hsu Lin were standing there, his hand on her shoulder.

"Please," I said to her, "sit with us. I'd like to know what happened between the time Mr. Small grabbed you and we reached the porthole."

"He spoke gibberish," Lin said.

"Can you remember any of it?" Phineas asked.

"Let me think. He was grunting and mumbling as we struggled. I asked him to let me go. He would not. I said, 'Why are you doing this?' He said, 'I was the man in the box. I don't know how—but suddenly it's not just the two of us, and I'm the man in the box, and the captain, he— how did he manage that? Everything's gone—unless...'

"I said, 'Unless what?' And he said, 'She had to go. I failed. So, you have to go. That's something. Enough? I don't know. It *must* be enough!'"

Lin caught a stray lock of hair at her temple and tucked it behind her ear. "I was confused. How did Mr.

Small know my brother's name? So I asked him. I said, 'Mr. Small, how did you learn of Chaos-in-a-Box?' And he said, 'Yes, that is *exactly* how it felt! I didn't ask to be the man in the box. But I was. It would have been different if I'd won, or if I'd killed her. But now *you* have to be enough.' Then there was the pounding on the door, and you know what happened next."

I put my other hand on hers and squeezed gently.

Phineas looked across me to where Toru leaned against the bulkhead. "It's time to talk to Captain Stowall."

Toru gave a slight lift of the chin toward the stern. I straightened and turned. Mr. Arnold was making his way along the deck, Robie in tow. Déjà vu, as my mother would have said. But whether Robie would be an escort or a guard, I didn't know.

Lin and I weren't up to going over the details with the captain. I needed food, a quiet place to think, and a change of clothes. My outfit still smelled of the spirits Small had imbibed.

"Miss Hsu's cabin is being cleaned to remove all trace of the incident," Arnold said. "In the meantime, may she rest and recover in your cabin, Miss Rees?"

"Of course."

Arnold and Robie escorted the four of us to my cabin, which required us to run a gauntlet of sympathetic murmurs, whispers behind hands, and sideward glances. As we walked, a thought struck me. I might need legal representation for having shot Small. I wasn't worried about Lin's vulnerability. She'd been abducted and was entitled to defend herself by any means necessary. Only she and I, and perhaps Phineas, had witnessed Lin's decision to plunge that hairpin in *after* the shot had hit him in the shoulder.

"Mr. Arnold, would you please send someone to find Mrs. Hartfield for me? If she's willing, I'd like to have her present at my guardians' meeting with Captain Stowall, in case there's a question as to whether firing to protect Hsu Lin makes me culpable in any way."

"I'll see to it. And Dr. Doyle will check on you both after he finishes in surgery."

Toru, Phineas, and Arnold left us in Robie's care. Clearly, the captain wanted to prevent further attacks, or restrict our movements. Fine. Seclusion sounded wonderful to me.

I rang for breakfast. Lin and I tried to sponge off all vestiges of Small's attacks. I loaned her my spare kimono, and handed off our clothes to Ah Jim when he arrived with our breakfast tray. I poured the tea, and Lin and I tucked into the food. Only then did I broach the question that had been lurking like the bad dream I couldn't shake. "Why use the hairpin when the man was already immobilized?"

She paused, spoon raised, and looked up from the boiled egg. "Because he touched me against my will."

"Remind me never to cross you, Lin."

She smiled. "Have no fears. And thank you for defending me. I hope to repay your kindness one day."

"It's not necessary. You'd have done the same for me."

She gave me a look I couldn't read. But a knock on the door prevented me from responding.

Dr. Doyle entered, closing the door gently after him. I had expected him to look tired, but surgery seemed to have energized him.

"Mr. Small is alive, but in a coma. The hairpin pierced his lung and heart. I managed to stop the internal bleeding and extract the bullet, but I don't know if he'll survive. Touch and go, I'd say. Shock from the wounds didn't help. Mrs. Small is with him, although I heard she chucked him out last night."

"Did he say anything before you began the operation?" I asked. "Anything that would explain why he attacked us?"

"Not a whisper." He shook his head, as if he'd seen all manner of strange things in his career. "Drink and drugs do that to some men, lassie, as if another creature lives inside them, waiting to be let out. I've seen timid men become bold, shy men turn garrulous, and others suddenly rage and destroy."

He took a deep breath, set his medical bag on the bed, and refocused on the matter at hand. He checked our eyes, pulses, bruises. Took off my bandage and examined the stitches, still neatly aligned. "All good here." He applied some salve that smelled of eucalyptus. "I'll take the stitches out the day before we dock. Just send Ah Jim with a note as to when you'll visit the medical bay, and I'll be there." Doyle studied us for another moment or two. "Are you able to sleep?"

"We haven't tried," I said.

"Well, you seem to be holding up remarkably well, considering a man tried to kill you both this morning. So, if there are any emotional effects, let me know. Sleeplessness, lack of appetite, listlessness, bouts of tears, that sort of thing. It would be natural, particularly if the brute dies from his wounds."

He patted our shoulders and left, carrying his energy with him. Neither of us returned to our interrupted breakfast. Lin sank onto a chair and closed her eyes. I offered her Annie's berth. She shook her head. I understood. Sleep could bring nightmares.

Yet we both drifted off, slumped in our chairs, waiting for the next knock at the door. It came from Phoebe Hartfield. Toru and Phineas had elected her to relate the results of their meeting with Captain Stowall.

"The captain decided the shooting was justified," she said, taking the chair I'd just vacated.

I moved to sit on my berth. "What did he say when my guardians recounted Mr. Small's ramblings?"

"Captain Stowall said he retired shortly after dinner, before the dancing and gaming began. He didn't see Mr. Small, and certainly did *not* discuss Miss Hsu's brother with him." She turned to Lin. "The captain is as confused as you are, Miss Hsu, but he has launched a separate investigation to uncover the reasons why Mr. Small attacked you and Miss Rees. He asks that if you recall any further bits of Mr. Small's ranting, that you please alert either him or Mr. Arnold. And the captain said that if you do not wish to reoccupy your cabin, he will find other accommodation for you."

"That will not be necessary, Mrs. Hartfield. I am sure the cleaners will have left no trace of last night's event. And the guard posted outside will ensure my continued safety."

"I'll relay that to Mr. Arnold." Phoebe Hartfield looked at me. "What are your plans for the rest of the day?"

I hadn't thought that far ahead. My mind was still attempting to make sense of the Small affair. I said, "I'll be keeping to my cabin for much of the day. I have my studies. And Lin, of course, may stay here as long as she wishes. But if you would be kind enough to help Dr. Nakagawa and Mr. Arnold discover Mr. Small's activities last night, I would be grateful."

"With pleasure. Perhaps I could bring you a report later?"

"Splendid," I said.

She left us, and I picked up my drawing pad. But for once it held no interest. Nor did my Latin translation, the chemistry and biology questions, or the math problems. Although I'd changed clothes, and washed my hands and face, the smell of whiskey and Mr. Small's body odors still clung to me.

"Would you help me wash my hair?" I said to Lin, who was drowsing again in her chair. "Annie used to assist me, but..."

She smiled. "If you will help me with mine. Wei Xi was not an ideal companion, but she was useful."

We filled the pitchers with hot water, lathered our hair with lavender-scented soap, and recovered the ability to laugh in the process. When we'd removed the tangles from our wet hair, I asked Lin if she wanted to try on Annie's hats.

"You do not mind?" she asked.

"I'm practical. If you don't want them, I'll add them to the pile of Annie's things I'm offering to the women in Third Class."

Lin tried on two hats, one with a veil, one without. "You know," I said, "with the veil lowered, and in Annie's clothes, you could blend in with the Europeans and Americans as we disembarked, especially if we dressed your hair differently."

She didn't respond, but considered the effect in the mirror, turning this way and that. She was still standing there when Ah Jim brought word that her cabin was in order.

She touched my shoulder lightly and left, carrying the two hats. When she was gone, I drew the curtains around my berth and slept. And did not dream.

A knock woke me. I dragged myself to the door, feeling disoriented and sluggish, although I'd slept for seven hours.

"I can come back, if this is a bad time," Phoebe Hartfield said.

"No, no. Come in. I hadn't meant to sleep so long. I'll send Ah Jim for tea." I waited for her to enter, then asked the guard, Cotton, to knock on Lin's door and alert her that tea was in the offing.

When the three of us were gathered around the tiny table and had served ourselves, I yielded the floor to my lawyer.

"The news isn't good, I'm afraid," Mrs. Hartfield said. "I've just come from checking with Dr. Doyle. Sick Bay is in an uproar."

Mr. Small had not regained consciousness after the operation, so they hadn't been able to question him. Mrs. Small, who had spent the morning by his bedside, had retired after luncheon for a few hours' sleep. Small died while Doctor Doyle was having an early tea. Mr. Kidd was on a short comfort break. Two minutes. No more.

Small had not struggled when his air supply was truncated. The pillow from Sick Bay's second bed covered Small's face when his wife returned to his bedside from an afternoon siesta. She fainted. Mr. Kidd found her.

"Captain Stowall is apoplectic," Phoebe Hartfield said.

I could imagine. I wasn't sure what I felt. Relief that the threat was gone, but sadness, too, especially for Felicity Small, so recently married.

Lin spread plum jam on a bit of toast, then set it on her plate, as if she'd lost the taste for food. She asked, "Does he suspect anyone?"

"He suspects everyone. No witnesses have come forward, although it's early going."

Everyone? I'd been asleep, with a guard posted in the passageway halfway between my cabin and Lin's. The captain must see that she and I could not have slipped out to finish our defensive efforts of the predawn hours, unless the guard was sleeping or had slipped away.

I stood and opened the door. A new guard stood at ease in the passageway. "When did you come on duty, sir?" I asked him.

"A quarter hour or so. Four bells, miss."

"And was Cotton at his station when you arrived?"

"He was at the steward's station, getting news of what happened in Sick Bay. You heard about that? But no worries, miss. Cotton had your cabin door in sight from there. Nothing out of order on his watch, he said."

"Thank you."

"Pleasure, miss."

I rejoined Lin and Phoebe. The latter said, "I couldn't help but overhear. The previous guard... Seaman Cotton, was it? Well, he was indeed near the steward's station, but a step or two around the corner, asking another seaman about the commotion. Cotton saw where I was going, and accompanied me back to his post. I'd say your cabin and Lin's were out of his sight for a bit."

I looked at Lin, whose eyes were focused on her food. Her fork chased a grape around the plate for long seconds before pouncing and piercing the soft flesh.

"If we alert Mr. Arnold that Cotton wasn't at his post," I said, "then we stand to lose our alibi for the time of Mr. Small's murder." I let the words hang there, the underlying question unasked.

"That is true," Lin said.

"I didn't leave my cabin," I said.

"And I did not kill Mr. Small."

It seemed a straightforward answer to my unspoken question. Her eyes held mine. I sensed I was missing something, that perhaps I should be asking a different question. But nothing came to me. Perhaps later tonight, when I was alone, inspiration would strike. Or perhaps I was missing information yet to be revealed.

I shrugged. Time would provide the answers. In the meantime, the captain would look elsewhere for Mr. Small's killer.

Phoebe Hartfield pushed her plate to the side and filled her teacup, wrinkling her nose when she tasted the lukewarm brew. "What I wouldn't give for a cup of strong coffee."

"Shall I—"

"No, don't bother. I won't be here long. I have one other piece of news for you both, something that bears on Mr. Small's movements last night, though the captain may have closed the book on that episode now."

"But Lin and I haven't."

"Right. Dr. Nakagawa talked to the steward on duty in the gaming salon last night. It appears Mr. Small was gambling on backgammon, not poker. Do you play?"

"My parents taught me." I stood and opened the drawer in the dressing table, removing a roll of quilted fabric tied with heavy black ribbons. Lin cleared our plates onto the tea tray, and I unrolled the cloth backgammon board I'd pieced in Japan from small squares of muslin and the torn pants my father had been wearing when he was injured. On the reverse side was a draughts board. I'd turned my father's pockets into bags, one of which contained smooth discs of sardonyx and black onyx. The other pocket held ivory and ebony dice. The pieces had been Toru's gift to us. My father had watched me make the soft game board as he slowly recovered in hospital.

The set enveloped me in memories. I shook them off and set the stones on the board in their proper arrangement for beginning the game. Finished, I gestured with my hand for Mrs. Hartfield to continue.

"Do you play, Miss Hsu?" When Lin shook her head, Hartfield continued, "Ah, well, perhaps Miss Rees will teach you. For today, all you need to know is that the white stones (red, in this case) and black stones move in opposite directions around the board, advancing upon the throw of the dice. In the conventional game, two people play against each other. They can wager on the outcome, of course. That is apparently what Mr. Small was expecting to do last night, playing against Mr. Lamb. But as they set up the board, Colonel Grayson arrived with three other men, and suggested that they join Mr. Lamb's side. Mr. Small was inebriated, and apparently unfamiliar with this form of the game, in which a team, headed by a 'captain,' plays against a single player. The team's player rolls the dice and moves the stones for his team. The team confers among its members and decides what moves should be made. The captain, Colonel Grayson in this case, conveys the move to their player. The single opponent is called 'the man in the box.'"

"Oh, no." My stomach lurched.

"Oh, yes. What Mr. Small didn't realize was that the wager he had agreed upon with Mr. Lamb had to be paid out to *each member* of the opposing team if Small lost. Which he did."

Lin had twisted her napkin into a knot during the story. She set it on the table and watched it spring open. "He did not have enough money to cover the bets."

"No, everything was gone, as he complained to you, Miss Hsu. The steward said that one in the group agreed to take his marker, but he doesn't know which one. Dr. Nakagawa approached the players, but none of them will discuss the game. They said it is unseemly, especially in the circumstances. They also returned most or all of the wagers to Mrs. Small, who otherwise would have nothing. Some of them may have been unwitting accomplices. All seemed to be ashamed. All except Mr. Lamb and Colonel Grayson."

"So, you couldn't find out which person, or people, put Mr. Small up to attacking the two of us, presumably in exchange for the marker. Or why they wanted us killed." I picked up the board and poured the stones into their bag, tying it closed. The silence stretched on as I rerolled the cloth and pieces. "Captain Stowall knows?"

"Dr. Nakagawa was going to inform him while I came here. There may be a delay, of course, because of Mr. Small's murder."

"Killing Mr. Small ensures that he can never identify the holder of his marker," I said, "the trigger for his actions."

"Colonel Grayson was the team captain. Mr. Lamb set up the game. For me, that narrows the field."

"Did Uncle T know any of the other three men?"

"He said he's seen them in the card room. Family men of middle age. Businessmen from New York and

Boston, traveling alone."

I pictured a band of coyotes, hunting a rabbit in the night.

Phoebe Hartfield turned to Hsu Lin. "Speaking of traveling alone, what will you do when we reach port?"

"I am allowed entrance to your country only to marry Wei Mu, Wei Xi's brother. I do not have a choice. He is a member of a powerful Tong."

"And they run Chinese society, I know. I've had dealings with the Five Families. A country within a country."

"So I have been told."

"Do you want to marry Wei Mu?" I asked.

Lin shook her head, the faintest motion, as if she would not, could not, say the word aloud.

The silence stretched between us. I broke it. "Does the family know what you look like?"

"Wei Xi's introduction was to be all the identification necessary. My grandfather sent a photograph of me, but... I will show you."

Lin retrieved the picture from her cabin, handed it to me, and slipped back into her chair. The formal pose showed her in profile, a large wedding headdress covering the front, sides, and crown of her head. From the tiara hung many strands of small pearls. They reached nearly to her chin, and threw her features into shadow.

I reached over and turned her head so that she was in profile. Her fork, halfway to her mouth, clattered back to the plate. I studied her as an artist would, looking for distinctive features. No moles. No scars. No deep laugh lines. Indeed, no laugh lines at all. "Smile for me, please?"

She smiled, and the smooth skin barely wrinkled. But I saw where someday, if her fortunes changed, those smile lines would incise themselves around eyes and mouth. The lips tilted up slightly at the corner, but were not full, not thin, not protruding. Average. Her chin and jaw line were more defined now than they had been when the picture was taken, her cheek less rounded. She had lost the softness of childhood and become a woman.

"When was this taken?" Phoebe Hartfield said.

"Last fall. My grandfather had arranged with the school for me to visit a studio. The wedding costume was theirs, except for the headdress. My grandmother brought hers for me to wear for the sitting."

"In my opinion, this photograph could be of almost any young woman your age," I said. "The pearl falls hide your freckles, brow ridge, most of the nose, and the cheekbones. The hair is swept back over your ears. I see no obvious identifying marks. And you're not smiling, so no one could tell if the teeth are crooked or straight. I would defy anyone to positively identify you from this photograph."

"Unless she has that tiara in her possession when her luggage goes through customs." Phoebe Hartfield was looking at the last wedge of cucumber sandwich on her plate. "I think it would be wise for me to leave you to your discussion. As your lawyer, Miss Rees, I do not wish to know if any shenanigans are afoot." She drew on her gloves, picked up her drawstring bag, and stood. "Thank you for tea, Miss Rees." She offered her hand, and Lin and I pressed it in turn. "I'll have a word with the guard to stay close. We're still eight days from port, and your villain is most creative."

When Hartfield was gone, Ah Jim collected the tea tray. I asked him to let my guardians know that I would not dine with them, but would like to take a turn around the deck in the morning. Then Lin and I tossed departure scenarios back and forth. Eventually we settled on a simple plan.

"You're welcome to bring your sewing here," I said. "Or to sit and talk, if you need company."

She declined, and I felt relief wash over me. I needed to mull over my lawyer's revelations—and her parting shot.

Yes, our villains had proved to be most creative.

Chapter 28

WE WERE MORE THAN a week out from port. I still faced unknown, but resourceful, adversaries. Yet I had more allies than when we'd set sail from Yokohama. I smiled to myself, finding the mathematics encouraging.

This evening and the next days stretched ahead of me like a long mine tunnel. At two hours past midnight, we would cross the International Date Line and repeat Thursday. As long as I didn't lose ground—or lose focus—I thought I stood a decent chance of reaching my fifteenth birthday alive and whole.

My studies would take up much of my time. Apart from those, I required exercise to maintain both sanity and health. Yet Society frowned on play during the mourning period. Ergo, croquet, shuffleboard, and badminton were *interdit*. Forbidden. I needed to find a physical activity that could be undertaken in private, as I'd already made a spectacle of myself (and put myself in danger) while shooting against Gideon Lamb. Not to mention putting a bullet into Mr. Small early this morning.

I considered the remaining alternatives. I could and would work off some of the excess energy by circling the promenade deck with Phineas while most of the passengers were asleep. As for other options, Toru and I had begun self-defense lessons last spring. Perhaps we could continue—if he was willing, and if we could find a private practice room, *and* if Lin agreed to join me.

A larder full of ifs.

But, *"Qui onques rien, n'enprist riens n'achieva."* He who ventures nothing, achieves nothing.

I sent Lin a note. A few minutes later I received a square of white paper with stick figures that appeared to be wrestling. They had long hair. Another, taller figure, stood off to the side, arms crossed, observing. I took her reply as assent.

My second note went to Phineas. He replied that Dr. Doyle had no objections, from which I gathered that Doyle was with Phineas enjoying port and a board game. Phineas also said that it was up to Toru, who could be found in the library.

I knocked on the adjoining cabin wall. Lin responded and we set off, guard in tow.

We did find Toru in the library, writing a journal entry in Japanese. The elegant black strokes, delicate yet firm, spilled down the page. He wiped his quill pen, stood, and smiled as he greeted us.

I reassured him that Lin and I were recovering well, and said, "With the captain's permission, and yours, I'd like to resume our *jūdō* lessons. With Lin, of course." I spoke softly, so that our guard and the library steward couldn't hear us. "After what happened this morning, it seems a wise plan."

Toru looked at Lin. "For many reasons," she said.

He waited for more information. A good sign. I added, "And I thought we could invite Mr. McGinn to join us. A one-armed man might benefit from your tutelage."

Toru studied a mediocre watercolor hanging above the desk, a passenger ship under sail. "I would enjoy the exercise. My muscles are starting to atrophy."

I grinned. "Uncle P told me that you practice daily in your cabin, though without a partner. He regrets that he's not up to joining you."

"You have considered where we would train?"

"I thought, perhaps, the captain's dining alcove? In the wee hours before sunrise and our morning promenade."

"That could work." He still hesitated.

"It won't take a minute to move the furniture. And I will promise Captain Stowall that we'll leave everything as we found it. Please, Uncle T?"

He gave a little bow of assent. "I will plead your case

to the captain. If he agrees, I will speak with Mr. McGinn."

Lin and I retreated to our cabins where Robie again guarded our doors, claiming to be feeling "in fine fettle." I inquired about the state of the investigation into Small's death. Robie said Mrs. Small claimed she was resting in her cabin at that time, but her maid couldn't confirm it, as she'd been bathing in her own cabin. Mr. Lamb and Colonel Grayson gave each other alibis. They were playing poker in Grayson's cabin, located immediately above Sick Bay.

Seaman Cotton, Robie informed me, had been reprimanded for leaving his post and going to the steward's station. But Cotton continued to insist that our cabin doors had been within his sight the entire time he was on watch. In fact, from his vantage point, he claimed he could see the entire passageway, including my guardians' doors. None of us had left our cabins. No one had witnessed anything or anyone out of the ordinary in the vicinity of the murder.

Captain Stowall, I gathered, would be glad when this benighted voyage ended. As things stood, he would arrive in port minus two passengers and one stowaway, and with one unsolved murder.

In the quiet of my cabin, I took out my sketchbook and pencil, intending to illustrate a cowrie shell I'd found tucked in my mother's sewing kit. But when I opened the tablet, I found the copy of Hundun's letter to me, followed by the notes he'd made in the hours before his death. I'd asked him to tell me what Wei Xi had shared about our father's long ago work in Shanghai. But other than reiterating the story Lin had related about their mother—albeit from the Wei family's standpoint—Hundun offered only one new detail: His mother had been tasked with killing Glen Rees.

Whether my father had sensed the danger or not, his decision to leave the same day he received Sabine de Keridec's letter proved fortuitous, at least for Glen Rees. But Hundun's mother had been punished severely for leaving the assassination too late.

I turned to a fresh page in the sketchbook and picked up a pencil. My fingers remembered my father's visage and brought him to life. He'd left us suddenly, irrevocably. I'd not had a chance to say good-bye, to prepare for a future without him. And in the few short weeks since his death, I'd been consumed with putting his affairs in order, collecting his ashes, having a mourning wardrobe made, booking passage home, dealing with Annie's loss, and trying to understand who had killed her—and why. There'd been no time to mourn Glen Rees. Now feelings of loss and abandonment swamped me.

I tore the drawing from the sketchbook and tucked it in the edge of the dressing table mirror next to the one I'd done of Annie. I yanked open the cabin door, startling the guards, and almost ran down the passageway and out onto the deck.

The sun was still well above the western horizon, bathing the ocean in light, in heat. I leaned against the railing, gulping air. Tears blinded me and coursed down my cheeks. I didn't even try to brush them away.

I'd buried my mother and baby brother in San Francisco. Lost my father in Japan. Then Annie, her passing so *unexpected.* And her murderer, my half-brother, had followed her into the deep. Death and I were on more than speaking terms now. We'd developed an intimate relationship. Staring down at the brassy water sliding past, I felt clammy fingers caress my cheek. I had the sudden urge to join my loved ones.

"Come away from the railing, miss. Come away, now." Robie's voice. Robie's hand on my shoulder.

"It's not your time, Miss Rees." He turned me with his big hands, tucked my head against his chest, and let me rest there as I sobbed and struggled for control. "It's not your time by a long shot."

I heard people pass by. Robie shielded me with his big body. When the shudders had ceased, he guided me back to my cabin. I thanked him, and he flushed bright red and told me, "'Twere nothin', missy, nothin' at all." But I knew I'd remember his kindness for a long, long time.

I rested, a cool cloth over my eyes. An hour later, Toru sent a note asking if I were recovered. Word of my lapse had spread to my guardians and, no doubt, to the entire ship. The note said Captain Stowall had granted my request, and Michael had accepted our invitation—after being reassured that the activity could be tailored to his physical limitations. The first one-hour class would take place at four the next morning in the captain's dining alcove, to be followed by several circuits of the deck with Phineas.

I smiled. I now had a plan that would help carry me through till San Francisco, barring more attempts on my life.

Why would anyone plan and commit murder? What drove one person to deprive another of the essence we husbanded from our first breath?

I answered my own question. Revenge. Crimes of passion, born of anger over stolen property or the killing of a loved one. Greed, too. Crimes of lust for fortune or power, status or land—for profit, or to remove obstacles to obtaining something coveted. Young as I was, I'd seen greed operate on four different continents. But which motive was operating here?

I realized that Lin and I, potential victims, were characters in an unfolding story. If I wanted to understand why someone was trying to kill us, I needed to consider the events as a dramatic plot developing around us and enveloping us. This story, carefully orchestrated, had begun before Annie's murder. Wei Xi had pointed the weapon, Hundun, but had not prepared him for capricious variables: In this case, Annie wearing my hat and coat. He'd failed, and the plot became less structured and more opportunistic. Hundun, nearly trapped, lashed out at Robie and me, and then took his own life. Wei Xi was imprisoned below decks. If she had been the force behind the killings, that should have ended the story.

It hadn't. The Force, or someone serving as its agent, had launched a new offensive, as if determined to finish what it had started. Call it Act III, with my father's murder being Act I. Lin and I were attacked by proxy, by someone outside the original plan: Mr. Small. The attack was disorganized, so vastly different from Annie's murder. The overall Plan had disintegrated, but the motive, the impetus, remained. Only now, the cool logic of premeditation had devolved into frantic thrusts and attempts to obliterate any links to the planner. Hence, Mr. Small's murder.

The next step might be to silence Wei Xi, who could reveal all that she knew in exchange for a lighter sentence. Or the agent—or perhaps the Force itself—might now seek a way to finish the job.

If I could discern the motive, I could foretell the ending of the story. All I knew for sure was that neither Lin nor I would be safe until we reached shore. And perhaps, not even then.

Chapter 29

DURING THE NEXT FEW days, while Lin made alterations to Annie's clothes, I escaped back into the solid reliability and security of my studies. As time passed and nothing untoward happened, I felt the tension mount. Sleep eluded me, and I welcomed Toru's pre-dawn instruction in "the art of defense."

We took the precaution of wrapping my wounded arm with additional buffers of cloth. I wouldn't want to damage Dr. Doyle's careful stitches.

Michael McGinn, long in torso and short of leg, took to the training as a fledgling hawk to the air. He was quick on his feet and had wrestled as a youth, so he understood the importance of leverage and balance. He helped Toru redesign moves that minimized his limitations, and their early morning bouts became ever more demanding.

In three lessons, Lin mastered the moves I'd learned in the spring. She was smaller, more graceful and coordinated than I. She focused intensely on Toru's demonstrations. When Michael tired, Toru taught Lin more complicated holds and throws while I watched. Michael held the door to prevent interruptions from the staff or our guard. If the crew discovered Toru was physically interacting with either Lin or me, no matter how innocently, Stowall would put an end to our sessions. So, we were careful.

After our lessons, as light began to spread across the sea, we took quick turns about the deck with Phineas. I circled the promenade again with Toru and Lin before retiring. Our guards remained alert to anything untoward in the darkness. Once, I thought someone followed us, but the shape slipped away down a ladder.

Dr. Doyle checked on me each afternoon, often staying to quiz me on biology: Linnaean taxonomy;

Mendel's laws; the Wallace Line; Darwin's natural selection; human anatomy; et cetera. Toru borrowed my copy of Henry Roscoe's *Lessons in Elementary Chemistry* and asked me to design procedures to solve chemistry problems. Phineas set me oral exam questions about world civilizations, conversed with me in French and Spanish, and checked my translation of Virgil's *The Aeneid*. Chaplain Colins discussed comparative literature and philosophy, both religious and secular. To rest my brain, I set myself pages of mathematical problems and proofs. And I finished drafting my father's last map.

Sometime in the third night, Wei Xi escaped from her confinement.

* * *

It was the hour of the bread-baking in the kitchen next door, and Lin, Toru, Michael, and I were practicing our holds and throws in the dining alcove, when we heard running feet and the voice of the night guard, Cotton, outside the door. Phineas had felt well enough to join us. He was sitting with his back to the door, fresh white neckerchief pulled up across his lower face, watching our progress.

Lin and I moved into the shadows thrown by the shifted furniture. Phineas stepped out to the main dining salon, leaving the double doors slightly ajar so we could hear.

"They're searching the ship for the Chinese woman," Cotton volunteered before Phineas could ask. "Don't know how she escaped. But Mr. Arnold's on it. He'll figure it out."

I'd stopped thinking about Wei Xi, feeling safer with her under guard down below. My mind had been occupied by menaces still at large, those responsible for killing Mr. Small. For convenience, I called them Mr. Lamb and Colonel Grayson. But I had no proof they'd either arranged for or committed Small's murder.

"Wasn't she well-guarded?" Phineas said, voice muffled.

"Guess not," Cotton said. "And from what I heard, nobody searched her."

"So she could have had drugs, weapons, or tools on her person."

"Yessir. Nobody wanted to touch her."

"Do the searchers need to check the alcove?"

"I told them I already had," Cotton said. "I helped you move the tables and chairs out of the way, remember? A mouse couldn't hide there."

I handed Lin a damp towel, wiped my face and neck with a second, and tossed the remaining two to Toru and Michael. Drawing aside the curtain over the porthole, I caught the faint easing of darkness on the horizon. Our practice session was over.

We repositioned the furniture and gathered up our things. Michael helped Toru carry the rolled mats Uncle T and Lin had fashioned out of blankets and a couple of woven cotton rugs. They'd eased our falls and softened the noises of our workouts. Mr. Cotton led us back to our cabins and then escorted Michael out of First Class.

I washed and changed quickly. When I opened the door again, Cotton said, "Miss Hsu says she won't be joining you on your promenade. Having a bit of a lie-in, she says."

Halfway to Toru's and Uncle P's cabins I stopped, struck by a memory. Circles had underlain Lin's eyes this morning, as if she'd spent a sleepless night. And she hadn't looked surprised at the news of Wei Xi's escape. Had Lin perhaps slipped out to free her former companion? Or had my sister returned to her cabin to find her "aunt" in residence?

"Couldn't be," I muttered to myself. "That's the first place they'd search."

"Miss?" the guard prodded.

"It's nothing," I said and completed the short journey down the passageway.

My uncles and I held our conversation till we reached the after deck. There, Phineas shared what he'd learned about Wei Xi from Mr. Arnold while Toru and I were changing.

Wei Xi had shown no signs of fighting her confinement in the hold. She'd continued to hold her peace and refuse food, surviving on water and tea, supplemented with some dried fruit Lin had brought her. The crew assumed she suffered from seasickness and would eventually recover. They brought her food, morning and evening. Her guards, not wanting to waste good rations, took to retrieving the trays while the food was still warm. Last night, after eating, the seaman on duty had fallen asleep. Wei Xi managed to pick the lock and slip out. Her absence wasn't discovered until the changing of the guard.

We had circled the deck once while Phineas related the story. Around us the search went on. Feathered wisps of silvery cloud curled within a cerise sky. The sea swells slid by without whitecaps, portending another fine day.

"I'd like to visit the chapel," I said.

"To pray?" Phineas raised an eyebrow. Toru tugged at his ear and tried to hide a smile.

I stopped, hands on hips. "I do contemplate the metaphysical, gentlemen. On occasion."

They greeted this with open smiles, but Phineas said, "Then to chapel we shall hie," and led off at a brisk pace.

The chapel was dark but for the single, ever-burning candle in a swaying hurricane lamp on the altar. I told the guard we'd need a few minutes for solitary prayer. Phineas and Toru, hiding smiles, nodded and closed the double doors.

I took a taper from a box near the door. Touching the wick to the altar candle, I set the taper in a small, glass-sided lantern and led the way to the sacristy. There I found the footlocker exactly where I'd left it days earlier.

Handing the lantern to Phineas, I pulled a knife from my pocket and threw open the box. Hundun's few possessions were folded and tucked neatly in one corner. Other books and papers, also carefully stacked, belonged to Colins. Hundun would have removed them when he used the trunk, but he'd chosen to replace them before Annie's memorial service.

For no particular reason, I took out the bundle of clothes, tucked them under my arm, and scanned the rest of the room. Opened the water closet door. Empty. Opened the cupboard. No Wei Xi.

I borrowed a French Bible from the bookshelf and

used it to mask the bundle of clothes now pressed against my chest. I didn't know what I'd do with them. But Lin and I could decide together.

"*Quo vadis*?" Phineas was in rare form this morning.

"I go to my cabin, Uncle P. I don't know about you, but I could eat a full English breakfast."

Lin was standing just inside her open cabin door speaking with Seaman Cotton when we reached our passageway. Her hair, wet from the bath, still held the furrows of her comb.

"Breakfast?" I said, careful to keep my tone light. "Or have you eaten?"

"I was waiting for you. I will join you in a moment," she said, followed by the *snick* of her cabin door.

My uncles left me at my door. I ordered a substantial repast. Lin arrived at the same time as the tray. I hadn't heard footsteps in the echoing passageway. Thinking back, I realized I *never* heard her coming or going. She moved like a slight breeze riffling the air. Our father, too, moved noiselessly. As did Toru. It was not a trait I'd mastered. My feet invariably scuffed, or dislodged pebbles.

We ate eggs, toast, and jam in silence, then replenished the tea in our cups. I stood and retrieved the things I'd brought from the vestry.

"Did you have a nice walk?" she asked, sitting back.

I turned back to face her. "Too short." I tipped my arms down, revealing Hundun's bundle.

"What is *that*?"

"Hundun's things... well, except for the Bible. I checked the chapel in case Wei Xi was hiding there."

Lin stood, but stayed next to the table, lips pressed shut as if to prevent any words escaping.

"I find it curious that the steward's uniform Hundun wore when he attacked Robie and me is missing," I said. "He was dressed in other clothes when he went over the side."

A flush touched her cheeks. "You'll find the uniform in my cabin. Will you tell Mr. Arnold?"

I gave her credit for getting right to the point. "That depends on why and where you wore it."

She waited, as if trying to gauge how much I knew, how much I guessed. I could have told her all was guesswork.

She must have decided it didn't matter, for she gave a little shrug and said, "I wore the steward's uniform, waited until a cluster of people came down the passageway after the evening's entertainment, and slipped out of my room carrying a tray."

So that's how she'd been able to come and go unnoticed.

"The guards cannot distinguish a Eurasian girl from a cabin steward." She smiled. "None of the British crew can. Nor the passengers, especially when I plaited my hair into a queue and wore a cap covering my forehead. How did you know?"

"I noticed the regular waves in your hair during our workout this morning. And the circles under your eyes."

"Ah."

I weighed my next words carefully. A step in one direction, and my conscience would be clear. A step in the other, and I'd carry a burden forever—and perhaps pay dearly for my choice.

"They're still searching for Wei Xi." I put her king in check.

"They won't find her." She toppled her king.

I sank down on my bunk. The Bible and clothes slipped out of my hands and tumbled to the deck. There was a world of difference between suspecting and knowing someone's dead. Between knowledge and complicity. I had no idea what to do with my information. Nor could I ask my guardians without putting my sister in jeopardy.

Lin rescued the book and set it on the bunk beside me. Then, one by one, she picked up and examined Hundun's meager possessions. Black cotton, wide-legged trousers. A linen undershirt. A small mirror. The stub of a pencil in a folded scroll of rice paper, tied with a piece of thread. And two flat discs of metal, perhaps three inches in diameter, each in a half-circle case of leather that dangled by a cord.

She handed me one. I removed the circle from its

case. In the center, the metal had been cut to form an eternal knot. I took my sketchbook from my pocket. The disc appeared decorative, until I touched the edge, honed so finely that one pass over my sketchbook cleaved ten pages.

As Lin examined the second disc, I slid the sketchbook back into my pocket, along with the rice paper-wrapped pencil.

"I have seen similar weapons," Lin said. She showed how the carved center of the disc slipped perfectly over a cloth knot on the shoulder of her silk jacket. Tugging off the weapon, she prepared to fling it at the metal bulkhead.

"Don't." My order stayed her hand. "The edge will be dulled by contact with metal. And it might make enough noise that the guard will come to investigate."

"We cannot have that," she said.

"No." I replaced my disc in its leather semicircle. Held by the sleeve, the disc could slice someone's neck, arm, or upper leg deeply enough to kill. I suspected that was the purpose. Silent. Decorative. Deadly. The tools of a young man raised and trained from birth for only one thing. Poor Hundun. Poor Annie. Poor Father, who, all unknowing, had set this chess game in motion.

The center carvings differed, I noticed. The one Lin held appeared to be a Chinese ideogram. I asked, "What does it mean?"

"Longevity."

"As in, long life to the bearer but not to the opponent?"

She laughed. A musical sound, unexpectedly rich and deep.

"You should laugh more often."

She raised one eyebrow, from which I gathered that humor had been in short supply in her life, let alone during this voyage.

I wondered how to direct the conversation back to a dangerous subject. After rejecting several overtures, I began, "About Miss Wei..."

Lin pulled back the porthole curtain, checked for listeners outside, then let the curtain drop. "Wei Xi had been caged like a songbird and had not been allowed to bathe since she was arrested. She literally *ran* for the deck, although we were careful not to be seen by the crew."

"You led her to the after deck. Did you ask who hired her to kill my family?"

She nodded. "She said it was more than her life was worth to tell me. So I showed her where Hundun had jumped into the sea. She loved him, in her way, you know. In memory of him, I gave her a silk flower I had brought along. And then I gave her a choice: the gibbet, after a humiliating trial, or the sea. She chose the sea." She noted the look on my face. "You would have treated her differently?"

I shrugged. I didn't know.

"Believe me, had she hesitated for more than twenty heartbeats," Lin said, "I would have dispatched her as our brother did your Annie."

There it was. Lin had acted as judge and jury. She'd been willing to serve as executioner. And she'd appointed me a keeper of that knowledge.

"Aunt Xi made Hundun into what he was," she said. "She took my brother from me, and nearly took my sister."

"And?"

"Are those not reasons enough to remove her?"

I just looked at her, sensing there was something more.

She turned away. Speaking so softly I barely made out the words, she said, "Aunt Xi was most pleased with the way I aided her escape. She suggested that their syndicate might have other uses for me once I became wife to her brother. She said I might take Hundun's place. I speak several European tongues. I can go where other Chinese cannot."

I felt breakfast turn sour in my stomach. But at the same time, I felt a fierce elation that the woman was gone from the world.

Lin noted the look on my face. "And she killed our father. Made us orphans. For that alone I would have ended her life."

"He would thank you if he could. *I* thank you. But why drug the food the guard ate *last* night?"

"We decided on the timing when I undertook a rehearsal the night before."

"You risked discovery twice."

"Little risk. I told you. Europeans ignore Chinese staff carrying trays. The tray held some dried fruit."

"And some sleeping draughts." Irony colored my tone. "No doubt provided by Dr. Doyle when you claimed sleeplessness."

That laugh again. "He was most kind."

All this had gone on under my very nose. I handed her the disc I still held. I had recognized the endless knot as a Buddhist symbol of the eternal cycle of birth, death, and rebirth, and of the constant struggle to achieve wisdom and compassion. It seemed to symbolize Hundun's short life and pursuit of knowledge.

She held the disc against her cheek for a moment before returning it. "That one is yours. The knot can represent good fortune arising from current situations. Our brother would have wanted you to have it—for protection, yes, but also to remember him by."

The metal was warm and alive in my fingers. "I could not forget him, any more than I could forget you."

"Will you tell Captain Stowall or Mr. Arnold about Wei Xi?"

"If I say yes, will I join the others in the ocean deep?"

She considered this for a full ten seconds. I counted.

"I think not," she said at last. "Toru reads me too well. He would know. And there would be hell to pay, as I heard one of our guards say. So, sister, my life and my future are in your hands."

I pondered this for as long as she'd taken. "I suggest getting rid of the steward's uniform. It's the only evidence linking you to Wei Xi's escape."

She stood on tiptoe and kissed my cheek, then slipped out with her bundle of Hundun's clothes and his disc.

Longevity. The charm hadn't worked for Hundun. I hoped it would prove truer for Lin, the disc's new owner.

I rang for Ah Jim. When he'd collected the breakfast

tray, I locked the door and placed a chair under the handle. I was on a ship in the middle of the ocean with at least one murderer. I had only Lin's word that Wei Xi was gone. And Lin herself had attempted to kill Mr. Small, knowing I was watching. She had denied smothering him later, but Hundun's uniform would have made her invisible then, too. Something to remember.

I made sure the curtain was drawn over the porthole. Satisfied I was unobserved, I took from my pocket the thin paper scroll I'd found among Hundun's things. Untying the crimson thread securing paper around pencil stub, I smoothed the paper out on my dressing table and weighted down the edges.

I'd half-expected the paper to be bare, but Chinese writing ran down the right side, top to bottom. The English text on the left was in Hundun's handwriting, but I had no way of knowing if it was a translation or transliteration of the characters on the right. I did recognize that the lines were passages from the *Tao Tê Ching*, as I'd read Balfour's English translation during my time in Tokyo.

> There was Something formed
> from chaos, which came into being before
> Heaven and Earth. Silent and boundless
> it stands alone, and never changes...
> I know not its name; but its designation
> is the Way... Being great, it moves
> ever onward; and thus I say that it is remote.
> Being remote, I say that it returns...
> The Breath of the Deep is imperishable.

> Sister, you are embarking on a perilous journey.
> Wherever and whenever you encounter water along the way,
> think of me. I will be there.

The signature was a tiny whirlwind above an open box.

I didn't know whether the message was meant for

me or for Lin. Both of us were embarking on perilous journeys. Neither of us might survive for long. But I knew that whenever I touched water along the way, I would remember not only Hundun, but my father, whose ashes went with him.

And Annie, who died in my stead.

But not Wei Xi, the architect of all those deaths. She did not deserve to be remembered.

Chapter 30

EARLY ONE MORNING A few days later, following our *jūdō* lesson with Toru and Michael, Lin and I returned to our cabins via the library. After previous sessions we'd been careful to avoid areas where early risers might congregate. We didn't wish our unconventional mode of dress to arouse curiosity about our activities. But as it was still very early, we chanced it. I was hoping for a word with Mr. Arnold, but he wasn't there.

The library steward nodded hello, then returned to perusing an old newspaper. George Mayweather occupied the desk under the porthole, intent on writing what looked like a formal report. Noting our arrival, he slid another piece of heavy paper over the finished lines and continued writing.

Lin, exhausted from our lesson, sank into an armchair and closed her eyes. I returned *The Aeneid* to the shelf and moved close to the British agent. I said softly, "Any news that you can share, Mr. Mayweather?"

He completed a word, added a period, then capped the quill pen and placed it in its slot. Scooting back his chair, he turned to face me. The pale-blue eyes took in my Chinese tunic and trousers. Lin had created the exercise attire from the skirts of two of Annie's dresses. I liked it as much as my travel costume.

"They have found no sign of Miss Wei," he said, "if that's what you're asking."

"It is. Miss Hsu and I have been keeping to ourselves since the memorial, with a guard or two posted nearby." I gestured with my chin toward the sailor who had stopped outside the door. "Per your recommendation."

"I noticed." He tugged at his beard and grimaced. "I also noticed that as soon as the guard was stood down for a day, you and Miss Hsu were attacked. Shameful business. Shameful. He won't be missed."

I caught a note of something—satisfaction? dry humor?—underlying the words. A counterpoint, as if he knew more about Mr. Small's death than had reached me through Toru and Phineas.

I prodded, "Have you learned of any progress in finding Mr. Small's killer? Last I heard, everyone with a motive either had an alibi for siesta time or was given one by the guard in the passageway."

"I've not heard anything different." He pulled more strongly at his beard. At this rate, he'd have no facial hair left by the time we reached port.

"Are you traveling in First Class, Mr. Mayweather?"

"Now, there's a thigh-slapper for you, since my employer believes in pinching pennies till they disappear. As it happens, my cabin's almost next door to Sick Bay." His lips twitched. "I was in my cabin at the time of Mr. Small's demise. Didn't hear or see a thing, erm, unexpected."

"How about expected?"

"Nothing I could swear to in court, mind you." He lowered his voice to a whisper. "Just the scent of a man's pomade, a hint of apple blossoms, drifting by my cabin door."

Toru. The shock must have shown on my face.

"You didn't know? Well, don't fret. I never mentioned it to the captain. Truth to tell, your guardian was a step ahead of me." In a normal tone of voice he continued, "Far's I know, miss, the captain hasn't a notion *who* killed Small. Can't even be sure Miss Wei didn't do it. She was that protective of Miss Hsu. Seems Miss Wei could have escaped *before* Small was killed. It's a right cock-up, if you'll forgive the expression."

It was my turn to smile. "I've heard much more colorful turns of phrase in the mining camps, Mr. Mayweather."

"I daresay."

I lowered my voice again. "One more question, if you don't mind?"

"At your service, Miss Rees. Now, and whenever you

need me."

The offer was unexpected. Tears gathered at the corners of my eyes. "Thank you. I don't know what I've done to deserve that promise, but I accept, gratefully. At the moment, I can think of only one way you can assist me: When last we met, you gave me a note. Can you tell me anything else that will help me to navigate the situation when we land?"

He nodded, applying stress to his side-whiskers. "You mean about Little Bo Peep and a certain sheep?"

It was my turn to nod.

"Well, when I left San Francisco, your grannie was keeping company with one Hubert Lyster. Bertie's an actor, on hiatus—a common state for him whenever he finds, well, erm—" He shrugged.

"A rich woman to support him?"

"Precisely. But *our* sheep's running with the same flock as Lyster, if I read the situation right. That's why he garnered the invitation to one of Bo Peep's *soirées.*"

"One of several reasons, more likely. I think the black sheep is more ambitious than any mere actor."

"You may be right."

"Will you keep your ear open to the gossip about town?"

"Gossip's my stock in trade, Miss Rees. Can I reach you at home in San Francisco?"

"I wouldn't trust a letter. But I'd trust my housekeepers, Tom and Mary Daly, with my life. Mr. McGinn, too. I offered him lodging and employment, at least until he has his feet under him."

"I'll use McGinn, then. You'll tell him?"

"Of course. And if I should have to go underground for a while—"

"Might be a good idea, leastwise till your father's will gets probated."

"If I should *voluntarily* disappear, and you can't reach Michael, try Dr. Nakagawa. And you will always be able to get word to me through our family and company solicitor, Charles Sutherland."

"Good man. Honest as the day is long. And smart. Knows everybody. Keeps his ear to the ground."

"He's worked with us from day one. My parents trusted him. And I'll also keep in touch with Mrs. Hartfield. She's handling my emancipation case."

He laughed. "Then that will give me another reason to visit her in the city. I find I like your Phoebe Hartfield."

I surprised him by leaning over and kissing his cheek. When he blushed, I whispered, "That's for protecting Uncle Toru. And me."

"And Miss Hsu," he whispered back. "Mustn't forget her."

I drew back, startled. His wink confirmed that he'd discovered her secret. How, I couldn't fathom. But he knew. Perhaps not all of it, but enough to prevent Lin from entering the United States if he chose to reveal her actions. Or if I did.

Mayweather watched my face, reading the conflicting thoughts his revelations had triggered. If I kept silent about Toru's and Lin's acts, I became complicit. A moral dilemma. This must be well-trodden territory for spies, whatever country or cause they served.

I asked, "What would my parents have done if they'd been privy to secrets such as these?"

"As for your mother, now, I couldn't say. But your father?" Mayweather smiled and his focus turned inward, remembering, "Glen Rees would have said you were serving the cause of justice."

"But not the law."

He chuckled. "That's a dog of a different color."

"You fight for a greater good?"

"Not on your life, missy. We're just mechanics, men like your father and me. We find ways to oil the hinges and grease the gears so that the world keeps turning and internecine conflicts are kept to a minimum. Involving the law only gums up the works and wastes time none of us has. Nothing more to it than that."

"So, the decision, in the end, is mine."

"Ain't no one can make it for you."

I sighed. I hadn't bargained on having to make momentous decisions for years yet.

"Did your mother raise you religious?" he asked.

When I looked surprised he repeated the question.

"I was baptized Roman Catholic as a baby. But, as my parents were scientists, we discussed all the philosophies we encountered."

He scratched his graying-red eyebrows. "A rational approach, you might say."

"You might."

"It's just a thought, missy, but most people I've met across the world don't look below the surface of things. Not like you and your parents. So, if you were to, say, carry a little Bible or prayer book when you went through the customs line, the agent might take you for a religious person, a truthful person. He might not see the need to question you much. Or those with you."

I stared at him. *How did he know? Was I that transparent?*

"It's what your father would have suggested."

"Thank you, Mr. Mayweather. I'll keep that in mind."

Lin opened her eyes, stretched, and rose gracefully. I went back to the bookshelves and selected a travel-size *New Testament*. When I turned at the door to look back, Mayweather was at work again.

Were Lin and I in his report? Was Toru?

I wished, not for the first time, that my parents had lived to guide me through this treacherous landscape.

A short time later I was standing on the forward deck with Phineas and Toru, watching light infuse the dawn sky, when a sailor in the rigging sighted land. It would be the Farallon Islands to the southeast and Point Reyes to the northeast. From deck level I could see only a thick mix of fog and low clouds in the distance.

For days, now, I'd known we were getting close to the continent of my birth. Drift logs and kelp floated by in the water. A lone pelican, blown off course by some storm, landed on the bridge and hitched a ride for an entire day. He was home now, or as close as mattered. A few herring gulls found us next, drawn to the garbage tossed overboard by the kitchen crew. The gulls vied with the fish for the leavings.

The visiting birds lightened my spirits. Whatever lay next, I longed to get off this ship, longed to be free of my cabin and the restrictions forced on me by circumstance.

After a short promenade with Phineas and Toru, we stood at the rail watching light infuse the dawn. I tucked my hands through my guardians' arms. I gave Toru's arm a gentle squeeze, but kept my eyes on the water. "Mayweather knows about Small," I said. "And he suspects about Hsu Lin and Wei Xi." I felt his forearm tighten, but otherwise he didn't react. "He recommends you change your brand of pomade."

Phineas laughed behind his neckerchief. His shoulders shook. He started to cough, and bent over, gasping for air.

"You do pick your times, Keridec," Toru said. But he, too, was smiling. He patted my hand. "Phineas and I spoke last night. We know you have never meshed well with strangers, no matter where you lived. You would retire to a corner to observe and draw and try to blend in with the surroundings. But we have seen a change in you the past two weeks. You have matured by leaps and bounds, become less reticent, more confident, more..." Toru searched for the word.

"Capable?" Phineas croaked.

"Just so. You make our guardianship a pleasure."

My tears began as he finished. Toru handed me a pristine handkerchief. A minute passed. I tucked the soggy square into Toru's pocket, then found my own linen. When I could breathe again, I said, "That means more than I can say. Thank you both. But I anticipate your guardianship will be put to the test when we reach port."

"Undoubtedly," Toru said. "But we will find a way to deal with whatever comes."

"Speaking of which," I said, "I think we need to alter our approach once we disembark." I explained what I had in mind.

"In for a penny," Phineas croaked. Toru nodded.

As if by mutual consent, we turned to go below; I to get my stitches out and then to finish my preparations for the next act in the unscripted drama. I hoped they'd feel as proud of me tomorrow as they did today.

* * *

Dr. Doyle was pleased with how quickly and cleanly

my wound was healing. "You'll have a scar, Miss Rees," he said, snipping and pulling out the threads. "But a good yarn to go with it, that's for sure."

"And how is Mr. Robie?"

"Good as new, and with his own story to share. No doubt the adversary will grow with the telling. Latest version has him fighting off two knife-wielding giants."

I laughed, though a part of me felt like crying. Hundun, our lone attacker, wasn't alive to contradict Robie's tale.

"I'll never tell," I said. I pulled down my sleeve, replaced my glove, and climbed down from the table. "I appreciate your care throughout the voyage, Doctor. And please thank Mr. Kidd for me."

"Treating you has been our pleasure, Miss Rees. I only wish the voyage had been less, er, eventful."

"As do I, Dr. Doyle. But it's one I shall never forget."

Chapter 31

Thursday, August 13

THROUGH MY CABIN PORTHOLE, I smelled San Francisco well before I sighted her. Terrestrial and marine scents intermingled. Mudflats and brackish estuaries. Fish from the market on the wharf. Manure from cattle, horses, and mules. Kelp caught up on the rocky shore. Dank, salty fog. The sun, behind the mist, was a giant white pearl. I caught only glimpses of the summer-yellow eastern hills as the offshore wind struggled to push back the fogbank.

Once within the harbor itself, sailors reefed and stowed the sails. The big screw engine throttled back. A pilot boarded to navigate the last leg of the journey. Sounds emerged. Foghorns, of course, sonorous and doleful as a bassoon playing a dirge. Officers shouted to their crews on ships putting out to sea or jostling for position at the docks. Sea lions barked on rocks and piers. Horses whinnied, mules brayed, and whips cracked as the longshoremen unloaded cargo onto waiting drays. Bells clanged from the mule-drawn streetcars.

Vendors plied their trade along the wharves and within the dark alleys of densely packed businesses and warehouses crowding right down to the shore. A teeming mass of humanity, confusing and chaotic, but with an internal order, my father used to say, that was as predictable as the order aboard ship. One just had to learn the rhythms, the ebb and flow of any seaport, large or small, whose lifeblood was commerce.

The fog was slow to withdraw from the lower reaches of the city. But above, in the sunlight, the houses of the wealthy clung to the tops of hills. Well below those citadels, like skirts trailed through the mud, circled the teeming abodes of those who worked for others and without whom a city would founder.

Home. I had lived in many places with my parents, from dusty and muddy mining camps to large cities. But the town before me was my birthplace. The only home we'd ever owned stood amid a cluster of buildings on Rincon Hill, farther south. My mother's body was buried at the foot of a mountain to the west. Some of my father's ashes would soon join her.

I went up on deck, guards at each elbow, to greet the diffuse light of morning. No shadows touched the gray water, roughened to whitecaps. Wind whipped at my hat, though the ship traveled slowly. The dingy, gauze mist muffled the clanks and thuds of cargo being loaded onto barges and coastal ships. Pelicans, gulls, and cormorants circled entrails tossed overboard by a passing skiff, remnants of a morning's fishing.

The sun broke through, turning muddy streets to plaited rivers of light. Market Street. Van Ness Avenue. California. Workers sang as they loaded a coastal packet ship. A row of taxi carriages and wagons snaked its way down the wharf. Longshoremen lined up to unload the ship—mostly white men, but a few with darker skin, and a couple of husky, muscular Chinese who were all torso and short legs. Spanish, German, Irish, and Scottish accents sang "Oh My Darling Clementine," though the words were more innovative than any I'd heard before.

I felt the *Oceanic* begin its maneuver toward an empty berth. The engine fell nearly silent. And now other sounds assaulted my ears. Hundreds of passengers crowded the deck, jostling for position, standing on tiptoe, leaning over the rail, searching for loved ones or their first glimpse of San Francisco. Sun-browned faces of the third-class passengers. A few pale-skinned women from First Class in hats and bustles. And their men folk.

Children chased each other between parcels and parents. Older siblings attempted to corral them, with little success. I felt again the keen sense of loss. My only close blood relatives were two foreigners: my half-sister and my mother's mother. The latter was ensconced in my home, and I didn't anticipate a warm reception. Quite the opposite. Now, the game would begin in earnest. I dreaded what lay ahead.

A cheer went up. We had arrived. Favorable winds had brought us home in near-record time.

Drawing back into a protective shadow, I lowered the veil on my hat. Watchers below would be unable to determine my age or identity.

I hadn't given Phineas or Toru details of my plan once on shore. This act was mine, and I was a minor. If I ran into trouble, I'd accept whatever punishment the law meted out. If not, well, I'd feel supremely lucky.

A hint of blue touched the water before the mist closed in again. I hoped the fog would linger at least until we were through customs and into our conveyances. My job would be easier in the half-light.

I was beginning to think like a spy, like the man my father had once been. Like Hundun. I'd left the old Keridec Rees somewhere under the ocean with my father and my dear Anne Bonney.

Part V

San Francisco, California, Thursday-Friday,
August 13-14, 1885

"What forms of crime are these? Tell me, maiden."
— Virgil, The Aeneid VI (translated by James Lonsdale
and Samuel Lee, 1871)

Chapter 32

11:30 a.m.

THE CUSTOMS HOUSE WAS bedlam, or appeared to be. Luckily, not much had changed in the two years since I'd been abroad. I'd been depending on that.

Lines snaked forward flanked by porters pushing carts piled high with trunks, valises, hatboxes, and assorted crates and cases. First-Class passengers received preferential treatment. Family groups and couples were in one line, singletons in another. A logical arrangement that allowed businessmen to move quickly out the warehouse doors at the far end, and soon freed up customs agents to help with the groups.

Hsu Lin was at my side, my guardians behind me. Lin wore Annie's clothes. We'd helped each other into corsets and bustles, arranged each other's hair. Silk veils fell from the brim of our hats to screen our faces. Fans fluttered in the dense, humid air to distract curious eyes.

I didn't want anyone to notice or wonder about my companion, so we found positions well behind Colonel Grayson, Gideon Lamb, the Pomfrews, and Felicity Small. Like me, the widows Pomfrew and Small wore black. Mrs. Small's hand rested in the crook of Lamb's arm. I could see her husband's coffin being loaded onto a plain wagon outside. I wondered what plans the young widow had made. I wondered how Lamb planned to juggle visits to young Mrs. Small and not-so-young Constance de Keridec.

I breathed a sigh of relief when the last of the people we'd spent time with on board collected their bags after the customs search and exited through the gate. But the buffer group of passengers still had to deal with the customs agent. I observed him interact with the young woman preceding us. She was heavy with child, and leaning on her husband's arm. The agent snapped his fingers. A runner brought a chair. I smiled, and made a slight adjustment to my plan.

I'd adopted Mr. Mayweather's sage advice and carried my papers and Hsu Lin's in the travel-size *New Testament* I'd nicked from the library. She carried a matching one that the nuns had given her when she left the convent school. The black leather stood out against our lacey white gloves, as if to say, young women carrying the Good Book must be above falsehoods.

Phineas had choked off a laugh when he saw me draw the book from my *réticule*.

"Don't look so surprised," I said. "You're my godfather, after all, as well as my guardian. You're supposed to be guiding my feet along the straight and narrow path."

"In that, I'm afraid, I've failed you."

I put out a hand and patted his arm. "I forgive you, Uncle P."

"This should prove to be a most entertaining hour," Toru said, but his smile seemed tense.

I attempted a haughty look. Failed. My facial muscles were too stiff.

"Are you nervous?" Lin murmured.

"I'm no actress."

Phineas patted my hand. "All will be well, Keri. No matter what happens, all will be well in the end."

I straightened my shoulders. "I'll keep that in mind. And you two—follow my lead, and try not to look surprised." I searched the cavernous room behind them. "Wait. Where's Michael?"

"He's directing the porter," Phineas said. "They should be delivering the bags in a moment."

Beyond him, in the entrance, I saw the ghost of my father advancing before a heavily laden cart. I shook my head, but the image remained. Squinting, I recognized Michael's wiry form. "Why, Father's tweeds fit him perfectly!"

Toru nodded at Hsu Lin, who gave a slight bow. "Not perfectly—there was not enough time. But he will pass."

Anne Bonney's fiancé arrived, out of breath. Toru said, "Miss Rees, meet Mr. McGinn, our new valet."

"How do you do, Mr. McGinn." I shook his remaining hand. "I'm delighted to make your acquaintance."

Michael entered into the spirit of our theater of the absurd. "And I yours, Miss Rees." He nodded toward the customs table. "I think the agent is finished with the couple in front of you."

I turned and stepped to the customs desk, while Michael directed the porter to take Lin's and my luggage across to the receiving area. The agent was making a final note on some papers. When he looked up at last, I said, "Why, it's Mr. Heyne, isn't it?" I looked at the carefully penned nameplate off to the side. "I thought so."

I lifted my veil, set the *New Testament* on the desk, removed my papers, and slid them across the waxed wooden surface. Heyne's eyes followed my every move.

"I'm sure you don't remember me, sir. When my parents and I returned from South America, you were kind enough to find my mother a chair. She was with child, then, and we'd barely escaped a war zone. A terrible time. Terrible. I remember that you saw how thirsty we were and had someone bring us water." I smiled. "The kindness of strangers, and a wonderful welcome home."

He opened the papers, looked from my description to my face. "Of course I remember," he lied. To my recollection he hadn't been on duty that day. "But you've grown some since then, eh?"

"Four inches," I said. "I do hope I've finally stopped. I'm already taller than most of the young men my age."

"Nothin' wrong with that. They'll catch up. How's your ma and the little one?" He stamped my papers then looked at Hsu Lin. I took Lin's papers from the book still sitting on the desk, and I passed them to him.

"I'm afraid neither survived childbirth, Mr. Heyne. That's why my father and I needed to get away. We went overseas to explore some mining prospects. Unfortunately, a few weeks ago I lost him, too." I opened my left hand and showed him the small glass bottle with my father's ashes. "I'm going to put them in my mother's grave. Together again, at last." I dabbed at the corner of my eyes with the tip of my gloved finger. I wasn't acting. The tears were real. "But Father had the foresight and the time to select guardians for me before he died." I half turned so that Heyne could see Phineas and Toru behind me. "Mr. Quade and Dr. Nakagawa, my father's business partners. They returned with me on the ship. I don't know what I would have done without their help... and my companion's." I nodded at Hsu Lin. "She's been a great support during this time."

On cue, Lin lifted her veil enough that Heyne could see her face. The brim and veil threw shadows on her face, accounting for the apparently darker eye color. As for the rest, Lin was more lightly built, but we obscured that by wrapping her midsection with a length of cotton fabric. She wore shoes with heels to approximate Annie's height. I was hoping that my story of becoming orphaned would distract Heyne enough that he wouldn't focus too closely on her.

"Naturalized citizen, I see," he said to her. "Born in Ireland?"

"County Cork." Her brogue was a flawless imitation of Michael's. "You, good sir?"

"Galway," he said, stamping her papers. "But, like you, this is my country now." He passed the papers back to us. "Anything to declare?"

I shook my head. "Our travel was for business, not pleasure. And then, of course, I spent my last months nursing my father. So I have his mining files, ore samples, and books, as well as my own textbooks. And a few bits and bobs for my grandmother. Some silk fabric, a few costumes for her collection, that sort of thing."

"Sorry to hear about your folks, miss. But seems like you're in good hands. And at least your old granny's waiting for your return."

"Thank you, Mr. Heyne. You've been very kind."

I released the breath I'd been holding. Lin and I replaced our veils and turned to go.

"Wait," Heyne called. I turned. Lin continued on toward where our cases had been checked, closed, and restacked. Heyne was holding out my *New Testament*.

"You'll be needin' this in the days to come, Miss Rees."

"Yes, Mr. Heyne... yes, I will. Thank you." I took the book from his outstretched hand, gave him a huge smile, and followed Lin.

But we did not exit the building. That doorway was a portal, both physically and metaphorically. Out there in the dockyard mists, people would be waiting for Hsu Lin and Wei Xi to emerge. To get by the watchers, Lin must be part of a group of Americans and Europeans. Westerners. That explained our masquerade. Michael, poor mourning Michael, had volunteered to play the part of "Annie's" suitor, though it would hurt him like the devil to do so. But it was even odds as to whether Lin would be able to slip through the web.

So, we waited for my guardians and Michael to catch us up. And while we waited, our eyes searched the milling throng outside, looking for enemies.

The men sailed through customs. I suspected that Mr. Heyne didn't want to leave two women unescorted for any length of time. When we reunited, Toru and Michael went out to scout for trouble and requisition two drays. It would look odd if Toru went alone. But what would be more natural than for him to venture out with Michael to hire a carriage large enough for four people (and the traveling cases of three) and a wagon for Michael, his goods, and mine? Once they had our goods loaded, Michael would accompany my bags to the house with one note for my housekeeper, Mary, and her handyman/chauffeur husband, Tom, and another note for my grandmother.

It started to rain as Phineas, Lin, and I watched from the cover of the customs house. The crowd milled about, shouting at children and servants and workers, shouting to make themselves heard. The echoing noise set my nerves on edge. I felt a tug on my *réticule*.

I grabbed a thin wrist and held it. A pickpocket, a boy, but he carried a short knife to cut the strings of my bag.

"Watch yourself," I said to Lin and Phineas, as the boy twisted in my grasp.

Lin's hand pulled Hundun's lethal disc from her pocket and slashed another urchin's suspenders. Then, with a second sweep, she parted the rope holding up my thief's torn pants. I heard a startled *Oy!* from one, and *Whotcha!* from his partner, before they jerked away and scuttled out the door, holding up their breeches as they ran.

It had happened so quickly that Phineas caught only the end of the action.

"Urchins." I grinned. "Nicely done, Annie. And welcome, um, home." I was going to say *Welcome to America,* but stopped myself in time. It would have scotched the entire production.

She smiled back. A real smile, like sun breaking through the clouds after a storm. "It reminds me of that time in Shanghai," she said, still in Annie's brogue.

"You're a born actress, you know," I whispered. *Or liar.*

"You should see my Portia," she said, just as softly. "'The quality of mercy is not strained,' et cetera, et cetera."

Portia. A woman imprisoned by her family and the strictures of society, expected to marry a man chosen by lottery. Little wonder Portia's predicament resonated with Lin.

"I'm going to miss you," I said softly. "It will be hard for a girl alone."

She gave a little shrug that reminded me of my mother. "It has always been hard. But I have education, a craft, and a stake to get me started. I will find my way."

It was raining harder now, which should work in our favor.

"You have the letter of introduction to Mrs. Hartfield's friend?"

Lin patted her waist. "And Michael has the letter to your housekeeper. I checked."

Phoebe Hartfield and I had settled our accounts and said our good-byes the previous night. I'd paid for the work she had already done and furnished a deposit against future work. Then I'd asked her if she knew of a rooming house where a young woman without family could live safely in the city. I couldn't take Lin home. That would be the first place the Wei family would look for her.

Mrs. Hartfield did not ask for details. Lin and I didn't offer them. Better all round to keep my lawyer in the dark.

"I know a place," Phoebe Hartfield had said. "A boarding house on Taylor Street that at present has only a few guests, all women. At least that was the case when I set out for the Orient last fall."

"Russian Hill? But that's not far from Chinatown."

"Admittedly. But the rooms are too expensive for the young women who work as day help, or as seamstresses or milliners. I shouldn't think anyone would look for Miss Hsu there."

"She will accept me?" Lin asked. Meaning, accept a Eurasian.

"I saved her from a ne'er-do-well husband and rescued her livelihood from being taken away in the settlement. She'll take you free of charge, if I ask her."

"That won't be necessary," I said. "We don't want to raise eyebrows or draw attention to Lin. Shall I send funds with you to book the accommodations?"

Mrs. Hartfield hesitated. "It might be better for me to bill you. No, that's no good. We don't want anyone to make a connection between you two. Perhaps two weeks payment in advance?" She named a sum. "However, if Miss Hsu leaves before then, you'll have to forfeit the remainder."

"That's not a problem."

I went back to the purser and drew more funds from my account. He didn't even raise an eyebrow. When I returned I found that Mrs. Hartfield had provided a name and address, and had written a letter of introduction to the owner of the boarding house for "the young woman who bears this letter."

At the same meeting, I had paid Lin the sum I'd promised when she'd agreed to be my companion, along with additional monies to cover living and travel costs until she found a safe place to live and work—if such a place even existed in the rabidly anti-Chinese America to which I'd returned.

Thus, we had a plan. But in order to begin this next phase, we had to safely pass through that custom's house door and the loading dock beyond. The ruse might be just enough to confuse any conventional Chinese men waiting for a girl in traditional Chinese dress to come off the ship with Wei Xi. When the men inquired as to the whereabouts of their relative, they'd learn that Xi was still at large on the ship, having escaped from custody, and that there was no record that Hsu Lin had left the ship.

I felt the web of tension tying up my innards. We had to move quickly. The ship's manifest must match the list of passengers disembarking. We needed to be long gone by the time it was discovered that Anne Bonney, missing passenger, had gone through customs in the company of one Keridec Rees.

What was taking Toru and Michael so long?

At the portal, I saw Phineas turn. He beckoned.

Chapter 33

1:45 p.m.

TEN YEARS BEFORE I was born, St. Mary's Hospital had been erected on the southeast side of the city, between First and Second Streets, Bryant and Harrison. The Sisters of Mercy staffed it, ran a nursing school, and worked with women and girls from the community who needed help, including employment of the legal variety. Just one year before I was born, north of the hospital, the nuns had opened Our Lady of Mercy Academy. I'd spent a semester there around the time my mother died. I didn't think the good Sisters of Mercy remembered me fondly. With good reason.

Even as a young child, I'd loved to experiment with chemical reactions. During the last such experiment, while I was studying at Our Lady of Mercy, I attempted to create a new form of safety match to rival the Swedish near-monopoly. The trial hadn't gone exactly as planned. I set my hair on fire. I'd had the foresight to have a bucket of water standing by, so I dunked my head. But the smells of sulfur, red phosphate, paraffin, and burning hair permeated the halls. The nuns had sent the other girls home while they aired out the school. I was sent down.

The good news was that my hair grew back. And I'd already tested out of every class they offered. Except Domestic Science. I still couldn't make a perfect, flaky pie crust.

Under the hospital *porte cochère*, Toru and I helped Phineas alight from the carriage. I trusted that the nuns at the hospital would be different, or wouldn't remember me after more than two years. But just to be sure, I had Toru, Phineas, and Lin precede me into the foyer. There, Lin and I sat with Phineas by a window while Toru took care of checking him in.

Toru was told that yes, there were both a men's ward and a private room available in the area set aside for consumptive patients. The receptionist, a lay person, quoted Toru three prices: a lower price for the ward; a medium price for a private room if Phineas had his own attendant and supplied his own alcoholic beverages; and the highest price, fifteen dollars, for a private room with full service. As Toru's time would be spent running the business, Phineas requested the higher priced private room. Toru registered him under an assumed name.

I got the impression that there was a high vacancy rate in this wing. The cold, damp San Francisco weather wasn't conducive to healing from consumption.

Phineas had gotten stronger on the ship. We didn't want to lose the progress he'd made. We all knew that as soon as he had rested from the effort and stress of disembarking and dealing with customs, that he must find a more felicitous climate. One where the air was dry and clear and warmer. A desert place.

I kissed Uncle P's cheek, not knowing when I'd see him again. "Please get well. I need you. Toru needs you."

"I'm working on it, my dear. And don't worry. I'll be keeping my eye on you from afar."

The words were blurred by the handkerchief covering his mouth and nose. He looked exhausted.

"Get word to me if there's anything I can do for you," I said.

He kissed my forehead and went off with Toru. But Phineas was leaning on his walking stick more than I'd seen since we'd left Yokohama. The battles aboard ship to keep me alive and safe had taken it out of him.

Lin slipped her arm through mine, an unusually cordial gesture, and we turned to find Michael McGinn and Tom Daly waiting at the entrance to the hospital. Joining them, we discovered our bags stowed, dock transport paid and dismissed. Toru and I had decided it would be safer if only close friends knew where we would be dropping off Hsu Lin.

Tom greeted me with a huge grin. "What a surprise, your turning up without so much as a by your leave, young Keri. Mary's changing your linens and readying Young Tom's room for Mr. McGinn here." He looked me over. "You've changed, girl. I'd hardly have recognized you."

"I know. I've grown. And I'm dressing a part, Tom, trying to look older and more assured since..." I couldn't go on.

"Michael told me about your father and Annie. Rough news, that, for all of us." Tom hugged me, and I inhaled the remembered scents of pipe tobacco and good wool and Mary's cooking. "We left Mary crying in the soup."

I stepped back. "Cock-a-leekie soup?"

"You guessed it. Though your gram still won't touch it. Eats like a sparrow, she does. It'll be good to have you and your appetite home again."

"Have any of my grandmother's paramours taken up residence?"

His face assumed a neutral expression. "A Mr. Lyster. Hubert Lyster. An actor. But there's a Mr. Lamb that was coming around last spring."

Home would provide no refuge. I felt the rain seep into my spirit as Toru stepped through the hospital door.

"Tom, we've offered transport to one of our fellow passengers who had no one to meet her at the dock. I hope you don't mind." I motioned to Lin, who'd waited by the wall for Toru. He escorted her to the carriage.

"Never you fear, Miss Keri. Young Michael filled me in." Tom nodded at Lin and said, "Pleasure," before handing us up and closing the door. I said, "New mules?"

"One. Call him Blinkers. Had to put Henry down last winter. Still got Barney. And the horses, of course. The Countess wouldn't be caught dead behind a pair of mules."

As we started off, Toru turned to Lin. "It would be best to keep your face covered until you are in private. It is dangerous sharing this carriage. No one must connect you with Keri now that you are off the ship."

Lin gave a brisk nod.

From my *réticule* I drew an object wrapped in a clean white handkerchief and tied with a ribbon.

"The handkerchief belonged to our father," I said to

Lin. "The ribbon was Annie's. What's inside is something Father gave me on my last birthday. Two small things, actually, but they will hold memories for you. And I hope they will give you strength to deal with whatever lies ahead."

I started to lay it in her lap, but she stayed my hand. "I have nothing to give you."

"You agreed to be my companion after Annie died. You didn't have to help me out. Things might have been easier if you'd said no."

A grin flickered to life for a moment only. "But not so interesting."

She untied the ribbon. Inside were our father's signet ring and the necklace with the green jade dragon she'd tried to pinch the first day we'd met.

"If you ever need help from Uncle T or me, send one of those objects by messenger, either directly to us, or to Mrs. Hartfield. She'll know what to do."

Her eyes glistened behind the veil. "Thank you, Keri. Did you know that jade symbolizes strength?"

I nodded. It felt like a period at the end of a very long sentence.

The mules dragged the carriage up Russian Hill and stopped before a three-story house on Taylor Street. I groped for Lin's hand. "We'll say good-bye here."

She exhibited the first sign of hesitation I'd ever seen in her. These were foreign shores, and she was Eurasian. Although she would continue to use Annie's papers, at least for a time, the climate was dangerous. But no more dangerous than if she'd married into the Wei clan.

She leaned forward and kissed my cheek. "Thank you, sister," she said, and gave her hand to Toru to help her down.

Chapter 34

3:15 p.m.

A MAN WITH LONG, iron-gray hair, a hat that had seen many winters, and a thick, gray beard stood in the negligible protection of the small portico fronting the house on Taylor Street. He was carrying a bouquet of flowers. As Toru helped Lin from the carriage, the man rapped on the door. No one answered. I wondered if we were at the right address.

Tom carried Lin's cases up the steep staircase. Toru and Lin followed close behind. The man turned from the door. "Afternoon," he said, his voice carrying. "There appears to be no one at home, I'm afraid."

"We're expected," Toru said. "Perhaps the landlady is at the rear of the house." He tried the door. It was unlocked, so he stepped aside for Lin to enter and gestured to Tom to bring her bags in out of the rain.

"Would you like to come inside and wait with us?" Toru asked the gentleman, whose sun-browned skin suggested he spent most of his time out of doors.

"No time, I'm afraid." He looked at the bouquet as if unsure of why he held it. Even at a distance, I recognized daylilies, variously colored roses, and poppies. Flowers of remembrance. "Mrs. Jackson died here yesterday. The flowers—" He cleared his throat. "They're from my garden. I wanted to mark her passing in some way. She was a great woman, a powerful force for good. I shall miss her." The old man fished something from his vest pocket. I saw a flash of white. A card.

"We'll deliver them for you," Lin said.

"Thank you kindly." He handed the bouquet to her. Fishing a pencil stub from the same pocket, he scribbled on the card and tucked it among the blossoms. "The landlady cared for Mrs. Jackson at the end. Please tell her that Mr. Muir thanks her."

Lin nodded. The man tipped his hat and jogged down the steps, opening his arms as if to embrace the rain. *John Muir.* I'd grown up reading his articles and essays about the Sierra wilderness—or having them read to me by my parents. *And Mrs. Jackson?* I wondered if that could be Helen Hunt Jackson. If so, then Lin was staying in rarified lodgings. I hoped she wasn't afraid of ghosts.

Through the still-open door, I saw Toru bend toward Lin, perhaps offering final counsel. A minute later a bustling figure came down the stairs from the floor above. Lin handed her the flowers, then Phoebe Hartfield's letter. Toru pressed the landlady's hand, stepped back out the door, and closed it behind him.

I felt as if I were abandoning an old and dear friend. Yet two weeks ago I hadn't known Lin existed. In the coming days, we each would be more alone than we had ever been. I wondered if she was as apprehensive as I, or if she simply relished her newfound freedom.

When Toru was back in the carriage, I asked, "What did you say to Lin?"

"That there will be difficult times ahead when the tensions around her cease and she is alone with herself. I told her that the way her father survived his darkest days was to focus his attention on the world around him. And to find something that surprised him. Not something big, mind you, but a person's story, a child's laugh, a cherry blossom. The taste of a ripe apple. Even the smallest of surprises can lighten those dark times."

"You are a poet, Uncle T. Li Po or Bashō could not have put it better." I thought he colored slightly, but he was pleased. "I don't know you at all, do I?"

"You know the important things."

Which was true. I knew enough to trust him implicitly.

"And some things you probably should not," he added.

"We will not mention Mr. Small again," I said.

The boarding house was at Taylor Street and Broadway. We set off east on Broadway and crossed through the hubbub of Chinatown. I held my breath, fearful of being recognized. But no one gave us a second glance. And no one seemed to be following us.

We turned southeast on Columbus, heading for the financial district. Charles Sutherland, Esquire, and the company I now owned with Toru and Phineas, occupied the upper two floors of a building near Montgomery and Jackson. A fashionable and popular restaurant took up most of the lower floor of the building, which stretched from Montgomery to Hotaling, a throughway no bigger than an alley. On the east side of this alley were smaller buildings that housed our rock and mineral samples and a laboratory for assaying. But the heart of the business was on the second floor of the office building.

We approached the block from the north. The carriage slowed, then stopped. The cacophony of street sounds swelled as the cries, laughter, whistles, and shouts of venders and draftsmen mingled with cracking whips, braying mules, and the clanks and creaks of all manner of wagons, carts, and carriages. The noise reverberated off buildings, assaulting my ears. I covered them as Toru called, "What is it, Mr. Daly?"

I couldn't hear Tom's reply. I uncovered my ears and leaned toward the window for a better view. "What did he say?"

"Cart overturned," Toru replied. "Spilled cabbage all over the road." His face and voice were tense.

The office building loomed just ahead. A welcome party half-obscured the entrance to the restaurant.

I shrank back against the seat. "It's Gideon Lamb." My voice stumbled on the surname.

"And at least two men. Chinese. Well dressed. Perhaps your age, or a little older."

Toru had to lean in front of me to see. "One of them is Wei Xi's brother."

The Wei family would now know that Hundun was dead, that Wei Xi was missing, and that Hsu Lin had not gone through customs as a Chinese national. They would have learned from Lamb that Hsu Lin was my half-sister. They would be looking for her. If they found her, would Lamb and my grandmother pay them to kill a possible heir, or would my grandmother be content to see Hsu Lin's wings clipped by a marriage she didn't choose?

Toru sat back, straightened his vest, and pulled a derringer from an inner pocket. "Mr. Daly!" he called. "We have company."

Michael scrunched down until his head was closer to the opening between the driver's bench and the compartment. "Problem?"

My stomach was a hard knot. I pointed to where Lamb stood under a canvas awning. Michael, holding an umbrella over Tom, craned his neck to see. I thought I heard him curse.

Tom looked, said something I didn't catch, then turned his head so he could speak to Toru and me. "Worse luck," he said. "The Countess is sitting by the restaurant window. Looks like she's sipping tea."

"Grand-mère Constance is here to identify the carriage for Lamb and the Wei clan," I called up to him. "Has she seen you?"

"Dunna think so. Seems to be talking to Mr. Lyster."

Bertie Lyster. The unknown piece in this chess game. Was he just background, to be replaced by Gideon Lamb, or was he the architect of the plan?

"Is there a way around the obstruction?" Toru asked.

"I've an idea." Michael scooted towards Tom, saying something that was buried by the hubbub and clamor. In the distance, St. Mary's bell struck the hour. Four o'clock. Tom nodded. Michael tilted the umbrella a bit more, and under its cover Tom switched hats with him. Then, tightening his grip on the reins, he whistled to the team and turned them to the right.

Curses flew from the farmer as our mules drove through the leafy litter. Children, emboldened by our action, darted out to snatch dirty vegetables, daring moving wheels and hooves. Tom yelled at them but pressed on.

I handed Toru my leather coin purse. He tossed it to the vendor to offset his losses. "Mr. McGinn," I called, "please ask Mr. Daly to continue on for a block or so. Then turn left, and double back. We'll use the tradesman's entrance."

"Gotcher, Miss Keri."

"My trunks can go on to the house," I added. "I only need my valise. Can you get it?"

"It's on top. I'll pull it off when we stop."

I thanked him and sat back to peer out the window. Lamb was leaning against the wall, studying our carriage. He must have seen my movement, even through the rain. He straightened and moved closer to the restaurant window. My grandmother's perfect profile, framed by a violet hat, turned slowly. Her glance sharpened as her gaze went from the mules to the carriage to the driver to the door. To me. She froze, fork halfway to her lips. I saw the fork fall, and then she was out of her chair, hands framing a heart-shaped face that was pressed to the glass. Our eyes met. I couldn't speak, couldn't breathe, couldn't shrink back from that pale visage contorted with venom. This woman wanted me dead.

I must have whimpered. Toru took my hands in both of his and shouted to Tom, who snapped the whip and drove the mules into a lumbering gallop. Up three blocks. Sharp left, which threw me into Toru. Sharp left again. Doubling back. Never slackening pace until Tom dragged the mules to a halt outside the barber shop at the rear of our building.

The tradesman's entrance was to the right of the shop. Most people didn't know the narrow, steep, evil-smelling, claustrophobic stairwell existed. It was devoid of light and not wide enough for two people to walk abreast. Lamb wouldn't expect me to use it. The Weis, however, might consider it.

Tom set the brake and got down to open the door. He didn't seem to have aged in the two years I'd been away.

I found my voice. "Tom," I said, abandoning formality, speaking rapidly, "I must hide out for a while. Tell the Countess that you let Uncle T off at his club and brought me home. Say I went out for a walk after tea. She won't be home for an hour or so, so you have time."

"You scared, Miss Keri?"

"As I've ever been, Tom. That man on the street, Gideon Lamb, threatened to kill me. Judging by what I just saw, he's working with the Chinese family that was hired to kill my father and me. They succeeded with Father. Annie's killer told me so. And he gave me an address in Chinatown where the hires are made. I'll give that to Mr. Sutherland."

"You think the Countess knows?"

"Her face said it all. It's no coincidence that she and Mr. Lyster are here. I fear I won't last a night if I go home. Until I'm free of Grand-mère, I have to let my lawyers fight this battle."

"You have friends—me and Mary, young Tom, your guardians..."

"I know, Tom. But you can't protect me twenty-four hours a day. You *can*, however, be my eyes and ears at the house."

"It'd be a pleasure, Miss Keri." He took my hand and helped me out.

"I was hoping to be home for my birthday." I managed a wry smile. "Tell Mary I'm sorry." I turned to Michael, who was holding my valise and watching the street. No sign of pursuit. Yet. I said, "Mr. McGinn, Dr. Nakagawa and Tom Daly will put together the list of people I trust. You've met all but Mr. Sutherland, my lawyer upstairs. Mr. Mayweather said he'd contact you if he learns anything. If you'll serve as go-between, I'll instruct Mr. Sutherland to pay you a fair salary."

"You can count on me, Miss Keri. They killed my Annie."

"Wait. Don't let my grandmother know you were engaged to Annie. It's too dangerous. And try to stay out of Mr. Lamb's way. He saw you at the memorial service." I knew we were short of time, but there was so much to say. "Tom?"

"Yes, miss?"

"Could Mr. McGinn stay with Young Tom for a while, instead of at the house? Work with him? I'll be paying Mr. McGinn's salary, and I'll add in enough to cover his bed and board."

He nodded. "Good idea. They've enough room, at least till the little one arrives. After that, we'll figure something out. In the meantime, Tommy could use the help."

"Then please make sure Uncle Toru has Young Tom's address."

Tom grunted assent. His eyes were damp. "We'll look after Mr. Michael, never you fear. And Mary will send soup and whatnot to the hospital for Mr. Phineas."

"If you do, make sure no one knows. Or follows. Uncle P needs to stay hidden while he makes plans to recuperate elsewhere."

I looked at the men surrounding me. I loved them all. "Don't let anything happen to you. It would kill me."

Tom patted my shoulder. "Don't worry about us. We've been taking care of ourselves since long before you were born."

"Mr. Sutherland's office will continue to handle all the family finances, and Dr. Nakagawa and Mr. Quade will take care of the business while I'm away. They're my legal guardians, and in almost as much danger as I am, I suspect. But at least we now know for sure who's after us. And why. Even if they can't be prosecuted for any of it."

"They'll pay, one way or t'other," Michael said. "Never you fear, Miss Keri."

I kissed Tom's cheek and hugged him. Michael handed me the valise. I kissed his cheek, too. "That's from Annie."

He grinned. "Naw, Miss Keri. Annie kissed much better than that."

"We need to go," Toru said, shutting the carriage door. That *snick* had a finality to it that I'd remember for a long time. Tom and Michael nodded and climbed back to their bench. Michael waggled the umbrella as the carriage set off at a sharp pace.

Toru took my valise, saying, "Let me go first." I followed him into the maw of the stairwell. He lifted a small lantern with a candle from a ledge near the door, lit it with a Swedish safety match from the adjacent box, and handed the lamp to me. "I need to keep one hand free," he whispered, showing me a knife sheath at his waist.

I tell of arms, and of a man. Virgil again. But immediately I rephrased it. *I sing of arms, and of a woman.*

"One moment." I handed the lantern back and took

Hundun's disc from my bag. I wrapped the thong about my right wrist and fitted the leather-sleeved edge of the disc against my palm.

Toru nodded, and I took the lantern in my left hand, holding it high.

The law office was on the third floor, our company offices on the second. The walls muted the sounds of the traffic outside and the restaurant kitchen. I smelled pork frying. And cabbage. And plums, I thought. And the sweet scent of lemon cake baking. I realized I was starving. I hadn't eaten since before dawn. Maybe we could have food sent up to Mr. Sutherland's office.

Toru's long legs had carried him well ahead of me. He was one step from the first landing, a counterclockwise turn, when I smelled the rankness of unwashed human, overlain by vegetables fried in oil.

I jiggled the lantern to get Toru's attention. Shadows broke and reformed on the walls and high ceiling. Toru stopped, turned, and that's when a solid shadow leapt on him, arm raised, stabbing downward. I heard a muffled thud as the knife pierced my valise and stuck.

Toru tossed the bag behind him. I sidestepped. More flickering light as I almost dropped the lantern.

I'd expected Toru to draw his own knife. Instead, he grappled with the man's clothes, seeking purchase in the tunic. I watched the nearby shadows, hoping there was only one assailant, not two or three.

Toru grunted, "Move."

I flattened myself against the right wall and set down the lantern. A man sailed past me, landing on his shoulder with a soft thud, then sliding down three stairs. He rolled. Started to rise. I was closer, so I grabbed his queue, yanked it sideways to expose the neck, and stomped with my foot. The man lay still.

Toru slipped past me.

"Dead?" I barely breathed the word.

Toru shook his head. Tried to catch his breath, to prepare for another assault.

"We can't leave him here," I said. "He'll report to the others."

Toru picked up the unconscious form and slung it

over his shoulder. I lifted the lantern to reveal a young man of perhaps twenty years, his face pockmarked from some fever. Forehead shaved. He'd lost his cap somewhere. I found it on the stair.

Toru went past me. Bent to take the valise he'd dropped. I stopped him. "One arm free," I whispered.

I hung the disc around my neck, picked up the cloth bag, removed the knife that had been plunged into its side, and slipped it into my waistband. I followed my guardian quickly, but carefully, up another half flight. The door to the mining office faced us. We would not go up another flight and arrive with an unconscious man, thereby jeopardizing my lawyer.

Toru gave a coded rap on the heavy wood. Waited two seconds. Repeated. They each had their codes. I had mine. But now was not the time to use it. Why tell anyone I was there?

Rhoderic Perry opened the door. "Toru?" he said. "And is that," he paused, squinted, "Miss Keri?"

"Shhh." I touched finger to lips. "We need to be inside, Rep. Quickly."

He jumped back and opened the door wider. Looked at Toru's burden, then over my shoulder, as if we should be more.

"Where's your da? Is Glen still in Japan?"

"He's dead."

I saw disbelief on Rep's face as he locked the door behind us. They'd been close.

"I'm sorry," I said. "I forgot that no one here knows. He was murdered last month."

"Murdered." Rep shook off his daze. Stared at the man Toru dropped on the wide pine planks of the floor. "I assume he's involved somehow."

"He was waiting for us," Toru said. "There are more out front, by the door."

"The broom closet will do for now," I said.

"For now?" Rep said. "What if his friends send reinforcements?"

"We'll deal with that when it happens."

Rep shook his head, then shrugged. "I'll take the shoulders, Toru. You take the feet."

I preceded them to the closet, a stout wooden room of generous dimensions used for storing field gear, recently collected ore samples, and weapons. Only two brooms. We removed everything from the floor but the boxes of rocks stacked against one wall. I checked the man's pockets. Found a second knife in a cloth sheath sewn into his jacket, made to lie flat against his upper back. Another was strapped to his right calf. The man meant business.

Toru stood up. "Can you do a likeness?"

"Yes," Rep and I said together.

I smiled, drew my sketchbook from my pocket, and offered it to him. "I'll help Uncle T truss him up."

A look I couldn't read touched Rep's eyes and then was gone. He said, "You're different."

I didn't know how to react. Settled for, "Growing up faster than I'd like, despite people intent on stopping me growing up at all."

It was his turn to search for words. He pulled the pencil lodged behind his ear. "Later, I'd like to hear the tale. Where's Phineas, by the way?" His eyes widened. "They didn't get him, too?"

"Consumption. He's hidden away at St. Mary's, though that's a bit too close to my grandmother for comfort."

"The *Countess* is involved?"

"She's downstairs as we speak, having tea with her latest conquest. And positioned where she could identify our carriage. She spotted us. That's why we used the back stairs."

"If this man's friends are coming, we need to move quickly," Rep said, and settled to capturing the prisoner's likeness.

I didn't know why Toru wanted the drawing, unless it was for evidence or leverage later. But I trusted his instincts.

I found rope carefully coiled and hanging from pegs in the closet wall. Chose the finest cord, not the heavy climbing ropes that were so expensive to replace. I pulled our attacker's knife from my waistband and held it up. The blade was beautiful, the haft inlaid with enamel in geometric designs of red and black and ivory.

"I'm keeping this knife," I said to Toru, cutting off enough line to hogtie our guest. "You and Rep can dicker over the other two." We gagged the prisoner for good measure, and stood up. "You'll call the police?"

"Once we finish at Sutherland's." Toru straightened his clothes and ran a hand over his hair.

"What will you tell the coppers?" Rep asked.

"Keri will tell them that this man attacked her on the stairwell."

"I won't say which stairwell, of course. And then I'll show them the rent in my valise."

Toru smiled. "And I will say that I was escorting you and came to your rescue."

"Which is true enough." I looked at our trussed bird. "He won't suffocate, will he?"

Toru shrugged one shoulder.

"I'd rather not have to dispose of a body," I said.

Rep cleared his throat loudly. He didn't look concerned, just perplexed. This was a side of Toru—and of me—he hadn't encountered before. But all he said was, "Surely he won't be in there long enough to suffocate?"

"I hope not," Toru said.

We locked the closet door, put the weapons and gear in Uncle P's office, and locked that door, too.

"Now what?" Rep handed my sketchbook to Toru. The likeness was accurate. I'd recognize him if we met again. But the prospect made me shiver.

"Next we meet with Mr. Sutherland," I said. "Having him come here would save us from showing ourselves in the hallway or dealing with whatever else lurks in the back stairwell."

"I'll deliver the invitation, but Emmons and King are upstairs," Rep said, meaning geologists Samuel Franklin Emmons and Clarence King. "They'll want to hear the news, too."

"They're welcome, of course," I said. "Please tell them it's important. No—vital. Life or death. Show them this knife." I offered Rep the blade, enameled handle first.

If Rep wondered at my issuing directions and generally appearing to be on an even footing with Toru, his only response was to take a revolver from a drawer in one of the specimen cabinets and tuck it into his belt. He carried the knife in his hand. "You remember my signal?" Toru and I both nodded. I followed Rep to the main door. He opened it a crack and checked the hall. I stood on tiptoe and peered over his shoulder. The wide staircase came straight up from the main door guarded by Gideon Lamb and the Wei henchmen. Three doors opened off this first landing and hall. They led into our company offices. The landing was empty, but noise rose like the buzzing of locusts from the restaurant below. The sound would cover his footsteps. But it might also cover the footsteps of others.

The disc around my neck slipped free and slapped against Rep's shoulder. He turned his head, caught the leather thong, and examined the disc. "Lethal."

I heard the humor in his voice, saw it on his face. I sank back on my heels and gently but firmly removed the disc from his hand. "You don't know the first thing about what I've been through the last two weeks, Rhoderic Perry. The last five *months*." My tone was soft, but the words were bullets that found their target.

His face sobered. "Sorry. You're right. I don't." He shook his head and slipped out, knife in hand.

I locked the door behind him, then walked through the U-shaped office to check that the other two doors were locked. We had always kept them that way to prevent thieves from entering one place while causing a distraction at another door. It had happened. Once. Once was enough.

Toru was standing beside one of the long, rain-streaked windows, peering down at the street. He went from window to window, always staying to the side. He returned to the drafting table in the middle of the main room. Looked at the geologic map in progress, at the ore samples weighing down the corners. Maps, cross-sections, mine drawings, and columnar sections of rock decorated all the walls, and even some windows. Rocks and mineral samples dotted tables and desks. But Toru's focus remained on the threat that might come from the street below.

I went into my father's office. Each partner had one. Father's was the largest. Now it was mine. But I would give everything I owned to see him here, sitting in the chair.

I left the office. "I'm going to get rid of this corset and bustle," I said to Toru.

"Can you manage alone?"

"Needs must."

I went to the large water closet on the other side of our office complex. The bustle was no problem. The corset defeated me. The laces had knotted. I used the knife to slit them. It was wonderful to be able to take a deep breath.

I tossed the bustle and corset in the refuse container. Fetched three more chairs to supplement those in my father's office. And then I sat in his chair. The leather seat curved to fit him, not me. The room was stuffy, unused, but I didn't dare open a window.

Below, in the street, I could hear rain thudding on canvas awning, washing the world clean. Inside, I sat with the ghosts of past conversations, of laughter, of stories. God, how I missed him.

And how I loved this place. Even more than I loved my home, I realized. No one had died here—at least not yet. But my home would forever be tainted by the deaths of my mother and my stillborn brother. And of Annie, whose demise, I suspected, was wholly or in part orchestrated by my grandmother, and whose winter clothes and baubles were still in her room.

My home was now the lair of the Minotaur. I could not venture into that labyrinth and hope to survive. No, this office was my real home now.

A single knock on the rear door. Pause. Four soft knocks. Pause. A single knock. Rep had been smart enough to avoid the back staircase on his way up. But four armed men would be enough to deal with anyone hiding there. And perhaps they'd relished the challenge.

Toru opened the door, knife in hand. I stood behind him holding the revolver I'd taken from my valise. Only when Toru saw the faces and counted heads did he return the knife to its sheath. He gave a short, sharp bow to Sutherland and Emmons as they passed him, wordless.

Rep brought up the rear. He must have told them about my father. Their eyes were full of pain and shock. Each one patted my shoulder as he passed. It was almost my undoing.

"Mr. King?" My voice choked on the K sound.

"He'd already left," Rep said.

"A meeting with financiers, followed by dinner," Emmons said. "Better Clare than I."

Dinner. Food. "Is there any food around? Biscuits? Cheese? Field rations? Toru and I haven't eaten all day. And coffee or tea?"

"I'll find something." Rep headed off toward Phineas' office. He always kept a supply of tea and crackers.

I started to remove the chair I'd brought for King, then stopped. Phineas, though not present, was a partner in this enterprise. Rep returned with a lacquered tray holding a large teapot, five cups, an unopened package of water biscuits, and two apples cut into slices. The men allowed me to take half an apple and a handful of biscuits before digging in themselves. Rep chose the least-chipped cup for my ration of tea, and set it in front of me. We ate in silence, appreciating food. I knew there had been times in the geologists' field excursions when fresh fruit, indeed *any* food, had been scarce. They never took it for granted. Sutherland knew them well enough to accommodate their need to eat first, talk second, although he'd have preferred the opposite order of things, I suspected.

As I sat in my father's chair, facing the four men and the empty chair across his desk, I had the oddest feeling that my entire life had been leading up to this moment, in this room, with these people. I wasn't a theological determinist, despite my Welsh father's Presbyterian roots. But I sensed this group—Sutherland, Emmons, Nakagawa, Perry, and the absent Quade—represented the major influences on my future, however long that turned out to be. And I was content to travel on with this not-so-merry band.

I sat back, replete. "Thank you for your patience, gentlemen. Toru and I need to report on what's happened the last few months."

I looked at Toru. He gestured for me to tell the story. I reviewed my father's accident on Mount Fuji, which wasn't an accident at all. His sudden death in hospital, right when we thought he'd be released to finish his healing at the Nakagawa estate. The listeners didn't interrupt, but I saw the glances they exchanged, the nods, heard the grunts of anger. I'd written letters from Japan, dictated by my father, to handle business and personal affairs. They'd all expected my father to come home.

I moved on to the shipboard adventures. For the first time they learned the names Hsu Lin, my half-sister, Hundun, her twin, Wei Xi, George Mayweather, and the Americans Gideon Lamb, the Smalls, Colonel Grayson, and Phoebe Hartfield. I set on the desk my copies of Hundun's confession and the address on Dupont Street, reported how he'd said the people at that address had been hired to kill my father and me.

They passed around the paper. Emmons looked at Toru for confirmation. "I checked the directory," Toru said. "It is a restaurant and shop owned by the Wei family."

"They own the entire block of buildings. And many others," Sutherland said. "They're a powerful family, with fingers in a lot of pies."

"And you think that's a Wei soldier we put in the broom closet?" Rep asked Toru.

"Correct."

"Broom closet?" Sutherland said. "Why?"

"I'll get to that as soon as I finish the shipboard adventures," I said.

I told them how Hundun had been raised to be a weapon. That he'd killed Anne Bonney by mistake, that he'd tried to kill me a second time. I showed them the pink scar on my forearm. And then I told them how he chose to go overboard with our father's ashes, all but the few he left me in a bottle.

I took the bottle from my pocket and set it on my father's desk. And my father was there with us, as he'd been since the beginning of their enterprise. I said, "Tonight, when it's late, I want to visit my mother's grave.

Will you help me?"

"Of course," Emmons said, very quietly. The others nodded.

"Thank you. Now, gentlemen, the tale gets even stranger from that point on."

I related the entire Gideon Lamb-Mr. Small sequence, including Small's attacks on Lin and me and his subsequent murder, Wei Xi's escape from the hold, and her disappearance. I omitted the part about smuggling Lin through customs and into hiding, as we'd broken several laws in the process, and I didn't want to make them accessories after the fact. I reported that Gideon Lamb was out front with two Wei soldiers, while my grandmother sat inside having tea with Hubert Lyster. I finished with the attack on Toru and me when we climbed the back stairs, intending to reach Mr. Sutherland's office.

"The man in the closet is the one who attacked Toru with a knife." I motioned to Rep and he handed me the enameled hilt. "This one."

"It would appear that your dear grandmama, and perhaps Mr. Lyster, have designs on your family fortune," Sutherland said. "No surprise, that."

"Mr. Lamb also may be aiming to get the company assets, one way or another. Grand-mère Constance is devious, but she'd be no match for him."

"And you are the stumbling block," Rep said.

"One of them. Dr. Nakagawa and Mr. Quade are, too. They're partners."

I heard footsteps on the main stairs. One set. And a faint rustling from the back stairwell. Emmons, Sutherland, and Rep drew their guns. I set mine on the desk in front of me. Toru had his knife.

"Two front, two back?" Emmons asked.

They started moving, but I stopped them. "How about four at the front door first, then move to the rear. I can cover that while you're busy. It would take time to batter down the door."

"She knows how to use the gun," Toru said when Emmons seemed about to object. "She shot Mr. Small a week ago."

"Well, I guess that answers my question," Emmons said. He was grinning. "This should be fun."

Someone knocked firmly on the front door. "Polite for a killer, eh?" Rep said.

They all headed to the main door, while I stepped out of my father's office, found a protected vantage point, and trained my gun on the rear door. I heard a faint scratching, then two thuds and a whispered, "Miss Keri, it's me. Mayweather."

And from the front entrance came Phoebe Hartfield's dry voice asking if four weapons were indeed necessary for Miss Rees' visiting lawyer.

Chapter 35

6:40 p.m.

REP OPENED THE DOOR to the rear stairs, revealing George Mayweather, each arm wrapped around the neck of an unconscious Wei henchman. Probably a hundred more where they came from.

I introduced Mayweather, then said, "I'll get the rope. And we'll need gags."

"And bags to go over their heads," Mayweather said. "Don't want them to be able to identify us."

Why hadn't I thought of that?

"The large sample bags should do," Toru said. When he opened the closet door, the man inside didn't move. He was still out. Or pretending to be. He didn't open his eyes, which was just as well.

Rep grabbed some canvas bags from his field gear, cut breathing holes, and slipped the bags over all three heads. We moved the new prisoners in with the old, after removing an arsenal of weapons.

I wasn't keen on spending the night explaining the prisoners' presence to the police. My grandmother would use the danger as ammunition to argue against my suit for emancipation. But how could we remove the men from the building without anyone knowing?

The solution was beyond me. I felt as if I hadn't slept in days. No—weeks.

Once the broom closet door was locked again, I led the way back to my father's office. I introduced Mrs. Hartfield and explained what she had been hired to do for me, then gave her the big desk chair. I sat in the Phineas Quade honorary chair, happy to relinquish my role as storyteller. Toru and Mrs. Hartfield filled in the blanks and completed the picture. I drifted off, giving my subconscious the freedom to consider my next steps. Or so I told myself.

I woke to the familiar sounds of the lamplighter in the street below, whistling as he made his rounds. The rain had stopped, and the setting sun found its way under the clouds. The city was golden, glistening like sugar, a place of wonder and magic.

Someone had carried me to the leather sofa in Phineas' office and covered me with a rough wool blanket that smelled of campfires and coffee and sage. I stretched, feeling refreshed, and visited the water closet. I encountered no one, although I suspected I hadn't been left alone. No lights were on, and I didn't dare light one to announce my presence.

When I emerged from the WC, I found Rep setting out dinner on the desk in my father's office. He'd tacked up a blanket to cover the window and lit a lamp. I could hear the music of a piano in need of tuning, the clip-clop of horses' hooves in the muddy street, drunken yelling, a woman's screams. Welcome home, Keridec Rees.

I closed the door to the office so no light leaked out into the main room. "It smells wonderful," I said, inhaling the scents of pork loin smothered in a brown sauce with grapes, new potatoes, and green beans cooked with onions, garlic, and bacon. "Where's everyone else?"

"The lawyers retreated to Sutherland's office to finalize a batch of legal forms for you to sign. Emmons and your Mr. Mayweather went off to solve the problem of the Three Chinamen in the Broom Closet. They've been removed, by the way. And Toru went to check on Phineas, and then spirit your half-sister—"

"Hsu Lin, but she's using Anne Bonney's papers at present."

"Miss Hsu will need to leave town quickly. Mayweather said that once they figure out the connection between the two of you, her life isn't worth a Confederate dollar."

He studied me to see how I was taking this news. I swallowed a chunk of potato before it was chewed, and coughed as it struggled down my gullet.

Rep would be twenty-four, I reckoned. He'd grown

since I'd seen him last, and now stood a couple of inches over six feet. And he'd filled out through the chest and shoulders. He had russet-brown hair, beard, and mustache, and eyes the shade of flax-blue my mother had loved. He was dressed in Levi Strauss denim jeans and a worn deerskin tunic sewn with fine rawhide strips. Indian-made, though I didn't know which tribe. Field clothes.

"What did everyone decide about me?" I asked.

"I didn't think you'd let them, us, just decide for you."

"You're right. But I expect you hammered out a plan anyway. You all know the risks I'm facing, at least till I can legally make decisions for myself and the company. The lawyers know that we'll have to go into a holding pattern while my emancipation case and my father's will work their way through the courts. My guardians... You did learn Father named Toru and Phineas as my guardians? Good. Well, they support my going to ground while the lawyers work. Only way to protect myself, since my grandmother seems to be involved."

Rep made a note in a small field notebook he always kept at hand. "Toru and Phoebe Hartfield said you want me to become a partner."

I put down my fork. "It's time—if that's what you want."

"I want. I have the money to buy in. Should be enough, since I'll be bringing two decent prospects with me."

"Toru explained where the shares you're buying will come from?"

"He did. But are you sure you want to lose that much clout in the company your parents founded with Phineas?"

"It's the only way I can see to protect it from potential takeover, to make sure any two of us have a majority of shares."

"In case something should happen to you or Phineas."

"Or both. Phineas has willed his shares to Toru. And vice versa. I suggest we keep your partnership a secret for as long as we can, to protect you."

He patted my hand, a gentle touch. "A pretty bleak picture you're drawing, Keri."

"Bleak, but not impossible." I turned my hand over. Trapped his fingers between mine. "Rep, you've held the fort these past months. But we need you now, more than ever."

"At your command, m'lady."

I smiled, releasing him. "Thank you." I heard the bell at St. Mary's and counted the tolls. Nine. "In one day and three hours, I'll be fifteen."

He took the cover off the remaining dish. It was a lemon cake. "Happy Birthday, a bit early."

We were finishing our cake and tea when a soft knock sounded on the rear door. Rep said, "That'll be Phase One arriving."

Phase One was the barber from downstairs, carrying a candle he blew out as soon as he was in the door. It appeared I was to have a haircut, my first ever, not counting the times my mother trimmed the ends of my hair to even them out.

"Good evenin', Miss Keri," said Pat Kenny, who'd cut my father's hair for years. "I hate like the dickens to touch your beautiful tresses, but Mr. Rep here, and Mr. Sutherland, too, assured me it's necessary. So don't ye worry none. I'll make a good job of it."

Pat retreated to the door to pick up a bag and carry it into my father's office. I looked at Rep and spoke in tones that wouldn't carry. "I'm to travel somewhere, dressed as a boy?"

He grinned, clearly delighted with the plan. "You are going by train, but not in the passenger car. You're the temporary head groom's lad, traveling with Emmons' horses. Didn't you notice the saddlebags Emmons and I packed while you were sleeping?"

He nodded toward the pile of field gear we'd removed from the closet. My mother's saddle, blanket roll, and saddlebags stood a little to the side.

"A groom? At some point in the not-to-distant future, Rhoderic Perry, I'll get you back for this."

"I look forward to the day."

"You do realize I'm still the majority shareholder in

265

the company? That means I can change my mind about the partnership."

"Yup. So I'll just have to take my fun where and when and how I can."

I realized that our repartee might have drifted from teasing into something else. "Rep, um, was I flirting just then?"

"First time you've dipped your toe in that particular pond, eh?"

"I think so. I may have done it before without realizing."

"Well, you might want to be careful till you're a mite older."

"What has age got to do with it?"

"In your case, everything."

"I'll try to remember, though I'm not sure it'll help." I'd been raised around men, and saw them all as colleagues or friends. This was unexplored territory.

Pat came out to tell us he was ready. He had set a basin on a chair, laid a cloth on the floor, and set another chair in the middle of the cloth. The basin was empty. The pitcher nearby, full of water. His hands held a shaving blade and a comb. "You ready?"

"I'd like you to save my braid, please. Can you have it made into an attachable hairpiece? Wherever I'm going, I might have to suddenly metamorphose back into a girl."

"I'll have it done. And deliver it myself to Mr. Sutherland."

"You're a good man, Pat Kenny."

He smiled broadly. "Sometimes," he said. "Only sometimes." The smile faded. "Your pa used to say that, Miss Keri. They told me he'd gone on to join your ma. The missus and I are very sorry."

"Thank you, Pat. I'm sure they'd think this adventure of mine was a grand lark." At least my father would. I wasn't quite so sure about my mother, who'd spent long hours brushing and plaiting my hair.

I sat in the chair. Pat moved behind me, draped a cloth over my shoulders, and picked up the braid. I reached back and put a hand on his wrist. "Not too short, now."

"Don't worry, Miss Keri—the way I cut it, the world will see what it wants to see."

I released his wrist. Felt a tug. Heard the unique sound of blade sawing hair. And then, while he washed and combed and trimmed the hair, I contemplated Phase Two.

If I were with Emmons' horses, I'd be bound for Denver, the headquarters of the Rocky Mountain Division of the U. S. Geological Survey. I could deal with Denver. Or Colorado Springs. Both had climates suitable for Uncle P's recovery, should he choose to follow me east.

Rep perched on the edge of the desk, head tilted to one side. I began a silent conversation, mouthing, *"Denver?"*

He nodded.

"When?"

"Tonight."

"I'll need clothes."

"Emmons."

"Emmons?" I clarified.

Answering nod.

That should be interesting. Mr. Em hadn't been a young boy in a very long time. "And I still need to deal with the ashes."

Rep frowned in confusion, then pulled the little bottle from his pocket. I smiled, grateful he understood. I crooked my finger to bring him close enough to whisper in his ear, "Can you give me a hint as to where I'll be staying, what I'll be doing?"

He whispered in my ear, "You'll have plenty of womenfolk around, even if some of them wear habits." He straightened, hiding a smile.

I mouthed, "A convent?"

The smile turned to a deep chuckle.

I said aloud, seemingly apropos of nothing, "Problem is, I've tested out of all the subjects. Except Domestic Science."

He leaned in and whispered again, "The Colorado School of Mines is just up the road. Ever hear of guided studies? Emmons might be able to put in a word so you can live in one place, do chemistry labs and take tests in another. Might work."

Barring that, I could always tutor some of the other girls. It would refresh my memory and cement my knowledge. I saw my world opening up.

Rep stepped back to see how I was taking the proposition.

"When did you get so smart, Rep?"

"Always liked to solve problems. That's why your da recruited me."

Not to mention sponsoring him at university, making sure he had field experience during the summers, and hiring him when he completed his studies. My father, his friends, and partners had been training Rep for years.

"Don't know what I would have done without Glen," Rep said. "Miss him like the dickens."

"You and Toru will need help."

"Already got two boys from across the Bay working for us. Seem to have potential. Been around some. Emmons took them to Mexico and Arizona to explore some properties. We'll whip them into shape or send them packing. We know what Glen wanted… what you want."

Toru and Mayweather knocked at the rear door as Sutherland and Hartfield came in the front. It was as if they'd timed their arrivals to coincide. Everyone crowded into my father's office, the only illumined room. Toru's clothes were rumpled, one pocket of his coat torn half off. Mayweather looked just as scruffy. Dealing with our three captives had taken a toll.

"Toru gave me Phineas' key," Sutherland said, explaining how he'd gotten in. "Can't we turn on some lights?"

"No," the rest of us said together.

"Emmons will be along in a minute," Toru said.

They all studied the effect of the haircut.

"You'll pass," Mayweather said.

Phoebe Hartfield nodded. "It's just long enough to be held back with a ribbon, once she gets where she's going."

I thanked Pat Kenny. Rep paid him with money from my father's safe. Mayweather shook my hand and then, derringer drawn, escorted Kenny down the back stairs to his barber shop. Mayweather would cover our departure, then slip away to his lodgings. I wondered if I'd ever see him again.

I collected my things into an old field bag of my father's. Steps whispered again on the rear stairs. Rep let in Emmons, wearing moccasins and his usual buckskins. He handed me folded clothes, and I retreated to the WC to change. I emerged wearing dark cotton trousers and tunic, a miner's jacket, and a cloth cap, all relatively clean.

The group turned as one. Rep whistled. "I wouldn't show myself, were I you—you'll have girls running after the train all the way to Denver."

"Know anything about horses?" Emmons asked.

"Enough to feed, saddle, ride, and curry them."

"It's a start." He put a callused brown hand on my shoulder. His eyes twinkled. "These ponies are my children. They've covered a fair bit of the West with me in the saddle. I'd appreciate if they arrived in good shape."

"Yes, sir, Mr. Em."

"That's the spirit, boy. Oh, and they like it when I sing to them."

"Any particular song?"

"Know 'Red River Valley'? I taught it to Glen around the campfire one time."

And he'd taught it to me. "It'll be my pleasure, sir."

Chapter 36

August 14, Midnight

WE **LEFT AS THE** clocks struck twelve, using darkness to shield us from curious eyes.

In a pack around my waist and in the field bag I carried all that was most important to me in the world. Word would be sent to Tom and Mary regarding my other things. I'd write out the list on the journey to Denver. For tonight, I would be just another lad on the streets of San Francisco early on a Friday morn.

I felt free, and as if a great weight had been lifted with the cutting of my hair. Justice would eventually be done to Gideon Lamb, Hubert Lyster, and my grandmother, but it would never make up for what they had taken from me.

As the back stairs had proven to be the more dangerous egress, I followed Emmons down the main staircase. He wouldn't be known to Lamb or his friends, and my disguise should protect me. The Chinese watchers outside the closed restaurant crouched against the wall, smoking. They didn't give me a second glance. Emmons called me "boy" and climbed into the closed coach. I tossed in my field bag and followed him inside.

We circled around to the back entrance to pick up Toru, Rep, and Sutherland. They'd brought my mother's saddle, saddlebags, and bedroll.

My mother was buried in Calvary Cemetery, at the foot of Lone Mountain, perhaps five miles away. The coach carried six men and one boy, all armed. After witnessing my signature on various documents, including an even newer will, Phoebe Hartfield had left, saying she had no wish to visit a cemetery during the witching hours.

The carriage was driven by young Tommy Daly, with Michael McGinn on the seat beside him. Tommy owned a growing transportation business: delivery wagons, one carriage, and one coach, the latter bearing no markings on the side to give us away.

Heavy gray mist blanketed the hills. A foghorn droned in the distance. Tommy drove the coach as far into the cemetery as possible, then turned it around and ground-hitched the mules. I alighted, took a lantern from the side of the carriage, and began to wend my way between the headstones. I heard a thud behind me. Turning, I held the lantern aloft. The men were rearranging Emmons' and my saddles at the back of the carriage. One must have fallen.

Noticing that I'd paused to wait, four of the shapes left the carriage and came towards me with silent treads, wraiths in the mist. When they caught up, faces grim as the graveyard, no one spoke.

I found my mother's grave by instinct, a homing pigeon returning to the cote. I'd taken an amethyst crystal from my father's desk. I knelt to place it in the soil before the stone. Then, using Hundun's disc, I excavated a hole six inches deep and poured in my father's ashes, mixing them with my fingers. I left the bottle in the hole, replaced the soil, and patted it down.

"I'll come back," I said to the damp earth. And to Toru and Rep, "You'll add my father's name and dates to the stone for me?"

"Of course," Toru said.

In the distance a church tower struck one. "Better get moving," Emmons said. "We've got to be on the early ferry to catch the train."

I hugged them, one after the other, including Michael. Rep was last. "Don't do anything stupid," he said.

"No guarantees."

Sutherland said, "My daughter Meg, the oldest one, attends that school. She's a senior this year. While you were sleeping, I sent a telegram to reserve a place for an unnamed student."

Things were looking up. I'd always liked Meg Sutherland.

"Keri," Toru began. I focused on him. "I cannot envision a scenario you cannot handle, not after what you have been through lately. Trust your instincts."

"*There* be monsters," I said.

Rep laughed. The others joined in. An odd sound in a cemetery in the darkest hours of the night.

"There be monsters *everywhere*," Rep said.

"My parents loved you all," I said. "I love you all. Please take care of yourselves while I'm away."

I was crying as we left the silent stones behind.

* * *

We made the ferry with thirty minutes to spare. One by one my companions had been dropped off by the side of the street, close, but not too close, to their dwellings. Each one pressed my hand as he left. Toru gave something to Emmons. A glance passed between them. And then we were two, except for our trusty drivers.

At the landing, Emmons and I hopped out. Tommy untied our belongings and draped our shoulders with saddlebags and field bags. Michael loaded me down with my mother's saddle, which knocked my cap askew. With a grin, he used his one hand to straighten it. "You'll do," he whispered. "Not even Annie would recognize you."

Emmons handed money to Tommy, as if we were regular paying customers. Tommy hesitated. Michael nudged him, and said, "Change, sir?"

"No. Keep it." Emmons picked up his saddle. "Thanks for coming out so late."

"Of course, sir. "

I spotted the glowing end of a single watcher smoking in the shadows. I kept my head down and trailed Emmons up the gangplank. The horses were already aboard.

In a stall that smelled of horseflesh and pipe smoke, Emmons introduced me to Isaac "Shorty" Simms. A little under five feet tall. Fudge-colored skin. Pale eyes caught the glow of the lantern hanging in the corner.

Three horses munched from feedbags under Shorty's watchful eye. One of them was Aster, my mother's mare. I saw the blaze on her chestnut forehead as she turned and nickered, recognizing my scent. I put my hand in her mane, my head against her neck. "Thank you, Mr. Em."

"Thank your guardians. And old Tom," Emmons said, feeding carrot chunks to his children. He handed me a carrot and said to Shorty, "Any messages?"

I wondered at the tension underlying the words.

"Newsy came by." Shorty's voice was a soft drawl. He didn't call Emmons "sir." I expected they'd covered a host of rough trails together.

"Well?"

Shorty slipped a folded newspaper from under a curry comb on the bench. "Gave me a couple of stories they're working on for the next edition." He passed the paper to Emmons. "Appears they found three men, Chinese, wearing hoods and nothing else, bound together in an alley near Chinatown." A brief flash of white teeth in the near darkness. "They'd been offloaded from a cart or wagon."

"Uninjured?"

"Except for an inked drawing on their wrists. Some kind of flower. An apple blossom, mebbe. Something like that."

Emmons twitched the blanket into place on one of his horses. "That all?"

"Newsy stopped in at the precinct house, like you asked. Heard gossip that someone had just reported a body in the Catholic Cemetery."

I lifted my head from Aster's neck. Saw the ghost of a smile on Emmons' weathered face. But I stayed silent, waiting.

"Was the body identified?" Emmons asked.

"A Gideon Lamb. Man arrived on the *Oceanic* only yesterday. A tragedy, sure enough."

Which explained the thump I'd heard as I wended my way to my mother's grave a few hours ago. We must have carried the body of Gilbert Lamb for miles through the heart of San Francisco to deposit him not far from my father's ashes. No wonder the men had been so ready to laugh in a graveyard. They must have been worried all the way that we'd be stopped.

I removed my arms from Aster and threw them

around Emmons' neck. "Tell Uncle Toru thank you," I whispered in his ear. "And I hope you give a bonus to that newsboy."

He *ahemmed*. Lads did not hug their employer. I stepped away. "It won't happen again," I said. "Can you tell me if my traveling companion got away safely?"

I could have asked Toru when we were together earlier, but I never found the proper opening.

Emmons handed me a note. "Toru said to destroy this once you've read it."

I moved closer to the lantern glow. The writing was clear, beautiful, the language precise.

Dear Sister,
We captured and removed the black bishop. The queen is still in play. Stopping her and her consort will require time and more complex moves. I have done what I could to help – for the present.
Travel safely. I will send word when I am able. Until then, thank you for my freedom. Be well.

The signature was a plum blossom, an echo of the golden flowers atop the bronze hairpins I'd given her. And of the markings on the wrists of the three Chinese men found last night.

Toru, Mayweather, and Lin must have taken care of that business before they dealt with Lamb—the "black bishop." Retribution had been swift. Toru had protected his ward. Lin had settled any debt that she felt she owed me. And Mayweather had avenged his colleague.

I heard calls on deck, the engines and wheels turning as the ferry drifted away from shore. I went up on deck for a moment, to say good-bye to the lights of San Francisco and all the memories the town held for me. The air was dank and still and redolent of smoke, cooked fish and shellfish, and refuse caught on the rocks and trapped under piers. Harbor smells.

I was leaving behind all that was loved and familiar. The graves of my parents and baby brother. Annie and Hundun, lost at sea. My home, left to the machinations of my grandmother. My family business, turned over to others to run. My guardians. My friends, old and new. Except Emmons, of course. But he could go with me only part of the way. I was, for all intents and purposes, as alone as Shakespeare's Miranda before the shipwreck brought strangers to her shore.

Turning, I faced the East Bay hills. Beyond sight lay an unexplored world—the Sierra Nevadas, the Great Basin Desert, the Rockies, the Great Plains, Denver. And whatever adventures that new life would bring.

Author's Note

One of my reasons for writing this book is to pay tribute to the lives and work of the geologists who opened the way for the rapid settling of the West.

The California Gold Rush, beginning in 1849, triggered the development of cities like San Francisco from what had been small ports. Twenty years later, the completion of the first transcontinental railroad routes facilitated rapid land-based commerce from coast to coast. The geological, geographical, topographical, and railroad surveys of the 1860s and 1870s were completed by the time this book begins. The published reports and maps of these surveys revealed the geologic underpinnings of what had been *terra incognita*. An excellent summary of the four greatest surveys can be found at https://pubs.usgs.gov/circ/c1050/surveys.htm.

Geologic exploration of the West came on the heels of gold and silver discoveries which led to boomtowns in the 1860s and 1870s such as Comstock, Virginia City, Montana, and Leadville, Colorado. Supplying the boomtowns and the railroad expansion teams led to cattle drives, cattle towns like Abilene, Wichita, and Dodge City, and ranch wars. Cowboy culture blossomed, helped along by unlikely exploits captured in penny dreadfuls and dime novels.

Many of the geologists who explored and mapped the West were educated in Europe. This included Samuel Franklin Emmons, a member of Clarence King's 40th Parallel Geological Survey team that mapped a swath of the West beyond the 100th meridian, including Mount Shasta. When Clarence King became the Director of the new U. S. Geological Survey in 1879, Emmons was one of his first hires. He and King had made history when they had exposed The Great Diamond Hoax of 1872. What allowed them to save the investors was Emmons' and King's intimate knowledge of the geology and topography of the western landscape. Emmons, who produced the first comprehensive geologic report on the origins and extent of the Leadville, Colorado, mineral deposits, headed up the U.S. Geological Survey office in Denver in 1885, when this novel is set.

Although Samuel Emmons and Clarence King were real persons, I have used them fictitiously here. Likewise, the Occidental and Oriental Company's steamship *Oceanic* did carry passengers across the northern Pacific from Shanghai and Yokohama to San Francisco in 1885. Although she was real, the characters I have placed on board her and the events I have envisioned are fictional.

Acknowledgments

This novel followed a long and winding road to publication. I'd like to thank the many friends who helped me along the way: Anne Hillerman and Judith Keeling, who both suggested I write a historical mystery; Wynne Brown, J. M. "Mike" Hayes, the late Elizabeth Gunn, Ray Ring, and Elizabeth Trupin-Pulli, who commented on drafts of all or parts of the novel; Liza Porter, who helped keep the writing flame burning during the dark pandemic time; and my stalwart extended family, too many to name, who encouraged and supported me along the way, especially Jonathan, Jordan, Logan and Vanessa Matti, and Hillary and Len Whitten. I love you all.

Lastly, I thank Geoff Habiger, editor Lisa McCoy, and the staff of Artemesia Publishing for giving Keridec Rees a landing place and a launching pad.

About the Author

Tucson writer Susan Cummins Miller holds degrees in history, anthropology, and geology. She worked as a field geologist and taught geology, paleontology, and oceanography before metamorphosing into a writer of fiction, nonfiction, and poetry. Miller has penned six Frankie MacFarlane, Geologist, mysteries, four of which were finalists for the WILLA Award in contemporary fiction; the nonfiction anthology *A Sweet, Separate Intimacy: Women Writers of the American Frontier, 1800-1922;* and two poetry collections, *Deciphering the Desert,* awarded the 2024 Will Rogers Medallion Award in Western Written Poetry, and *Making Silent Stones Sing,* a finalist for the New Mexico/Arizona Book Award, the Western Writers of America Spur Award (Poem), and the WILLA Literary Award. Her short fiction appeared recently in the anthologies *Trouble in Tucson* and *SoWest: Wrong Turn.* She has been affiliated with the University of Arizona's Southwest Institute for Research on Women as a SIROW Scholar, and has been writer-in-residence at the Djerassi Resident Artists Program, Woodside, CA and the Pima County Public Library, Tucson, AZ. Currently, she's working on her third poetry collection, the seventh Frankie MacFarlane, mystery, set in Arizona and Sonora, Mexico, and the second Keridec Rees Historical Mystery, set in the Great Basin and Rocky Mountain West of 1885. Website: www.susancumminsmiller.com